—7 EAR 1121 .

WILD BEAUTY

Also by ANNA-MARIE MCLEMORE

When the Moon Was Ours
The Weight of Feathers
Blanca & Roja

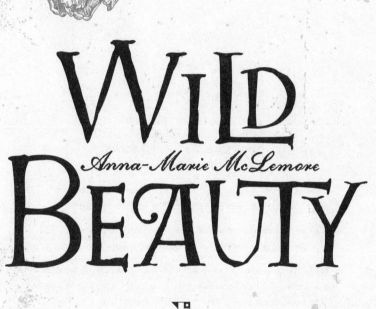

WILD
Anna-Marie McLemore
BEAUTY

SQUARE
FISH

FEIWEL AND FRIENDS
New York

For the women in my family,
for all women who hold the light for their families.
For the girls who've become my sisters,
for all the girls with the misunderstood hearts.

SQUARE
FISH

An imprint of Macmillan Publishing Group, LLC
175 Fifth Avenue, New York, NY 10010
fiercereads.com

Square Fish and the Square Fish logo are trademarks of Macmillan and
are used by Feiwel and Friends under license from Macmillan.

Our books may be purchased in bulk for promotional, educational, or business use.
Please contact your local bookseller or the Macmillan Corporate and Premium
Sales Department at (800) 221-7945 ext. 5442 or by e-mail at
MacmillanSpecialMarkets@macmillan.com.

Library of Congress Cataloging-in-Publication Data is available.

ISBN 978-1-250-18073-5 (paperback)   ISBN 978-1-250-12456-2 (ebook)

Originally published in the United States by Feiwel and Friends
First Square Fish edition, 2018
Book design by Danielle Mazzella di Bosco
Floral border © Nata Slavetskaya / iStock.com
Square Fish logo designed by Filomena Tuosto

1 3 5 7 9 10 8 6 4 2

LEXILE: 830L

If you look the right way, you can see
that the whole world is a garden.

—FRANCES HODGSON BURNETT

Quiero hacer contigo
lo que primavera hace con los cerezos.
I want to do with you
what spring does with the cherry trees.

—PABLO NERUDA

ONE

Later, they would blame what happened on the little wooden horses.

Estrella had found them when she was five, the set of them dust-frosted and forgotten on a high shelf. They had been small enough to fit in her hands, carved wooden wings sprouting from their painted backs.

No one could tell her where the little horses had first come from, or who they'd belonged to. Estrella took her mother's shrug as permission to keep them. She dusted them off, lined them up by colors, their wings rounded and splayed like stouter versions of a dragonfly's. At night, she counted them like sheep. She trotted them along her bedspread like the folds in her quilt were hills.

Now, eleven years later, they were more charms than toys. When she couldn't sleep, she ran her fingers along their wings like her grandmother did with her rosary beads. And tonight, she lay in the dark, turning each one in her hands, trying to ignore that hundreds of blue borraja flowers had sprouted from the ceiling of her bedroom.

Outside the door, she heard her cousins talking. Whatever they were whispering about was good enough to keep them awake; they were all worn down from work. Today they had finished bringing La Pradera into its spring bloom. The gardens were thick with lilies and irises. Morning glories covered the arbors. The blossoming trees floated their clouds of lilacs and mimosa.

There would be more work, of course. At La Pradera, there always was. Keeping up the bulb gardens, stopping the borders from overgrowing, filling in the flower beds. But it wouldn't be the same task they had each spring, forcing their fingers down into the hard earth, bringing the ground back to life after the cold months. Their hands were raw from it. They had called up new flowers so many times that the crescent moons of dirt under their nails seemed as much part of them as their skin.

Each spring felt like all of them, not just the gardens, coming back to life. They spent winters giving their flowers to ceramic pots they kept indoors, or pulling snowdrift roses out of patches of land soft enough to grow. But now all of La Pradera was theirs. They had every acre to let out the blooms that had been waiting in their hands all winter.

Estrella looked up at the ceiling, all those starflowers crawling over the rafters. Now that the season was coming on warmer, she had hoped she could wring herself out, give the ground all the flowers she had in her. But this still happened, borraja painting the space above her bed blue, no matter the season.

She left the little horses on her quilt and found her four cousins in the hall, all of them eyeing one of Azalea's ballet flats. Estrella couldn't tell why until she looked closer, and spotted the three letters Azalea had inked into the lining, where the writing would follow the lower curve of her anklebone.

Bay. Those three letters were as damning as a confession to a priest.

They all rushed into Azalea's room, Azalea calling protests after them. Now that they knew to look, they found the same three letters in her clothbound journals. In her books, as though they belonged not to her but to that name she had written on the fly leaves. On the pale inner satin of a velvet choker.

Then, there was no stopping them. They raided one another's rooms the same way their mothers checked for bottles of violet liqueur, or the dark-dyed lingerie they weren't supposed to have until they were older.

In Gloria's room, they found the creased photo she had pressed against the bottom of her middle drawer. The back looked sponge-painted in the lightest pink and coral of her lipsticks, the faint imprints of the hundred times Gloria had kissed the picture's backing.

The length of yew in Calla's closet told the same story. Bay, the girl those three letters and the face in that photograph belonged to, had been showing her how to carve her own bow. They had been sanding down the wood together, smoothing it in the last daylight hours before dinner.

Azalea eyed Estrella, willing her to be the next to confess.

Her glare reminded Estrella of the story neither of them had ever told. How Estrella had once kissed Bay under the flowering trees, how Azalea had seen it and, that night, gone after her like a lynx. Both of them had grabbed each other's hair until Gloria pulled them apart, demanding to know what this was about. They had traded stares, understanding that they would not tell the truth, instead piecing together some lie about a dress borrowed without permission.

Now Azalea looked ready to grab Estrella by the hair again. She must have assumed Estrella had grown out of that small, fierce love that made her kiss Bay under the mimosa trees. Estrella had thought the same thing about Azalea, that she was done with wanting Bay, or at least that she'd gotten distracted. She'd seen Azalea flirting with the young wives who grew bored at La Pradera's parties, their husbands talking of business they thought women couldn't understand.

But Azalea had been caught, and that stare was her way of telling Estrella that if she, too, didn't confess, Azalea would do it for her.

So Estrella opened her jewelry box to her cousins, showing them the collection of thick ribbons coiled together like a nest. They were each lengths of satin that had fallen from Bay's hair during La Pradera's summer parties and winter balls. When a ribbon slipped from the end of Bay's French braid without her noticing, Estrella lifted it from the flagstone courtyard before it got trampled.

Gloria's eyes slid upward, where the thick blanket of blue starflowers coated the ceiling. Her gaze made the rest of them follow.

Each five-pointed bloom was the deep, clear blue of a new night, the twists of vines flashing sea green between the flowers.

Dalia shook her head at Estrella, not in disappointment but in sympathy. Gloria gave her a small smile, gentle and sad, like Estrella was a child they were looking after. As though Estrella, not Calla, was the youngest Nomeolvides girl.

Calla, for her part, studied the flowers, asking if Estrella could remember what she might have been dreaming this time as blue stars opened over her bed.

"No," Estrella said, the same thing she said every time Calla asked.

Calla let out a disapproving hum, like a doctor being denied the satisfaction of making a diagnosis.

Azalea shuddered, the way she always did when Estrella grew a dark sky over her bed. Estrella didn't take it personally; Azalea had more superstition in her heart than she'd ever admit. It was the rest of them that worried Estrella, their concerned faces, like she was a child suffering night terrors. The rest of them drew flowers from the earth and over wooden arbors only when they wanted to.

Azalea drew her eyes away from the ceiling. She nodded at Estrella's jewelry box, those nests of ribbon, satisfied she didn't have to tell Estrella's secrets for her.

Dalia had been smart enough not to keep any evidence. But

her cousins knew, as soon as they saw the color bloom in her cheeks. Dalia, too, had fallen a little in love with Bay Briar. With Bay's laugh, reckless as any boy's. With how she dressed like a character from one of Gloria's old novels. Satin trousers to the knee, cinched coat, ivory stockings. On anyone else, it would've been a costume. On Bay, it seemed as ordinary as her fine, straw-pale hair, as though she'd been born in a waistcoat.

All five Nomeolvides girls loved Bay Briar. They didn't just flirt with her to needle their mothers and grandmothers. They didn't just admire her as some ornament that moved through La Pradera's gardens. They didn't all harbor crushes on her just because she was there.

They had all fallen in love with her. With how she could beat her grandmother's friends at card games, stirring their roars of cigar-smoke laughter as she took their money. With how she swirled and sipped the red-black wine at La Pradera's parties. (Estrella and her cousins stole bottles and passed them around behind the hedges, seeing how fast the wine could make them feel warm.)

It took only a few minutes standing in the unlit hall for them all to realize what this meant, the love held between them for a girl named Bay Briar.

For as long as anyone had memory, longer than the Nomeolvides women had been at La Pradera, each generation had borne five daughters. Only daughters, always five, like the petals on a forget-me-not. And ever since La Pradera had gotten its hold on them, sure and hard as a killing frost, every generation of five daughters had been trapped in these gardens, like their hearts were buried in the earth.

But Estrella and her cousins couldn't have five daughters if they were all in love with the same woman.

If they all loved Bay Briar, if they were too lovesick over her to sleep with men, their wombs would stay empty as their hearts were full.

They could be the last generation of Nomeolvides girls. The last ones bound together like forget-me-not petals. The last ones who could not leave La Pradera unless they wanted to die, spraying their pillowcases with bitter pollen they coughed up from their lungs as though it were blood.

The last to see their lovers disappear.

Then dread passed between them.

Nothing good came from the love of Nomeolvides women.

Five years ago, Calla's father had vanished. Before him, the traveling salesman who'd stayed at La Pradera longer than he'd stayed anywhere in a decade, all because he'd fallen in love with Abuela Flor's bright laugh. And before him, a man who collected old maps, and who became more of a father to Gloria than the man who'd given her half her blood.

If the love of one woman in this family was enough to make her lover disappear, what would the obsession of five Nomeolvides girls do to Bay?

"No," all five of them said at once, quiet as whispers, at the thought of Bay vanishing under the weight of their love. Not Bay, who visited the stone house where they all lived by ringing the doorbell, bowing, and announcing herself as *the Briar bastard, at your service.* Bay, whose mother had left her husband for Bay's father but had not bothered to take Bay with her. Bay, whose heart always stayed a little bit broken no matter how often her grandmother told her *Bay Briar, being rid of the two of them was the best thing that ever happened to you.*

And now, with her grandmother in the ground almost a year, the Nomeolvides women gathered around Bay like she was some fragile egg. Estrella's mother and her cousins' mothers brought Bay to their table at meal times, expecting her there as much as their own daughters. When Bay was sick, their grandmothers took bowls of blue corn pozole up the hill to the brick house Bay now slept in alone. They set cold cloths under her neck, changed her sheets when her fever soaked them through.

Estrella and her cousins saw the brittle sorrow, the grief drifting off Bay like a mist, and they all wanted to set their lips against her forehead to warm her.

They could not let their hearts destroy this girl they had all secretly loved.

Then Gloria had the idea for the offerings. She whispered into the space between them. "Why don't we ask it"—here she looked at the floorboards under their feet, as though staring into the ground below the house's foundation—"to protect her?"

The tilting of their heads turned to slow nods, all of them drawing closer to this hope.

The only thing stronger than the curse of their blood was

La Pradera, this flowering world that possessed the Nomeolvides women so deeply it killed them if they tried to leave it. If they did not want Bay vanishing, they needed La Pradera to guard her. From them. If anything could save Bay, it was the force and will of this place. Bay had grown up here the same as they had. This land must have fallen in love with her light footsteps and loud laugh, too. So they would beg La Pradera to give Bay its charm against the venom of their hearts.

In return, they gave the ground everything else they loved. Not just the photo at the back of Gloria's drawer, or the ribbons Estrella had collected. They took down lockets they admired so much they hung them on walls instead of keeping them in boxes. They gathered copper-backed hand mirrors and tins of apricots they'd sugared on Easter Sunday.

Gloria volunteered her best earrings, the color of champagne, bubbles embedded in the small globes, and her favorite apron—the ruffles in every shade of purple, from lilac to blackberry. She had worn it so many times to candy rose petals that even after she washed it, it smelled sweet as meringue.

Dalia chose the best perfume from her collection, a heavy bottle that held the scent of lavender and dry wood and bergamot oranges. Then, the fondant rose Bay's grandmother had saved for her off a princess cake from a summer party. She had kept it under a drinking glass so it wouldn't gather dust, and it had stayed as perfect as when it had topped the cake's green fondant.

Azalea gave up the spoon she ate dessert with every night, the pewter handle ending in a spiral like the curled tip of a fiddlehead fern. Then she surrendered her favorite candles, the wax as bright pink and red as the flowers she grew.

Calla offered the candy hearts she'd saved over the years, the big kind they carried at the shop in town. She'd collected ones with single words etched into the sugar. *Dream. Honey. True.* Next, she tore down the tissue paper flowers that hung on fishing line in her room; she had saved them from being thrown out after a spring ball.

Estrella parted with her favorite dress, the sheer layers of the skirt ending in points like the petals of starflowers. From her collection of carved horse figurines, wooden and winged, she chose her favorite, one with just enough color left to show the indigo it had been painted.

They scattered Gloria's earrings and Calla's candy hearts. They poured Dalia's perfume onto the flower beds. Into the thick hedges, they tucked her fondant rose and Calla's paper flowers. Azalea buried the pewter spoon, and Estrella planted the little indigo horse deep in the ground like a bulb.

Then they gathered at La Pradera's lowest point, a dark pond at the center of the sunken garden.

Gloria's apron and Estrella's dress floated in the water for so long the cousins all shivered, the ruffles waving as though they felt the loss of the girls who'd once worn them. Azalea lit each of her candles before throwing them in, the flames flickering before they went out.

Later, they would all swear they had seen something bright

in that water. A few trails of light swirling around the things they gave. A glow buoying up the apron and dress. An echoing of the candles Azalea lit and then let go.

It was this that let them sleep that night, this sign that La Pradera had heard them.

TWO

When he realized he had hands, and a body, he crossed himself. Even before he could open his eyes, he lifted his fingers to his forehead and prayed the words. *En el nombre del Padre, y del Hijo, y del Espíritu Santo.*

He could not remember when he had last had hands and a body, so thanking God for them seemed the thing to do if he didn't want to lose them again. *I exist. I thank God for my existence.*

It was too cold to be el Cielo. If he was with God in Heaven, why would he feel so cold? He wondered if he was in el Purgatorio, the place he would pay for his sins.

But the air. The air smelled too sweet for this to be Purgatory, like the sugar of fruit and the green of trees. These scents came to him as familiar, but he didn't know why.

He could not remember dying. He could not remember where he had been before this either.

A damp chill soaked his back, and under his fingers he felt the wet brush of grass. He opened his eyes to columns of white sunlight. Those fingers of sun spread out over a world that looked like a single garden but stretched as wide as a valley. They cut through a gray mist turning a little blue at the edges.

Everything else was color. Trees rose toward the sky, letting the pale sun through their branches. Vines crawled up the walls of the valley. The grass was so bright it looked polished. The flowers stood sharp against the green valley and the blue-gray morning. They grew in pink and orange and violet. It was vivid and beautiful enough that it hurt him to look at it, and again, he wondered if maybe this was el Cielo.

A figure floated through the light so slowly he did not flinch or startle. The blurring of mist and sun fell away, and he saw her, a dark-haired girl in a green dress, the mist collecting into drops on her hair. The brown of her shoulders looked familiar, not because he knew her but because the color felt like something that was his, too.

He looked down at his own hands and forearms, remembering this body he once had and now had again. He and this girl were not the same brown but close, like the bark of two different trees in this garden.

She spoke to him, but he did not hear her. She sounded as distant as the far-off call of a bird echoing through the valley. His own heartbeat, a thing he had not understood to be there until that moment, grew louder in his ears. The pressure in his rib cage made his chest feel like it was hardening into wood. He hadn't realized he was trying to get to his feet until the act of sitting up and trying to stand left his lungs raw and worn.

The girl knelt near him. Her skirt spread around her, the hem lapping at his thigh. He tried to breathe, but the shame of realizing how dirty his clothes were made the feeling of weight on his chest worse. The stains on his shirt matched the soil caught under his fingernails, like he'd been raking his hands through the ground. Flecks of earth fell from his fore-arms but dampened and stained his collar and the hems of his pants.

They could have come from sleeping and waking on this ground. But each dulling stain felt like the sign of some trans-gression he had yet to confess. Maybe this girl had come to give him a chance to unburden his soul, but how could he confess the things he had done if he couldn't remember them?

Again, the girl spoke to him, this time with light hands on his shoulders, like she was telling him not to move so fast.

The wonder of her struck him still. He wanted so much to both run from her and be in her presence that she must have been some saint he did not recognize. She had been sent there to find him, and now she would judge his spirit.

But she was not dressed as some angel of Heaven, in the golds of saints' light and the blues of la Virgen. Nor was she the flame colors of the damnation he knew to fear; she was not some beautiful demon who would turn to fire and ash when he touched his fingers to her dress. Instead, there was the dark brown of her hair and her eyes. The lighter brown of her face and her hands. The faint red of her lips, and the soft green of her dress.

She was warmth but not fire, light but not sky.

"Fel," she said, and because he did not understand, he shook his head before he realized he was doing it.

She touched his shoulder.

"Fel," she said.

He followed the line of her arm down to her hand. Between her thumb and forefinger she grasped a scrap of cloth sewn to his shirt. She pulled it until the end came free from under his suspender strap.

Three letters, *F-e-l*, had been scrawled onto the cloth.

It looked like there might have been more letters, but the scrap had been torn, and those three were all that was left. The loss of the other letters felt as heavy as a prayer unsaid, like they were a map to this garden valley.

"Is that your name?" she asked.

He opened his mouth to say no but then realized he did not know what name to tell her instead. He didn't remember what he was called any more than he remembered where he had been before this garden.

If this was el Purgatorio, maybe it was his first test to resist her. The quiet force of her made him want to tell her things he did not know. It made him want to make things up, lie just so he could give her something that sounded true. And maybe she knew this and was waiting to see if he would lie in this way, or if he would admit that he knew nothing.

But her dress, green as the trees that softened the edges of this garden valley, her dress made him think of something.

Some understanding about the color drifted toward him but then skittered away before he could grasp it. And because he wanted to follow that understanding, to see if it would come back to him, he let this girl take his hand.

THREE

This boy was La Pradera's answer.

Estrella found him in the same corner of the sunken garden where she had buried her little wooden horse. But she wasn't telling her cousins that. If they thought the indigo horse had been the thing to do it, they'd look at her the same way they looked at her on the nights she woke with starflowers covering the ceiling. Like she was a girl whose dreams and favorite childhood toys were things they had to protect her from.

What they knew, all they needed to know, was that the five of them had brought their nighttime offerings, and the gardens had given them something back.

Gloria tried to hand the boy the phone and asked, "Is there someone you want to call?"

He blinked at the phone like it was something not only unknown but unknowable.

He reminded Estrella of the partridge chick Dalia had as a pet when they were little. That was before the old cat Azalea had started batting at it, and Dalia got worried the cat would eat it. Dalia had long since given it to an old woman who now fed it peaches and read it the Psalms, but Estrella remembered it. Scrawny and funny-looking and made presentable only by its fluff, a mix of brown, black, and gold.

Instead of fluff, this boy had his hair, coarse and dark as Estrella's, but uncombed, and his loose clothes. Brown pants, and a shirt that had once been cream or tan but that the earth had darkened.

Dalia whispered something to Calla about his clothes.

The rough shirt, trousers, and thick suspenders were work clothes, but ones as out of place in this century as Bay's waistcoats.

While Bay made the clothes of some other time seem as natural to her as her hair, everything about this boy seemed misplaced. He had an underfed look made more pitiful by the lost way he studied everything from that phone to the windows. He seemed like he had wandered into a world he did not belong to.

"How old do you think he is?" Gloria asked.

Dalia shrugged, looking at him as though he could not see her staring. "Seventeen? Eighteen?"

Dalia glanced at Estrella, and Estrella knew she was not saying the rest. He seemed about seventeen or eighteen, but he had the diminished sense of a boy the world had worked hard.

It made them all feel a little guilty for having not just mothers who plaited ribbons into their hair but grandmothers who read to them when they had all had the chicken pox at once.

Being a Nomeolvides girl, living so closely with generations of five women each, meant they all had not just their own mothers, not just their own grandmothers, but five.

"Who loved him?" Azalea asked.

They all turned to her, understanding even with just those three words.

Azalea wanted to know which Nomeolvides woman might have once loved this boy into disappearing, and how La Pradera had returned him from whatever cursed place lovers vanished to. She looked at him like he was a spirit, despite Estrella leading him by the hand and showing him to be as solid as the flowers they made.

"I don't like this," Azalea said, shivering as though a draft had come through the house.

"Well, we can't leave him like this," Dalia said, her voice low in case the boy could understand her. "Look at him."

Azalea flitted around the hall like a bird caught under the rafters. "I still don't like this."

Estrella let go of the boy's hand. She felt the slow, shared breath in that always came before they started arguing.

To her and to Dalia, La Pradera had given them this boy, and they were asking for its wrath if they did not take care of him. If they ignored him, they risked La Pradera stealing Bay Briar, that girl they all loved, out of spite.

To Azalea, he was a lost lover returned from some disappearing place, and to touch him was to provoke La Pradera's curse.

Before Gloria and Calla could choose their sides, all five of their mothers gathered around this boy the way they did around Bay. Gloria's mother put her hands on either side of his face like he was a child, not an almost-grown man who stood a head above her.

"Pobrecito," Estrella's mother said.

The boy shuddered, eyes opening with recognition.

"¿Comprendes?" Calla's mother asked.

Dalia's mother shoved between them. She spoke better Spanish than any of her cousins, swearing she had learned it all by reading la Biblia in two languages. Now she spoke to the boy in a low voice, reassuring him in words Estrella and her cousins could neither hear nor understand.

When she caught the younger girls staring, she took them all in with one sweep of her eyes.

"He's not stupid," she said. "He just speaks a language none of you bothered to learn."

Estrella's grandmother and her cousins' grandmothers had no time for the pity with which their daughters greeted this boy. They led him upstairs, stripped him out of his earth-darkened clothes, and put him under a shower. Estrella heard the water turn on, and the old women's calming murmurs told her that the spray had startled him.

Estrella floated between rooms, listening outside doors and catching scraps she could piece together.

Her mother and her cousins' mothers whispered that maybe this boy was a sign from God. The lovers they had lost would reappear. The grandmothers, who now left the boy alone to wash himself, agreed that he was a gift from the land. The Nomeolvides women did not have sons, so this boy was the son they would never bear themselves. He was a son, a nephew, a boy cousin, a brother.

He was all these things this family did not know.

"The land doesn't give us gifts," Azalea said when Estrella told her cousins.

Even Estrella had to admit she was right. The land did not give anything without stealing something else. It had given their family a home, but in return it demanded the women stay. It insisted with such force that if any of them left, they weakened and grew sicker until they either came back or died.

"Watch your tongues," Abuela Magnolia said, and both Estrella and Azalea jumped to realize she was alongside them. "You don't know what it was like. You weren't alive before we came here."

"Neither were you," Calla said under her breath. The Nomeolvides women had been at La Pradera for a hundred years. And despite Abuela Flor and Abuela Liria's jokes that they were old enough to have seen the birth of Christ firsthand, no one alive in this family today had memory that far back.

Abuela Lila set her hand beneath Calla's chin, gentle but still correcting. "Do you know what it was like for our family before?"

Calla nodded. She could have recited, half-asleep or deep in a fever, all that Abuela Lila was about to say. They all could have. Before La Pradera they were las hijas del aire. Children of the air. Children who, on paper, did not exist, and so were considered invisible and formless as the air beneath the sky. It had been an insult thrown at their family as they moved from place to place, after new treaties had declared their land now belonged to another country.

So they wandered, with no birth certificates, no paperwork proving their names and their homes, no proof they had ever been born except the word of their mothers and the parteras who helped bring them into the world. Some—a girl who grew Mexican sage, another with a gift for tulips—tried to bury their last name and the lore of this family. But when their legacy was discovered, when blooms they never intended sprung up without warning, when their cursed love claimed the lives of adored sons, they were marked as witches, or killed.

Some had tried to suppress their gifts for the ground. They'd tried to pretend they had no flowers waiting in their hands. They looked for job listings like *secretary* or *shopgirl*, nothing to do with anything growing or blooming. They rented apartments in cities, or houses in towns too small to be printed on maps. They tried to act as though they had not been born with petals in their fingertips.

The blooms inside them always found their way out. Pushed down, they rose strange and spiteful, in ways as unexpected as they were dangerous. The girl christened after the purple velvet of Mexican sage had woken up to find a hundred thousand vines splintering her house apart.

Another with a gift for the petaled cups of ranunculus accidentally grew enough to flood the schoolhouse where she worked. The children ran from them like snakes, and mothers and fathers drove her from town.

The one with a blessing for tulips had resolved not to grow a single bloom, not even in a window box or flowerpot. She had not wanted to flaunt her gift in the middle of the drought-parched town where she hid.

Then, one morning, the yard in front of her rented house turned from the bristle of dried grass to tulips so thick she could not find the ground. Cream and orange. Lipstick pink and pale green. Color-broken red and frilled peach. All with smooth leaves as green as algae on a pond. And before she could clear them, her neighbors saw. They thought she was a witch who'd stolen all the water, and a group of barely grown sons shot her like a scavenging bird.

"La Pradera may keep us here," Abuela Lila said now, "but we had a worse life before these gardens."

They all knew. Their mothers never let them forget.

The legacy of disappearing lovers made the Nomeolvides women reviled, called the daughters of demons. They had endured the taunts and threats that came with being considered witches. Towns cast them out, not wanting them near their sons and daughters for fear Nomeolvides women would love them and they would vanish.

"And now the land is softening toward us," Abuela Flor said.

Estrella could almost hear the unspoken hope hovering in this house.

La Pradera had given them back a boy a Nomeolvides heart had once loved out of existence. His presence in their house held the enchantment and wonder of making a vanished love reappear.

If La Pradera could bring back a boy lost a hundred years ago, maybe it could break this curse they had carried here in their hearts. Maybe it would give them back other vanished lovers. Maybe it would lift the awful legacy from this generation of daughters.

That hope calmed Azalea, quieting her for as long as it took the boy to wash himself.

But then Abuela Liria volunteered clothes that had once belonged to her vanished husband.

"You're putting him in the clothes of the dead," Azalea said, paling.

Abuela Magnolia and Abuela Mimosa handed him the trousers and pulled the shirt over his head.

"Fine," Azalea said. "You don't care what you're bringing down on us. But what about him? You could be cursing him."

"Enough," Gloria said. The word came low, Gloria not wanting the boy to hear. But she hit it so hard it turned rough. Her eyes flashed to each cousin, first Azalea, then Dalia, Calla,

Estrella. "If there's any chance he belonged to one of ours, we treat him like one of ours."

They all hushed under her logic.

If he had been loved and made to vanish by a woman in their family, no matter how long ago, then in some way he belonged to them. His lostness was, in whatever far-removed way, their fault. Every woman in this house had inherited it, the same way they had inherited the loss and broken hearts written into their blood.

This was Gloria, quiet, her posture straight and unyielding. She held back so often that sometimes her voice startled them. But when she thought the four of them were acting like children, she took certain hold of their whispering and wondering and she decided.

"So until we have a reason to say otherwise, he's our brother." Gloria caught each of their eyes again. "Understand?"

The pride in their mothers' and grandmothers' faces was so open and full that Estrella thought it might lift them off the floor, each of them floating to the rafters and bobbing beneath the ceiling like balloons.

In the easing of their shoulders, Estrella saw their faith that, one day, this family could be left in Gloria's hands.

With the same rough efficiency as they'd gotten the boy naked and clean, the grandmothers went about feeding him. They fried eggs and tortillas for huevos divorciados, Abuela Mimosa spooning salsa verde over one egg and salsa roja over the other, and they sat him at the kitchen table.

Tía Hortensia and Tía Iris told him to "Eat, mijito, you're so skinny, mijito," as though it was his own gaunt frame, and not the legacy of this family, that put men at risk of vanishing.

"Gracias," he said, the first word Estrella heard him say. Then he bowed his head and said grace as though he had been speaking the whole time.

FOUR

They asked him if he wanted to sleep. He shook his head; he felt as though he had been sleeping, or dead, for a long time before this.

They asked him if he wanted to read, and handed him an age-softened Biblia. The insistence with which they pressed it into his hands made him wonder if they could see into his soul, if this was in fact el Purgatorio, a softer version of it than any he could remember hearing of.

He set la Biblia on the kitchen table.

What he wanted most was not to be a bother to these women who acted as though they were all his mothers and grand-mothers. They had already taken off his clothes like he was a child, put him under water that washed the earth off his skin, given him clothes that did not belong to him, fed him without asking if he was hungry because they seemed to know he was.

In the same soap-bubbled water where the pan soaked, he

washed the plate he'd eaten off of. Then the pan, scouring the cast iron with a stiff brush. He knew these things. His hands knew how to wash his face and knot the laces on his shoes and scrub an iron pan. He understood that around him in the garden valley were flowers, and he knew what flowers were, even if he could not remember the last time he saw them. Even if it seemed impossible that so many could crowd together in one place.

He was grateful for his hands, how they acted without waiting for him to tell them how. But they did not know what he wanted to know. He wanted to know things held not in his fingers but in memories so dull and tarnished he could not make out what they were.

He dried the plate and pan, and then stood holding them, realizing he did not know where to put them away.

A girl swept into the kitchen and whisked the pan and plate from his hands. She looked a little like the girl who had first touched him, but younger, and both taller and thinner.

"Did you disappear?" she asked.

He didn't know what she was asking. He hadn't gone anywhere but across the kitchen.

She put the plate away in a cupboard. "Did you disappear and come back?"

He shut the cupboard for her. Instead of risking giving her a wrong answer, he pretended he hadn't heard.

"I know you can understand me," she said, hanging the pan on the wall. "Don't pretend you can't."

On his back, he felt the pinprick of telling a lie.

The girl pulled aside thin curtains, letting pale light in through a window above the sink. "Do you have any sisters?"

She gave him the time it took for the dust to settle in the streams of light before adding, "Do you want sisters? Because we'll all be your sisters if you want." She opened a drawer and gathered up a handful of forks. "But if you fall in love with the same woman as us, we'll have to kill you. Five is already too many."

He tried to keep the shock off his face. If the five younger girls were all in love with the same woman, who was she? He imagined a figure twice his height, her saint's halo bright as the sun off the forks in this girl's hand, some divine being only those who lived in this place could stand to look at.

The other girls filled the kitchen. The one in the green dress, and three others who looked a little older than she was.

The light through the kitchen window fell on the girl's forehead and collarbone like it had in the valley, before she led him to this house. The hem of her dress brushed the leg of the wooden table.

"Azalea, no," the girl in the green dress said to another girl.

"You told me to be nice to him." The other girl—Azalea, he guessed—opened the cupboard. "They always make *me* feel better."

"Yeah, and they make everyone else feel worse," another, one of the two who looked oldest, said.

Azalea took down a thin box, shook it at her, and set it on the counter.

"Yes, perfect," one of the oldest ones said. "Thank you for your valuable contribution to this situation."

"Dalia," the youngest one said to one of the oldest girls, but neither of the oldest girls turned. "He can hear you."

Fel picked up the box. The words *Instant Mashed Potatoes* arced across the front, over a picture of swirled white fluff.

"But how do they get the potatoes in there?" he said to himself, jumping a little to hear the words in his own voice. Low, quiet, but spoken.

They didn't seem to hear this voice that startled him. His own voice, which he had not yet used except to thank the grandmothers.

But the girl called Azalea noticed him looking at the box and brightened.

"You've never had these?" she asked.

"Azalea, don't," the girl in the green dress said. "Nobody likes those but you."

"And maybe him," Azalea said. "We don't know yet."

"Bay settled this last week," one of the oldest ones, the girl called Dalia, said. "They're disgusting."

"She said she liked them," Azalea said.

"She was being polite," the other oldest one said.

"Don't let them scare you off," Azalea said, to him this time. "They're the best thing to come in a box."

She filled a pot with water from the sink.

This family had its own taps that ran inside. When he'd washed the pan and plate, he'd done it in the filled sink, one side soaped, the other clear, and hadn't noticed.

Whatever place this was between death and the next life had water that ran inside houses.

Azalea added salt and butter to the boiling water. The girl in the green dress and the two oldest girls kept talking. The youngest one hopped up on the counter, smirking at him like she was enjoying catching what the other girls missed.

"What do you want to tell Bay?" one of the oldest ones asked.

"The truth?" the girl in the green dress said.

"All of it?" Dalia asked. "Really? Even the part about why we did all this?"

"Why don't we just let Bay talk to him?" the other oldest one asked. "She can get anyone talking."

"You could get him talking too," the youngest one said, "if any of you were paying attention."

She hopped off the counter. The slap of her bare feet on the ceramic tile drew all their attention.

"He just read that"—she pointed at the box—"so I think he can understand you."

Azalea's hand paused, a snow of white flakes falling from the open box.

"You can understand us," Azalea said.

The youngest one nodded at him, slowly, leading him to imitate her nod and admit that, yes, he knew what they were saying.

That cautious nod started the questions.

"Where did you come from?"

"Where were you before this?"

"Did you disappear and come back?"

"Did you love somebody who looked like us a long time ago?"

"Who are you?"

"What are you?"

And, from the girl in the green dress, the question so soft it sounded breathed more than spoken, "What's your name?"

"I don't know," he said, with the full, slow breath of telling the truth. Wherever he was, he had this on his side, that each of these questions could be answered with the same truth. "I don't know."

FIVE

Estrella had worried that the boy might resist the work of her grandmothers' hands. But he had not fought. He had not wrenched out of their hold as they took his clothes or gotten up from the kitchen table when they told him to eat.

She wondered if he could feel in their hands how many times they had done this before. Not for boys who turned up in the sunken garden, but for their daughters whose lovers had vanished. For their mothers. For one another.

For Bay Briar.

After Bay had buried her grandmother, she had let go the men and women who kept up the great brick house, giving them a year's pay on top of what Marjorie Briar had left them each in her will. Then Bay had gotten into bed in the same black pants and waistcoat she'd worn graveside. She'd stayed there, face pressed into the pillow, no light in the room but a seam between curtain panels.

She lay there, dust graying everything in the house, her stillness mourning the woman who had been both mother and father to her when her own mother and father had not stayed. Marjorie Briar, who never sent invitations to her midsummer parties and Christmas balls, because on those nights everyone in town was welcome at La Pradera. Marjorie Briar, who lured wealthy men to invest in businesses that were weeks from closing.

The curtains in the windows of that brick house had stayed drawn. Estrella and her cousins worried Bay was starving. Their mothers feared she would wither from lack of sunlight.

But the Nomeolvides grandmothers had climbed the grass slope to the brick house. They threw open the curtains, ignoring Bay's groan against the light. They shoved her out of bed and toward the shower, dusting her room and changing the sheets in the time it took her to dress in clean clothes, shower steam curling off her skin.

They told her she would eat with them from then on, and even though Bay had inherited the land they all lived on, she obeyed. She bowed to the gravity of belonging to these women.

After a thousand meals at the Nomeolvides table, Bay Briar still came to the front door. The Nomeolvides girls crowded onto the sofa that let them see, between curtain panels, Bay waiting on the front step. For months, they had each assumed that the others only wanted the first look at Bay's newest outfit.

Now they knew better. They flushed at the fact that she waited to be let in, like a boy picking one of them up.

Tonight, Bay wore riding boots over plain trousers, but with a satin coat that looked like a smoking jacket. Her hair was so pale that, against the burgundy lapels, it glowed.

She stood against the deepening blue of the evening, and she bowed low, saying, "The Briar family bastard, at your service."

Pulling back up to her full height, she caught sight of the boy, and said, "Oh," as though a few blinking moments would help her understand.

Fifteen Nomeolvides women and Bay Briar and a nameless boy ate their cazuela in the quiet of the evening and the cool air of the propped-open windows. They stirred spoons through the potato and sweet corn and green chiles.

Estrella and her cousins felt their mothers' observations passed like the cazuela. A boy who would be a little bit handsome if he weren't so starved and nervous sat at their dinner table, and the mothers worried that their daughters would all be pregnant from him by spring.

But when Estrella caught her cousins checking their lipstick in the backs of their spoons, she knew it wasn't for this boy but for Bay. If they were watching the boy, it was for how Bay would react to him.

They waited to see if Bay would speak to him, which language he would thank her in when she passed the water pitcher or the salt.

To Estrella's cousins, the boy from the sunken garden was a curiosity. Bay was an obsession.

Tía Jacinta leaned toward Estrella. "I think it's a good thing," she said, adding chili to her cazuela. Nothing made in this house was ever spiced enough for Tía Jacinta's taste. "Pobrecita could use a friend."

This time, *pobrecita* was Bay.

Abuela Magnolia gave a slow nod, looking toward Bay. "She's lonely, that girl."

Estrella tensed at how Abuela Magnolia did not lower her voice. But they were far enough down the table that neither the boy nor Bay could hear them.

Abuela Magnolia shook her head, clucking her tongue. "Sleeping alone in that house."

"I'll go and sleep with her," Azalea whispered without looking up from her bowl, and both Calla and Estrella bit their napkins to keep from laughing.

"No, you won't," Azalea's mother said, not looking up from slicing her knife through pieces of potatoes.

Heat twirled through Estrella's face and forehead. She looked around, her cousins all in the same posture, faces bent to the table, shoulders a little hunched.

Their mothers had known about their crushes on Bay. Of course they had known. But now the fact that Estrella and her cousins saw their love mirrored in one another's hearts made her worry about how much their mothers knew, if they could see into their daydreams.

After dinner, the grandmothers passed plates of coyotas, and they all cracked the sugar cookies in two, revealing the ribbon of brown sugar in the middle.

The boy looked at the soft, damp center with the wonder of having broken open an egg filled with confetti.

In the noise of the table and the breaking of sugar cookies, Estrella did not catch what her grandmother told Bay. But under the chatter of her cousins and their mothers, Estrella heard the thread of Bay's voice.

"Stay with me," Bay told the boy.

Not a question, or an offer. A command no less final than five grandmothers shoving the boy up the stairs.

"I live over there," she said, glancing at the windows as though the Briar house was across a dirt road instead of up a grass-covered hill. "I have the room."

Estrella felt the hearts of every mother and grandmother at the table fill. This was a thing Bay's grandmother would have done, offer a place to a strange boy.

The boy did not answer Bay Briar. He lowered his head, studying the deep amber inside the coyota. Estrella felt his shame like a palm on the back of her neck, his embarrassment that a pale-haired woman had to offer him a place in her house.

But he did not say no. He did not shake his head. And for a boy who said little more than grace for the things put in front of him, this was a *yes*.

After dinner, the boy stood in the kitchen doorway, hands in his pockets, looking like he wanted to pace but didn't want to get in the way. Estrella's mother handed him a dish towel and made room for him at the counter. Drying plates and spoons seemed to calm him as much as watching the snow of Azalea's flaked potatoes.

Bay had just brought handfuls of silverware to set the table for tomorrow's breakfast when she stilled, her eyes fixed on the window.

"Oh no," she said.

"What?" Dalia asked.

Bay set down the forks and the spoons.

She made a line for the front door so certain that none of the Nomeolvides girls dared to cross it. She threw the door open, and in the seconds before she pulled it shut again they saw him. A man on the grass in front of the stone house.

Reid, Bay called him. Reid, said in a way meant to make it sound like a greeting. But Estrella caught the apprehension under the name. The wavering in her voice stretched the single syllable.

He looked a little older than Bay, closer to thirty than twenty. He wore pressed slacks, the kind Estrella thought men wore only to church, but a shirt so wrinkled he looked like he'd slept in it. He kept his hands in his pockets, not in the way the boy did, as though he did not know what to do with them. This man seemed to rest his hands in his pockets as a way of reminding anyone watching how at ease he was in the world.

He had a frame not so different than the boy's. A few inches taller if Estrella had to guess, and almost as thin. But while the boy looked underfed, this man, Reid, looked like he had come this way. Ash and red wine stained his wrinkled shirt. Her grandmothers would have done something about that, fearing what became of young men who drank and smoked more than they bothered with proper meals.

A knot grew in Estrella's throat, turning harder with each thread she drew between this man and Bay.

They both had that pale hair, the color of sand and shells. It held fast in the Briar family no matter how many brown-haired men and red-haired women they married. They both had eyes so light that a shift of sun could turn them from blue to gray. Fine freckles crossed the bridges of their noses like a dusting of nutmeg. Their noses had shapes so similar that, if it weren't for the difference in their jawlines and foreheads, Estrella would wonder if he was a brother Bay had never mentioned.

Estrella and her cousins spied between curtain panels.

"Should we invite him in?" Gloria asked.

Azalea laughed. "What do you think?"

"Look at her," Dalia said. "I don't know who he is, but I know her, and right now she wants to push him down the steps of the sunken garden."

They all saw it, the tightness in Bay's neck like she was trying to swallow a tablespoon of black pepper honey that would not go down.

Bay led Reid around to the side of the house, so Estrella and her cousins could not see them.

"Then maybe that's why we invite him in," Calla said. "To find out who he is."

"I have a better idea." Gloria pulled on the end of the

embroidered cloth Bay had just fluffed out for breakfast. The silverware clattered to the wooden table. "Let's do some laundry."

"What?" Estrella asked.

"Laundry," Azalea echoed, the word as light as a sun-bleached sheet.

Estrella listened for the sarcasm but didn't find it.

They followed Gloria to the laundry room, the tablecloth spilling from her arms.

The window gave them a framed view of Bay and Reid, walking the grass slope up to the Briar house. Calla sat on the windowsill, Azalea on the dryer, helping Gloria refold the tablecloth they had pretended needed a wash.

Dalia sprinkled lemon juice onto stained napkins. Estrella checked the pockets on their aprons and sweaters. Their mothers would let them spy on Bay and Reid only as long as they looked like they were doing something.

Estrella lifted the boy's clothes from the woven basket. The smell of iron was so strong on his shirt that she touched it lightly, cringing, waiting to find it starched with dried blood.

"It's the dirt," Calla said.

Estrella looked up.

"It's not blood," Calla said. "It's the minerals in the dirt."

Estrella shoved her hands into the boy's pockets, the second-nature checking that kept lipsticks and hairpins from going into the wash.

Her fingers found the rounded edges of something small. Wooden. She drew it out from his pocket.

A carved horse. Painted wings sprouted from its rounded back. The same as the ones she kept on a shelf and the one she had buried.

But this one was green. She had never seen one painted green. The ones she had left on her shelf were painted yellow, red, violet, orange, white. And the one she had buried, her favorite, had been indigo. This winged horse was as green as the trees of life in the sunken garden. Green as the dress she had worn when she found this boy.

Azalea's eyes held the same worry as when she stood under a ceiling of Estrella's starflowers. She fixed her stare first on Estrella and then on the green winged horse.

"What did you do?" Calla asked, shaking her head.

"Nothing," Estrella said, her voice pitching up. It was a lie and not a lie, a word said more in reaction than because she meant to say it.

Even though they'd found it in the boy's pocket, they all counted that horse as a thing belonging to Estrella. It was as much hers as the blue borraja clinging to her bedroom ceiling.

Her cousins fell quiet. They all watched the carved horse, as though it might beat its rounded wings and flutter from her cupped hands.

Whether all this was Estrella's fault or not, whether it was the fault of those little horses or not, they all understood this as she understood it. That wooden horse was a small, painted sign that if they wanted to keep Bay, they had to do as Gloria said and care for this boy the land had given them.

Estrella had buried a blue wooden horse under the earth, and La Pradera had answered with this boy. A lost brother or son or lover who had turned up with a green wooden horse in his pocket.

SIX

When she first set the small thing in his hand, when she said, "Here, I found it in your clothes," he did not recognize it as something that was his.

He turned it over. A tiny horse with wings on its back, chipped paint coating its body in green.

The wings were not the great feathered wings of a bird. They were simple and rounded. His fingers skimmed over the curved edge.

Green, the color of trailing vines in the garden valley. Green, the color of the dress the girl had worn. A cold shock of familiarity made him understand that this was why he had followed her.

He had barely taken into himself the knowledge that this little green horse was his, when the girl reached into her apron and pulled out another, yellow. Then another, purple. Then three more. White, orange, red.

She put them in his hands, their small bodies crowding the green one. "You can have these ones too, if you want."

But he could not answer. He could not nod to thank her or shake his head to refuse them. With each small weight into his hands, these tiny horses broke him. Each new color cracked him open a little further. He knew them. The feeling of the worn paint, their colors, the shape of their wings all pulled him back toward something he could not reach.

These were things he had touched and held before. But between where he was and the place where that understanding lived stood a border as heavy as the stone of this house. It was the same feeling he'd had in the garden, wanting to speak and not remembering how to ask his tongue and lips to make the words.

He knew what this girl wanted. She was giving him these small, winged creatures, and in return she wanted things he could not tell.

He could not give her his name, because he did not know it. He could not say how he had come to the garden valley, because he had no memory of a time before. He could not even admit to her that he was lost, because lost meant there was somewhere he would not be lost if he could just trace a path back.

There was no path back. He reached past the moment of opening his eyes, blinking against the pale sun in the garden, but beyond it there was only the dark, heavy blanket that felt as open and empty as a dreamless sleep.

He could remember having this body. He could remember things like oceans and ice, leaves and the smell of lemons, but he could not remember what any of these things meant to him. He knew plates and spoons and how to use them, but not where he had first learned how. He felt the certainty that this little green horse had lived in his pocket, but he could not remember why, or where he had gotten it.

He felt like he had woken up from a dream he very much needed to remember, but the harder he thought about it, the more it faded. The few fraying threads he could grasp weren't enough to suggest the whole cloth.

The girl watched him, her blinking slow. The brown of her eyes deepened and warmed. Her sympathy was so heavy and covered in thorns he didn't know how to hold it. The compassion of these women and girls did not come without pity, and he bristled against it.

He could not remember if the three letters sewn to his shirt were the beginning of a verse, or the start of a name, or a warning declaring the thing he had done, the reason he had been sent here stripped of memory.

If it was a mark, he should wear it. Or as much of it as he knew, the three letters that had not been torn away.

"Fel," he said.

"What?" the girl asked.

"You thought my name was Fel," he said.

"Is it?" she asked.

"I don't know," he said. "But that's what I want you to call me. That can be the name you call me." It would be the name he called himself. *F-e-l*, the three letters left on him.

"Estrella," she said, fingers on the doorframe.

It was only after she left that he understood it was her own name.

This place, this house filled with women who treated him like he was a son, these gardens that spread out as wide as a sea, they were all too soft and too beautiful to be where he would pay for his sins.

Instead, he had done something he could not remember, and to punish him for it, to punish him for forgetting, God had taken the things he knew.

God had left him just enough to be sure he had existed before he had come to these gardens. Enough to leave him reaching for things he could not know.

His back felt hot and damp. He reached to take off his shirt.

On his back, his fingers found veins of harder, raised skin.

He turned to the mirror on the inside of the door.

Thick, pale scars crossed his back, like strikes of a knife over clay. With the sight of them, pain traced along each one, not alive in his body now, but remembered.

Even the memory of how much they'd hurt sank under the shame of realizing they marked him.

The grandmothers had seen them. When they'd taken off his clothes they had sucked air in through their teeth and echoed the word *pobrecito*. He thought it had been about his ribs showing, or the way his hair had gotten messy enough to make him look like a stray animal.

But it had been this.

He put his shirt back on.

He found the grandmothers with their Bibles, laughing together in a way he had never thought was allowed over those onionskin pages.

Their eyes all found him at once.

Their gazes made him silent.

He could not ask them to keep his secrets.

"Thank you," he said, realizing that they could have already told their daughters and granddaughters if they wanted to. They all could have driven him out of their house as a criminal or a heretic or whatever they decided had gotten him these scars.

That night, behind the door of that room they had put him in, he broke open. All the color, all the things he did not know, the paths of scarring under his fingers, broke him open. He bit the backs of his hands so he would not cry onto the wooden horses.

He had done something wicked enough for God to carve out the center of him, and bad enough that men had marked him with it. If that was true, these women were showing him kindness God would not have wanted for him. But God had hollowed him out, and now he was not strong enough to refuse as firmly as these women insisted.

He could not even confess his sins to them because he could not remember the ways in which he had fallen.

As he slept, he held all those wooden horses in his loosely cupped hands, hoping he would dream of the things he had lost. But he woke up with nothing but the feeling of a dreamless night, empty and unyielding. He surfaced to the feeling of petals brushing his skin and realized they were falling from the ceiling like snow at midnight. Blue, dark, and shimmering.

The marks of his own teeth had cut into the knuckles of his forefingers. The salt of his tears had dried pale on the winged horses, like frost coating their bright backs.

SEVEN

Without the horses to turn over in her hands, she didn't sleep easily. Without them to count like sheep, the night streamed out in front of her, smooth and endless.

There was magic to things that were familiar and ordinary. The way they were known was a kind of enchantment, and when they were gone, the spell broke.

Estrella had given him the horses because it had seemed like the kind thing to do. It had felt like returning something he had lost. But they had made him sadder, like their wooden wings opened something in him. That made her wish she'd hidden them all in her dresser, tucking them under her slips and sweaters so this boy, Fel, wouldn't have to see them. But she had offered them, and he had accepted them—more like a responsibility than a gift.

Each time she woke, Estrella checked the ceiling for the

green of vines and the blue of starflowers. But the space above Dalia's bed stayed clear, the wood bare. That was something.

In the morning, the man called Reid had not left. Estrella and her cousins knew because three of their grandmothers had gone up to the brick house. They had pretended they were there to clean it, and because men who stood so proud in pressed slacks and wrinkled shirts were used to having brown-skinned women wait on them, he seemed not to notice.

Worse than not leaving, he had unpacked his things into an empty room. Not Marjorie Briar's. Estrella was thankful for that. If he had stuffed his clothes into her inlaid dresser and slept in her four-post bed, Dalia would have slit his throat in his sleep.

In the old carriage house, he had parked a gleaming car, all leather and shined chrome. Gloria almost spit onto the steering wheel, and Calla asked if they could drag an old key across the paint.

"You're not doing anything," their mothers said. "You don't know anything about him yet."

But they didn't need to know more than that Bay did not want him there. They saw in how tightly she held her shoulders, like they were a wooden hanger and the rest of her was dangling loose like a coat. They saw it in how she set her back teeth as Reid walked across the grounds, pointing out retaining walls that needed repairing or rose trellises that seemed a little overgrown.

"Why don't we just go welcome him?" Azalea asked as the light was falling that afternoon.

Calla and Gloria looked ready to throw ice water on her, to break her out of the spell of this man's polished car and gold-banded watch.

"He's probably used to having girls like us fixing his drinks," Azalea said. "He won't give it another thought."

The pinched corner of her smile told the rest.

"So we get him drunk enough that he forgets his own name," Estrella said.

Azalea drew up one proud shoulder. "Then maybe we go through his things."

"Okay," Gloria said. "But how do we get him that drunk?"

"I know how to do it," Fel said.

Their eyes all found him. He'd been quiet, drawing so close to the edges of the room he seemed like a panel of wallpaper. Estrella hadn't noticed he was there.

"You know how to make drinks?" Gloria asked.

He blinked, like he was pulling back from his own words, surprised he had said them.

He had said them without thinking.

This would be how Estrella would get him to tell things he either would not say or did not believe he knew. She would get him to speak without thinking.

"I know how to make a drink that'll make a man like that get drunk quick," he said. "But it's not Christmas, so I don't think we have what we need for it."

He spoke without hesitation, but he had the slight edge of an accent that reminded Estrella of her grandmother's. But her grandmother's was both fuller and sharper, more certain. He seemed unused to the sound of his own voice.

"What do you need?" Dalia asked.

"Sherry," Fel said.

"Done," Azalea said. "We'll steal it from Marjorie's liquor cabinet."

"We don't steal from the dead," Gloria said.

"Why not?" Azalea asked. "She's not using it."

Dalia cut through their arguing with a sweep of her hands. "What else do we need?"

"Oranges," he said, wincing, like he was asking for the moon to pour out into cut crystal. "And sugar. Ice if you have it."

Azalea's look was tinged with pity, but brightened with her own amusement. "I think we can manage that."

Estrella wanted to pinch Azalea so she would not laugh at him. Whether this boy had loved a Nomeolvides woman a hundred years ago or not, they had his clothes and his wonder about phones and showers to tell them this was not his time. He had come from a time when poor men could not easily get sugar or oranges. These were things boys like him knew only on holidays.

The six of them went up to the great brick house. They filled the empty kitchen. Azalea and Fel went to work on the drinks, him pouring sherry and sugar and her slicing oranges.

Azalea set curls of rind on each glass. She grabbed one and took a sip. "You can't even taste the sherry." She passed it to her cousins.

"That's the idea," Fel said, with no trace of pride.

"I like you," Azalea said. "You're smarter than you look. I've decided you can be our brother."

Fel gave her a cringing smile.

A chill spun through the kitchen. Every time one of them declared him a brother or a cousin, or their mothers and grandmothers pronounced him a nephew or son, they remembered that they did not know what the gardens wanted.

Estrella was sure the gardens were asking them to care for him, proof that they would do anything, even look after a strange boy, in exchange for La Pradera saving Bay.

But that was only the part they knew. There would be more. The gardens never let themselves be understood this easily.

Azalea brought the drinks into a damask-curtained room. Bay and Reid sat talking on antique chaises, each upholstered with different color brocade.

Fel handed Reid a glass, and Azalea leaned down to Bay and whispered the reminder Gloria had asked her to pass on, that she should drink slowly. For a few seconds, the dark curtain of her hair shielded both her face and Bay's.

"It's expensive, Bay," Reid said as the Nomeolvides girls listened from the hallway. "All those parties."

"Those parties"—Bay struck each syllable hard—"kept this place going. They kept this town going. And they made sure the town loved us. That's more than I can say for any other estate this family has."

Reid let the insult fall. "I know they meant something to Marjorie. But now that she's gone, we have to think about the books."

How dare he.

Estrella felt the words rising in all of them.

This man couldn't dream to be even a shadow of Marjorie Briar.

Marjorie had loved this place like it was part of her own body. She had grown up at La Pradera because the Briars had exiled her father here for crimes she never spoke of. When she grew up, they mocked her investing money into bakeries and dress shops, whispering that the businesses of women would not give her the same returns as banks or silver mines.

But later, when the Briars had spent more money than they had, when they had almost ruined themselves trying to look wealthier than any other family, they tried to sell La Pradera.

Marjorie wasn't having it, not the sale of her childhood home. She prodded and stoked the rumors about the Nomeolvides women haunting the land, about their disappearing men, until no buyer would come near the property line. So the Briars had no choice but to let her pay the overdue taxes and declare the land hers.

Marjorie did not fear the lore of this place or the Nomeolvides women, the stories of disappearing men. These gardens were the home of her girlhood. She and the grandmothers built a steady business selling seeds and bulbs to rich men on the promise that they held a little of La Pradera's enchantment.

"We?" Bay asked. "'We' have to think about the books? I haven't seen you here for, what, ten years?"

"I came to help you," he said. "This place could be making more money than you know what to do with."

No.

Again, a word passed between the cousins like a breath.

No.

For months, Bay had lived with her shoulders a little rounded, made small not just by the loss of Marjorie Briar but by the understanding that she was expected to replace her. She would be the one the town looked to for those grand parties that kept the shops open. She would be the one to spin tales of what beautiful gardens wealthy men could expect if only they bought a little Nomeolvides enchantment for their own estates. She would be the one expected to remember a thousand names, the ages of children, the favorite books or colors that Marjorie recalled as easily as her own birthstone.

For months, Bay had been choking. Her flourishes had grown stiff, her smiles more nerves than charm. But with every meal in the Nomeolvides women's stone house, with every plate of mole poblano, Bay sat up a little straighter. A thread of light in her came back. Bay was coming alive again. "You watch, mijas," Abuela Mimosa said a week ago. "Three months, she'll be throwing an autumn ball as good as her grandmother's."

And now, this man was shoving his way into this house and deciding Marjorie's place was his.

And Bay was letting him.

Reid took another swallow of his drink, his posture a little looser than a few minutes before.

Azalea nodded to them. The other four took off their shoes so their feet would be silent. They rushed up the dark wood staircase and tore through Reid Briar's things.

Estrella and Dalia threw aside clothes and cuff links, books and boar-bristle shave brushes.

"Don't go so fast," Gloria said. "We have to put everything back where it was."

Dalia found a stack of papers in the lining of Reid's suitcase. She let out a whispered but triumphant, "Yes."

The heavy sheet of the cover page was printed with a lawyer's letterhead. Estrella caught several copies of a court seal. But the sentences, thick and dry, were slow to give up their secrets.

"It's in legal," Azalea said.

"Give me that." Calla snatched the papers, dividing them between her and Gloria.

They skimmed the pages, leafing through.

Their glances flicked up at each other at the same time.

They caught each other's eyes and fell into laughter so heavy they tumbled onto the thick duvet covering the bed.

"What?" Estrella asked.

The two laughing cousins tried to sit up, but one look at each other, and the laughter pulled them both under. The papers scattered over them like leaves.

Dalia grabbed at a sheaf of papers.

"Hey," Calla said, still laughing.

"As best I can tell," Gloria said, swallowing her own laughter, not looking at Calla in case it started her up again, "this shining tribute to the Briar name"—she consulted the papers again—"attended a party at another family's estate and started a fire that caused a fortune of damage before they could get it out."

Calla giggled, handing Dalia the letters to and from the lawyer's office. "He was trying to show off by lighting a cigar with a candelabra."

"That's not funny," Estrella said. "What if somebody was hurt?"

Gloria passed Estrella one of the papers. "Nobody was." She leaned on her elbow, the duvet fluffing up around her. "Unless you count the Briars' bank accounts. They paid for everything."

Dalia shook her head at the papers. "So that's what he's doing here."

"What do you mean?" Estrella asked.

"He thinks he can make money here," Dalia said. "He wants to repay it. Get back in their good graces."

"Fat chance of that," Calla said. "Did you see the amount?" She fell back onto the bed. "All those priceless books."

"Irreplaceable artwork," Gloria said. "Antique furniture."

"And the piano," Calla said, still lying down but lifting a finger into the air. "Don't forget the piano."

Dalia still shook her head. "I knew it."

"Knew what?" Gloria asked, dabbing tears from the corners of her eyes.

"This is where Briars get exiled," Dalia said. "No one ever came here because they wanted to. They sent him here."

The truth settled over Estrella.

La Pradera, as beautiful as the gardens made it, was the place the Briars banished relatives they wanted out of the way. Marjorie's father, with his shameful legacy she would never speak of. Bay, a child made by a Briar daughter's affair. And now Reid, who had cost his family more money than Estrella thought books and a piano could be worth.

A hundred years ago, this land was the ugliest of the Briars' estates. The great house stood on rocky ground overlooking a barren ravine. The Nomeolvides women had been making a home in town but were a few Sundays from being driven out as witches. Anywhere they tried to live, peonies and flowering willows broke through rafters. Water lilies choked ponds and streams.

So the outcast Briars issued to these women an invitation: *If you can grow anything on this land, you can live here, too.* The Nomeolvides women answered by turning this place into La Pradera, acres of blooms and flowering trees, a barren ravine coated in vines and blossoms until it was worthy of being called a sunken garden.

The only reason the other Briars didn't move in and take this place for themselves was the shadow of the Nomeolvides legacy, their fear that anywhere the women had touched was a place men disappeared.

"She's right," Estrella said. "He wouldn't be here if he had a choice."

"Maybe Reid's not as stupid as he looks," Gloria said. "You know what Marjorie used to say. When they're about to run you out of town . . ."

"Get in front of the crowd and make it look like the parade," Calla said.

Reid Briar meant to turn a punishment into an opportunity.

The four of them put everything back, smoothing the duvet, hanging the clothes up, sliding the papers into the suitcase pocket. They slipped back down the stairs and into their shoes.

Azalea and Fel were still keeping Reid's glass full. Estrella and her other three cousins stopped in the doorway so fast they bumped into one another, skirts brushing.

Reid, his eyes reddened from the sherry that did not taste like sherry, looked up. His gaze caught Fel's.

"I thought it was all girls here," he said.

Fel stilled.

"They're not girls, Reid," Bay said, "they're women. And he's theirs."

"Who is he?" Reid asked, as though the boy he was looking at could not hear him.

"He's our brother," Azalea said. And it felt true, like the land had given them a brother when they had never had one.

"He's our cousin," Gloria said at the same moment. And this too felt true, even though they had never had boy cousins, either.

The words spoken at the same time made Gloria and Azalea whip their heads toward each other.

Reid might not have known they did not have brothers or boy cousins, but they had wavered, and now he watched them all.

Fel looked at Estrella. The terror in his face was as clear as a spoken question. *Please don't tell him. Please don't tell this stranger what little you know and how I know even less.*

"He's with me," Estrella said. Not only because she had been the one to find him. Not even because her cousins blamed her little wooden horses for the appearance of this strange boy. But because this was an explanation for their nervousness that Reid might believe. That what they were hiding was how a boy none of them were married to lived with them. "He goes with me."

Reid looked from each of their faces to the next.

"Why didn't you just say that?" he asked. "There's no rule against that. That's allowed."

The tension came into Bay's jaw so fast Estrella could see it. She felt it in her own bones, the muscles around her mouth hardening.

Azalea looked at the rest of the cousins, one eyebrow lifting, her open-mouth smile showing how she was too disbelieving to be angry yet.

Under Reid's friendly permission was the rough ground of what he wanted them all to understand. He was here now, so he was the one who would say what was allowed.

Dalia leaned into Estrella. "I guess we get to keep him."

A breath fell from Estrella. Dalia was right. Now that Estrella had claimed Fel as theirs, they couldn't put him in this house, no matter what Bay had offered.

"Fel or Reid?" Calla asked.

"Both," Gloria said.

"Give it two days," Dalia whispered, with a flick of her eyes toward Reid. "Bay'll be sleeping with us to avoid him."

EIGHT

The man looked through Fel as though he were branches. As though he were leaves and the sun found the cracks in him.

The man called the Nomeolvides women, even the older ones, *girls*. To this man, Fel was probably *boy*. That would be his name. *Boy*. The man might not bother to call Fel anything else. If Fel bringing the man orange and sugared sherry in a heavy glass did not seal it, then the brown of his face and forearms would.

Fel could not remember where he had learned to make the thing Azalea had watched him pour into glasses. The sugar and ice, the orange and sherry. It was a trick, a way to get a rich man drunk. A thing someone had taught him.

Sherry tasted sharp and strange, but the bite of alcohol, that was familiar. Fel remembered a few spoons of red wine swirled in water, to make it safe to drink. He remembered the dark color tinting the water. He remembered holding the glass in hands smaller than his but the same brown. His own hands, but younger.

He was sure of this memory, but he could not find the edges of it. It was a sense so distant, so faint and worn that light came through it. It faded like a scrap of paper disintegrating, and then there was nothing but these gardens, and the brick house where he'd sliced oranges, and this stone house where the women told him he would stay.

It was Estrella's room he had slept in the night before. It was her clothes in the dresser he did not look inside. Her fingerprints on the brass lamp he did not turn on, and the window he neither opened further nor closed. He had not known it was her room, but his fingers prickled with the sense that he should not touch anything.

He knew now that it was hers, when she told him he would sleep there again.

"You don't have to do that," Fel told her, but she had already disappeared down the hall.

He tried telling her mother and then her grandmother that he could sleep anywhere. He could sleep on the woven rugs that softened their floors. He could sleep on the worn sofa downstairs. He could sleep outside, he told them, the feeling coming to him that he had done it many times before.

But the women laughed at him.

"I've seen those girls watch a lightning storm for a whole night," Estrella's mother said. "If there's not a door to stop them, they'll stare at you so hard you won't sleep."

He didn't know why he'd be worth staring at. The youngest one, Calla, studied him like he was something she meant to name and classify. Azalea had seemed wary of him until she saw he knew how to mix a drink, and now her wariness seemed to have passed to the oldest, Gloria. Dalia seemed not to notice bumping into him as they dried dishes, and this made him feel like she really did think of him as a brother, some relative who had always been here.

But Estrella. Estrella looked at him like he was something more than the awkward figure he saw in the mirror. That reflection, wearing borrowed clothes, seemed both odd and familiar in its oddness. But she watched him like he contained some kind of hope too fragile to name.

"I'm sorry," he said when he found Estrella. "I don't want to turn you out of your own room."

She shrugged one shoulder, an identical gesture he'd seen on her cousins. That shrug almost made him sure it didn't bother her.

"Don't be sorry for her," Dalia said, passing in the hall with her arms full of clothes. "I'm the one sharing a bed with her, and she drools in her sleep."

Fel tried not to laugh.

"Hey," Estrella said, following after her cousin. "I do not."

"Estrella," Fel said.

She turned around.

He let a question rise through him, one he hadn't been steady enough to ask until now. "Where am I?"

NINE

The sun fell below the trees. The shadows deepened, leaving just enough light for Estrella to lead Fel through the gardens.

They passed the Briar house. When Estrella was little, that long front of brick gables and dormer windows had seemed like a storybook castle. In the courtyard of blossoming trees, the grandmothers' magnolias and lilacs ringed a wide stone fountain, filling the air with the smell of sugar and wet petals.

Wooden lattices and rose trellises screened the beds of hyacinths, irises, and lilies. Tía Hortensia's hydrangea bushes grew clouds of blue and violet blossoms.

Behind the trellises, Estrella caught her mother's shadow. Through the crosshatch, she watched her mother setting palms to the wood. Her thin fingers gripped the lattices, and rose vines climbed the frame. Brambles twirled up toward the arbored ceiling. Leaves spread, finding the sun. Buds opened into tea roses so pale pink and peach they were almost white, and into wide blooms the yellow of candle flames or the deep red of black pearl peppers. They came in the soft tints of a shell's inner curves, and in colors as deep as ink and indigo.

Through the rose lattices, her mother watched her with something between observance and disapproval. Estrella wondered if she was already falling short of the task of showing this boy the gardens.

Estrella stood up straight as they passed through the checkered shadows of the trellises.

"It's called La Pradera," she told Fel.

"The Meadow?" he asked. She saw the thread of confusion slipping into his wonder.

"The Briars named it, not us," she said.

There was a kind of false modesty to the rich Estrella still didn't understand. An estate thick with gardens was called a *meadow*. Women in cream silk tipped a hand toward their dresses and said they'd *just thrown something on*. Even Marjorie had called her midsummer balls *little parties*.

"My family's been here for a hundred years," Estrella said. "Before that it was just rocks. Nothing grew but brush and wild grass."

Fel walked with her alongside a low garden bed. Fireflies lit the flowers, drawn by the damp air and the mild scent of azaleas and dahlias. During the hottest summer months, Estrella and her cousins slept in the afternoons and woke at dusk, gardening by the lightning bugs' glow.

The sunken garden opened in front of them. When the Nomeolvides women first came here with flowers waiting in their hands, it had been nothing but a jagged ravine.

Estrella led Fel down the sloping path to the sunken garden's floor. The deep, wide well sat several stories below the rest of La Pradera. The basin, lined with trees and hedges, ran down toward a carpet of green. Bright curving flower beds and cypress trees swirled through, the color softening in the morning and deepening in the evening. Blue hyacinths and morning glories made the shadows under the cypress trees richer. Globes of hydrangeas grew in the purples and fuchsias of sugar plums. Pink day lilies and burgundy calla lilies followed the waves of hedges. Flowering trees sprinkled petals over the stone paths.

At the sunken garden's deepest point, a pond went down forty feet. The number dizzied Estrella. Branches of trailing willows almost met at the water's center, so the thought of a pond that went down as far as it was deep made Estrella feel like she was looking into the night sky.

"We made it our home," Estrella said. "So now we live here."

Fel stopped on the stone path, looking at the color rising around him. His lips were a little parted, like his lungs were held in the place between taking a breath in and letting it out. The border between wonder and fear.

"You made all this?" he asked.

She nodded. "About five generations of us."

"How?" he asked.

She felt a smile coming to her. She knelt, grabbed his forearm, pulled him down so he knelt next to her. The sudden cool of the ground came through her skirt.

She plunged her hands into a flower bed, clutching palmfuls of dark ground. This was as second nature as shaking her hair out from a braid, but the shiver of it, the feeling of something living in her becoming visible, never faded. And Fel shuddered as though he could feel it.

Small sprouts broke through the dark ground. They twisted out of the dirt, the single point of green becoming four rounded leaves. The leaves lengthened, veins deepening. The green grew richer, more textured. Stalks appeared from the point where the leaves met, and from those stalks, purple-red stems curled out from the center. Pear-shaped buds weighted the purple stems, covered in faint down, like the bowing heads of swans.

She held on to the earth, and the buds opened into the bright purple-blue of borraja flowers, five-petaled like stars. Five thin fruit petals unfurled purple-red between the blue ones.

"Does it hurt?" Fel asked. "When you do that?"

She drew her hands from the earth, untangling her fingers from the new roots.

"It hurts more if we don't." She brushed her hands together, raining dark soil over the leaves.

Her fingers drawing out these blooms felt like letting out the force in her. It brought the comfort not only of releasing these petals from her hands but of deciding where and when they appeared.

She couldn't do anything about the confetti of starflowers

that grew over her bed some nights. It worried her cousins and their mothers and grandmothers. Not like she was a witch; the Nomeolvides women were used to being painted as witches. More like she was a girl who needed watching, a girl whose own gifts might betray her or give her away. But here, kneeling on the ground, Estrella could decide.

"Things growing just live in us," she said. It was true for all of them. For Estrella's cousins, for her mother, her cousins' mothers, all their grandmothers, there was order to it, lilies and irises growing only where they asked them to. But their inherited gift still put a kind of desperation in them, a need to grow what was in them. They all had it. It was a drive rooted as deep in each of them as it was in Estrella.

It was just that sometimes Estrella's appeared, unwelcome, as she slept.

"It's like words we need to say," she told him. "If we don't say them, it hurts."

Estrella could see Fel trying to keep the confusion off his face. Her family was its own language, its own country, and she knew it. She laughed, the wind throwing a ribbon of her hair across her cheek. When she brushed it away, she felt her fingers leaving a damp streak of earth across her forehead.

Fel reached for her, so slowly she could have leaned back and stopped him. He brushed his fingers over her forehead, his thumb warm on her skin. That one point of heat spread through her face. It bloomed in each of her cheeks.

The pad of his thumb on her forehead felt as rough as

unfinished wood. Callused. She had felt the calluses on his hands the first time she had led him from the sunken garden, their grain softened by wet earth. She'd registered the coarse brush of his fingertips when she'd set the little winged horses in his hands.

But it wasn't until now, with his thumb set against her skin, that she realized how hard and solid those calluses were.

She took light hold of his hands, turned them over. The calluses covered his fingers and palms, thick and pale as a dusting of sand.

"How did you get these?" she asked.

"I don't know," he said.

"Do they hurt?"

"No. Not now."

She brushed her fingertips along the center line of his palms, and he flinched.

"Sorry," she said.

She felt him pulling his hands back. It was so slight it felt like something he was doing without thinking, rather than him asking her to let go. In the slight closing of his eyes, she found the shame he felt over these calluses. She wondered if seeing Reid's hands on the cut-crystal glass had made it worse, the long, smooth fingers, the nails filed and squared off.

But to her, these calluses were things he should wear with pride, the way Estrella and her cousins showed off the half-moons of dark earth under their fingernails.

His calluses were beautiful things both because they were

signs of the work he had done, and because if he could remember what that work was, he would know a little more about what he had once been.

Who he had once belonged to.

Estrella let go. She sifted through things that might distract him. She shouldn't have turned over his hands, showing his rough palms, and now she wanted him to forget them.

"Have you ever heard the fairy tale about the red shoes?" she asked.

"No," he said.

"It's a story Tía Azucena used to tell us when we were little," she said. "I don't remember all of it, but there's a girl who loves dancing, and one day she wears her red dancing shoes to church when she's not supposed to, so the red shoes make her dance until she dies."

"That's the story she told you when you were little?"

"It was something like that," she said. "I don't remember all of it, and anyway, that's not the point. The point is, think of it a little like that."

"The flowers kill you?" he asked.

"No," she said. "I mean it's like dancing. We have to dance because it's in us. We can't not. But if we dance too much for too long it would hurt, because our bodies couldn't take it. It's like that with the flowers. We have to make them because it's in us. But we couldn't make this whole garden overnight. It would kill us if we tried. That's why it took a hundred years."

"Like a horse," he said.

"What?" she asked.

"You're like a horse."

"I'm telling my cousins you said that."

He smiled, and it looked so true she wanted to take it apart and see how it worked. How she could draw that smile out of him again.

"No," he said. "I mean if horses don't have the chance to run, they wither. If you keep them in stables, they end up kicking at their stalls. But if they get worked too hard, they get sick."

She didn't know about the comparison, this boy likening her and her cousins to animals. But before she could object, an idea flickered on with the garden lamps.

"How do you know about horses?" she asked.

He looked at the grass beyond the flower bed. "I don't know."

"Did you work with them?" she asked.

"I don't know."

Estrella slid her hands back into the earth, as much habit as a way to make him less conscious of her watching.

"Fel, I'm going to ask you something, and I really want you to think about it," she said.

"Okay."

"Were you ever in love with anyone?" she asked.

"I don't know."

"Anyone who looked a little like all of us?" There was no softer way to ask this. She wanted to know if he had belonged to a Nomeolvides woman neither she nor her cousins nor their mothers had been alive to know. Their grandmothers had no memory of a boy like Fel, even in stories.

"I don't know," he said.

"Did you ever love anyone?" she asked.

He shut his eyes. "Yes."

"Who?" she asked.

He shook his head. She was learning this was his short-hand for *I don't know.*

"Someone who took care of me," he said.

"Do you remember anything about her?"

He watched the borraja, the blue bright against the earth.

"No," he said.

She let the silence draw out. This was a place she couldn't press too hard. He was soft here. He would feel the pressure as pain and turn quiet.

"Did she give you the horses?" Estrella asked. "The wooden ones."

More borraja sprouted, first leaves, then stalks, then down-covered purple stems and sharp-petaled flowers.

"I don't know," he said.

"Do you know anything about them?"

"I know I loved them very much," he said. "But I don't know why."

He looked wound, coiled, even when he breathed out.

"It's okay," she said. "This isn't a test."

"Yes, it is," he said.

Now he looked at her. The light had turned from gold to blue, and the warmth in the brown of his eyes cooled.

She picked a borraja flower. "You can eat them, you know."

She held it out on her palm, the five petals opening into darker blue.

"Try it," she said.

"I don't think I should," he said.

"Why not?" She ripped away a handful of them, the star-flowers breaking from their vines. "I do it all the time."

Fel cringed like she'd torn out a lock of her hair. "But they're yours."

"And I'm giving these ones to you." She took his hands and let the confetti of blue petals rain into his palms. "So now they're yours."

TEN

He did not sleep, not more than a little at a time. When he did sleep, it was shallow and dreamless, the darkness reminding him of all he did not remember.

If he did not dream of this empty place, he dreamed of a cord of heat breaking him open, marking him with all he had done.

When he woke in the dark, his fingers found the blue borraja Estrella had set in his hands, and that he'd left on the bedside table. He grasped at them like they were slices of water. He felt struck with the certainty that they would let him sleep, make him sleep. It overcame how odd he felt putting into his mouth something she'd grown in front of him. He set the first flower on his tongue, the taste clean and cold, more like ice than something living.

He fell asleep with one in his mouth. But it only made him dream of her fingers brushing his lips. He startled awake, shivering like the air had fallen into winter.

How little he slept left the daylight hours in a haze as heavy as smoke. Maybe it was because he wasn't doing enough for these women who were looking after him. He wasn't wearing himself out enough by the time night came. His hands wanted to thank them in ways more than peeling potatoes or drying forks.

But the mothers shooed him away from helping them with the laundry, flapping dish towels at him and reminding him that he did not know how to work the machine. The grand-mothers took brooms out of his hands in ways that made him remember that this was their house, not his.

His hands still wanted to work. So he worked on things that had gone unnoticed. A crosshatch of wood was crumbling under the weight of rose vines, so he strengthened its base until it did not wobble. The paint on a bench was peeling away, so he searched through dust-covered cans until he found the shade that matched. He replaced a few flat stones that had come loose from a path.

"You're a good boy, mijo," the woman who insisted he call her Abuela Magnolia said. "Bay's grandmother never missed a stone out of place, but ever since she died"—the woman clucked her tongue—"that girl . . ."

Fel waited for her to finish the sentence. She didn't. He understood. That was the weight of Bay losing her grand-mother, a loss too heavy to name. Bay was mired too deep in it to notice small things falling apart.

He knelt at a crumbling stretch of low wall, checking

whether any bricks were missing or if they were just out of place, when Calla grabbed his arm.

"I need a favor," she said.

She was the first to notice that he understood what she and her cousins were saying. So he didn't dare stop her when she pulled him toward the house up the hill. When she shoved him through the door and into the hall, he didn't resist.

The inside of the Briar house looked more museum or palace than home. Portraits of white-haired men and gown-wearing women stared down from the walls. The rugs had been woven so finely Fel didn't want to walk on them. Even the ashtrays looked like some kind of glittering stone, maybe marble or quartz. Did people really stub out live embers in there?

Everything in the Nomeolvides house looked handled and used. Cast iron pans. Books with worn edges. Even the brass of an old kaleidoscope shined with the oils of their fingers. He liked this about them, about their home.

Calla shoved him down the hall, where Reid was coming toward them, eyes on a set of papers in his hands.

"Go talk to him," Calla whispered.

"What?" Fel asked.

"You're a man and he's a man," Calla said. "So just talk to him."

"About what?"

"Do I have to do everything?" Calla took Fel by the shoulders, which made him feel like he was a child she was crouching down to, even though she was younger and shorter. "I just need you to distract him for ten minutes while I go look at something."

She dashed out of the hall, leaving him in the path of Reid's stare as soon as he lifted his head.

"Oh," Reid said. "Hi."

The space of the few seconds made Fel forget what to do with his hands. Before he'd been sent here, what had he always done with his hands?

"I was"—as soon as the words came, Fel wished he hadn't said them so fast. If he'd waited to start the sentence, he would've had a few more seconds to think of the end—"just looking at these." He tilted his head up to the portraits.

"Oh," Reid said again, but this time a laugh brushed the word. "They're something, aren't they?"

"Are they all people you know?" Fel asked.

"Sort of," Reid said. "If our family had a charter, it would have a line about every Briar getting their portrait painted before they die. A few are here, but most are scattered around the other estates."

Scattered around? Fel imagined paintings left at odd angles like pieces of a shipwreck on a shore.

Reid stood next to Fel, eyes joining his on a painting of a standing woman. Against the wine red of her dress, her neckline looked pale as a pitcher of milk. Her fingers rested on a dark wood table. Her chin tipped up, like her eyes were following a bird the painter did not show.

"It's an old tradition," Reid said. "But I guess there's something charming about it. Thank goodness for pictures, right? Can you imagine the days when you had to stand there that long?"

Reid's words rushed past Fel. He couldn't imagine any of this, a family with enough money that every son and daughter was painted onto canvas as tall as they were. He thought most families could not afford a single photograph of themselves, or even mirrors to see their faces in.

He could not remember any photographs he had seen before La Pradera. He could not remember the details of faces caught in shades of brown. But he remembered how rare they were, the silver-plated copper, the flashbulb. And here, on these walls, in every space not covered with portraits or paintings of ships, there were photographs. Dozens just in this hallway.

"Is the one of Bay here?" Fel asked.

Reid's eyes left the portrait. "Bay?"

"The woman who—"

"I know who she is," Reid cut him off, the laugh coming back into his words. "Why do you ask?"

Fel shuddered under the feeling that he'd just failed some test of how well he was listening. "I thought you said you all had your pictures painted."

"Nobody told you?" Reid asked. "She's not a real Briar."

He said it without cruelty.

"But I thought," Fel started, and then paused. "Her last name."

"Her last name is Briar," Reid said. "She has some of our blood. But she's not one of us."

It was a plain correction, a statement of fact as simple as naming the woman in the dark red dress.

"She acts like she owns this place," Reid said. "But don't let her tell you what to do." He set a palm on Fel's back. "She has no business ordering anyone around."

The force of that hand made the hallway seem like it was folding in on itself. The dark walls were crumbling and collapsing toward them, the paintings scattering like shards of a broken window.

Fel shuddered away from it before he could stop himself.

"Okay," Reid said, lifting his hands as though to promise he would not touch Fel again. "You're all right."

This man was lying. Fel wanted to tell the old women this, show it to them like a lost, shining thing he'd found in the grass. But he didn't know what this man was lying about, and he had no way to prove it other than his own body acting faster than he could think. So the glittering thing he wanted to give the old women evaporated from his hands.

ELEVEN

They decided they would scare him off, this man who did not know these gardens. In the cupboards of the Briar house, Azalea grew green leaves that crowded the space between plates and bowls. Gloria's vines clung to the inner walls, dense as mulch. Dalia's fingers left flowers in the colors of fall trees, spilling off bookshelves and rising out of Reid's dresser drawers. Calla crowded his marble sink and enamel bathtub with lilies, their whirls of white shielding yellow centers.

They hid flowers in their mouths, parting their lips when Reid passed and showing the petals like white or blue tongues. When he turned his back, Estrella planted starflowers in his food. Pink blossoms poked up between the ice cubes in his drinks. White blooms dotted a plate of dry-sherry scrambled eggs. They drew vines up through the floor of his bedroom. The starflower stems, fuzzy and purple, came in so fast and thick they buckled the aged wood.

But he drank the coffee, ate the eggs. From their hiding places in the hall, Estrella and her cousins saw him crouch to the split floorboards, pinching stems between his fingers and shaking his head as though witnessing a wonder. When they flashed the flowers hidden under their tongues, he said, "Extraordinary," with the half-breathed reverence of seeing a saint's relic.

They had not frightened him.

They had impressed him. Each flower that grew where it did not belong, each petal flashed between their teeth, deepened his interest.

Marjorie had loved seeing princes and ambassadors stride onto La Pradera, sure that no country gardens could match their own walled grounds. She loved watching them struck silent by the sunken garden opening in front of them, a ravine of flowering color and rich green.

Now that wonder worked against Estrella and her cousins.

That night, Estrella flopped down onto Azalea's bed. "Now what?"

"We try something else," Gloria said.

Azalea sat at her mirror, brushing pins out of her hair. "Like what?"

"Can we send him back to whatever corner of the world the Briars threw him out of?" Dalia said.

Calla's shape appeared in the doorway, outlined by the hall's light. "That might be harder than we thought."

Estrella sat up. Gloria, Azalea, and Dalia shifted toward the door.

"We might have a legal problem." Calla sat on the edge of the bed. "Well, Bay might."

"What are you talking about?" Azalea asked.

Calla sighed. "Marjorie's will."

"Marjorie left La Pradera to Bay," Estrella said.

"It might not have been hers to leave to anyone," Calla said.

"How do you know that?" Azalea said.

"I read the deed."

"When?"

Calla shrugged. "When Reid wasn't looking."

She gave them the words, assuming they would recognize them. *Fee tail. Devise. Line of succession.* Some Estrella caught. Others slipped from her hands. She felt herself settling between her cousins. She was not Azalea, who was too bored to listen and so skipped to being outraged. Nor was she Gloria, her lips pressed together in a way that meant she registered all this a little faster than the rest of them.

But Estrella understood enough for her worry to gather with her cousins'. It was so thick in the air they were breathing it.

"If it's a legal problem, why can't Bay go to court?" Dalia asked.

"Yeah." Azalea nodded into the mirror. "If we can't get him out of here, a judge can."

"It's not just that," Gloria said, and that look, that apprehension over the things she understood that they did not, drew their faces toward her like trumpet flowers finding the moon. "It's that Reid and the rest of the Briars decided she's not one of them."

"But she is," Estrella said. "It's her last name, too. Her blood."

"The Briars consider her illegitimate," Gloria said. "Because she was conceived in an adulterous union."

"Stop it." Dalia rubbed her temples. "You sound like a priest."

"Not a priest," Calla said. "That's exactly what the Briars would say. They've probably already said it."

"But she was raised by Marjorie." Azalea held up a hand. "Marjorie's as much a Briar as any of them."

"And Marjorie paid the taxes on this place when they were about five minutes from losing it," Dalia said.

"It doesn't matter what's true," Gloria said. "It matters what the Briars think. If Bay fights this, they will ruin her. They'll not only throw her out of here. They'll cut her off. And if she isn't afraid of that, she's afraid of them making her life miserable. I would be. They could tell any lie they want about her and everyone would believe it, because they're the Briars. They make things true."

"They would do that to their own family?" Estrella asked.

"Did you hear anything she just said?" Calla asked. "They don't think she's family. If they did, she wouldn't be here alone."

"She's not alone," Dalia said. "She has us."

Azalea's eyes found each of theirs in the mirror. "So can we kill him?"

"Anyone falling for him?" Gloria asked. "That'd be one way to do it."

Azalea looked at them one by one. "Well?" she asked, cocking an eyebrow at each of them. "Any stirrings of love?"

Their shared laugh was small, but it was clean and rare

enough that it rang. In the days since Reid had come to La Pradera, they had not heard this laugh, the sounds of their voices threading together like they were singing.

It tasted sweeter in their mouths for being a shared joke about the thing they feared most. The way the force and poison of a Nomeolvides woman's heart was enough to make her lover vanish. How their love was a kind of killing frost.

Another shape cut through the light in the doorway. Not Calla, who was still swinging her legs off the edge of the bed.

Bay.

Estrella and her cousins shuddered, as though they had drawn her here by holding her name between them.

"I thought you should know," Bay said. "Reid and I are hosting a ball."

Estrella felt all their hearts rising to the possibility of what this meant. It was as sudden as the smell of lilacs in March. Maybe Bay had broken through the worry that she could never follow after Marjorie Briar. Maybe she was ready to hold her own parties where they sold rich men seeds and brought new health into town shops.

But Bay's smile was pinched. The name Reid twisted her lips like the bite of a fruit rind.

This was not a summer party to sell seeds. This was not some evening glowing with fairy lights, meant to stir the town's love for this odd, flowering place.

This was a thing Reid had demanded. He had forced Bay into it.

Marjorie had died, and ever since, the line of Bay's posture had slumped a little, even as she laughed. Reid would not wait for her to rise from the low valley of Marjorie being gone.

The Nomeolvides mothers and grandmothers had fed and cared for Bay for months, and a little at a time, sureness had straightened Bay's shoulders.

Now it was falling away like a dusting of snow.

TWELVE

He dreamed, and the tiny horses became things that were alive. They flicked their wooden manes. Their carved legs and wings came to life. A saffron-colored one darted across Estrella's dresser. A green one flew toward the windowsill. An almost-white one disappeared into the sheets. They cantered into the cracks between floorboards, falling into dark places his fingers could not reach.

They were scattering, and he would lose them, these carved wooden horses that meant something he could not remember.

Their names. Their names were drifting through his dreams, but when he reached out for them, they flitted away from his grasp.

He had to round them back onto the shelf. If they left him, they would never tell him their names. If he lost them, he would never know why touching them made his heart feel both hollowed out and so heavy his chest could not hold it. He chased them toward the windowsill, across the floorboards, behind the dresser.

But he could not find them. They were too fast, and too small. By the time he noticed each flash of color, it was gone. One appeared in the air in front of him, wings beating like a hummingbird's, but he reached out for it, and his hand found nothing.

Those little horses were so much part of him that losing them emptied him. They were organs that had chosen to leave his body.

A blue one shook its mane and turned blue violet. It skittered off a shelf and landed on an outstretched hand. That palm stood pale against brown fingers.

He followed that hand, the wrist and arm, looking for who they belonged to. He found a girl who looked like Estrella but who was made of petals. She had Estrella's dark hair, loose and unbrushed, but dotted with blue violet. Her body was covered in forget-me-not petals, like she was growing them from her skin. They caught on her eyelashes. They stood in for fingernails. They followed the curves of her breasts.

Only a little of her showed through. Her lips looked red but unpainted, like she'd bitten them. Her eyes shone brown black. Forget-me-nots covered her body in blue that, on her hip or shoulder or the small of her back, blushed purple.

She laughed, and it sounded like an echo. She lifted the carved horse to her face like she was talking to it, and the world sank underwater. Through the window, the silhouettes of trees against the dark sky turned to streaks of paint. The floor looked like wood-colored waves.

But the petals on this girl's body, those sharp, papery edges, were clear as a bird's waxed feathers.

Flickers of forget-me-nots fell past the window, like a rain of blue flames. Those purples and blues softened and brightened. Light from inside caught in their curves. In one minute they looked soft as new snow. The next, hard as slices of a frozen river.

They were her body, her skin, her name. The girl covered in forget-me-nots spoke. But her voice sounded underwater, or like she was calling him across this valley made of flowers.

He woke enough to feel her hands, and know that, this time, he was not dreaming her. But he did not wake up enough to open his eyes, or to speak.

Her touch left the taste of that borraja flower on his tongue, sweet, a little like honey, but also clean as frost. What he imagined it would be like to taste a piece of the sky.

His palms were hot and damp against hers. The heels of her hands pressed into his, pushing him down against the bed, giving his body enough gravity that he would stay and not dream.

She did this first with his hands. Then with his shoulders, her palms weighting him down. Then his forehead, the sweat on his hairline cooling in the spaces between her fingers.

This is where you are, she whispered. *Stay. Don't go off where you're going.*

Through the blue-gray veil of sleep he understood. She was stopping him from drifting away. She was anchoring him to this bed so his dreams could not draw him up into their current like dust into the air. She was pulling him back from the place where he dreamed about scars appearing on his back, that feeling like he was being cut open with a rope made of embers.

The petals went dark, one at a time like blown-out candles. Then there was nothing but night sky, and her hands, and these whispered words.

Stay. A thing she told him to do for no other reason than *This is where you are.*

THIRTEEN

In the morning, Estrella did not find her mother's shadow behind the rose trellises.

Her mother found her first, catching her by the hair.

Her mother's scent, a combination of the roses and the perfumed powder she sprinkled on the back of her neck, drifted over her. It was a scent that matched her name. *Rosa.*

Her mother's grip on her hair was hard, a few strands caught on her nails and pulling at the roots. But even that slight pain was as familiar as her great-grandmother's woven blankets. It was a thing that seemed to calm her mother, grasping Estrella's hair like she was a doll.

She did it when Tía Azucena went through her closet; she'd held Estrella's braid while whispering, *If she borrows another of my skirts without asking, I'll grow thorns through all her dresses.*

She did it when Abuela Mimosa would not stop refolding

the sheets Estrella's mother had put away; she clasped her hands on either side of Estrella's head and whispered through clenched teeth, *Que Dios me ayude, if she does it again, I'm hiding them, all of them.*

She did it when everyone was arguing about whether there should be one or two services for Bisabuela Mirasol and Bisabuela Luna, the sunflower and moonflower cousins who'd died within a week of each other. Her mother had come into her room in the middle of the night and whispered, *They're going to argue themselves into their own graves. Then I'll have to plan everything for them, too!* She had said it with such dramatic weariness, collapsing onto the bed in a way Estrella knew was meant to make her laugh.

But now there was a sharper cut to the way her mother held her hair.

"If you spend another night in his room," her mother whispered, "I will wring your neck like a chicken."

"I didn't spend the night in his room," Estrella said.

She had heard him through the door. The soft noise held at the back of his throat had been half groan, half whimper, like he was choking on the sound.

"He was having a nightmare," she said. "I woke him up."

"Don't," her mother said. "Don't go near him at night."

"You thought he was a good sign." Estrella turned her head, her mother keeping a hold on her hair. "You all thought that."

Her mother pressed her lips together, a look Estrella had seen on her own face and on her cousins'. Even through generations, she and her family were all such copies of one another. But her mother's fingers were so much longer than Estrella's, her face so much thinner, her arms floating with a kind of grace Estrella could only stumble after, that they looked alike more in their expressions than their features. Azalea and Gloria looked more like her mother than she did.

"That was before I realized he doesn't sleep," her mother said.

"He does so," Estrella said.

"He dreams but he doesn't sleep."

"If he dreams, he's sleeping."

"He doesn't really sleep." Her mother let go of her hair. "He doesn't go to that still place where everything is quiet. And that means there's something that won't let him sleep. With men, it's almost always their own guilt."

"If you're so worried about him, why are you letting him stay?" Estrella asked.

"Because he means something. And we don't know what he means yet."

They didn't know, but they all had their hopes that it wasn't just this one boy. They all hoped he meant more than himself. He was the possibility of lost loves found, of legacies broken, of their hearts being built for something other than sorrow. He was the chance that the raw will of La Pradera was stronger than the curse they passed down like antique lace.

Fel was the glimmer that let them imagine that others might

reappear after him. Even the most wary and superstitious among them could not turn their backs to this.

Especially not Estrella and her cousins. None of them spoke of their own wish that La Pradera might break the curse of their five loves, that it might protect Bay. But Estrella could feel it mirrored between their hearts, fragile and identical.

"Gloria said we should show him the kindness we would show our brothers if we had any," Estrella said. "So did Abuela Lila. So that's what I did. I did what I'd do for a brother."

It's what she and her cousins had all done for one another, when they were children who did not understand that it was falling in love, not just any love at all, that could end in vanishing. They had clutched one another, shaking each other out of their nightmares that the way they loved their mothers and grandmothers could make them all disappear.

Gloria and Dalia had held Azalea while she wailed, wondering if giving her grandmother a birthday present was too much love, and would it make her turn to air? And then, years later, Azalea had stroked her fingers through Calla's hair and whispered that, no, loving their family would not make it all turn to dust.

That's never happened, Azalea whispered, in a gentler voice than Estrella thought she could ever hold on her tongue. *Not in a hundred years of being here. Not in a thousand years of being everywhere else we were before here. We keep our mothers and abuelas. We're stuck with them.*

Under her mother's gaze, the soft memory iced over.

"Wait," Estrella said. "This isn't about him, is it?"

Her mother looked away.

"This is about me," Estrella said. "You didn't say you don't want all of us around him at night. It's just me, isn't it?"

Her mother surveyed the ground at her feet.

"I think you could bring out the worst in each other," she said. "He doesn't sleep, and when you sleep, things happen."

"'Things happen'?" A laugh broke from Estrella's lips. Her mother wasn't one for softening the names of things, but even she couldn't leave bare the truth of starflowers growing from ceilings. *Things happen. Things* meaning Estrella's name wrapping around the rafters at midnight. "You named me for those things."

Other Nomeolvides girls were christened with flower names, guiding the form their gifts would take. Gloria covered the sunken garden's walls with morning glories, the leaves brilliant green as the flowers were blue and purple. The cream and soft rust petals of Dalia's blooms grew wide as dinner plates, and Azalea's bursts of flowers turned whatever sunrise color she wanted. Even as a baby, Calla got her hands around fistfuls of earth until the bells of lilies sprouted toward the light.

But Estrella's mother had instead christened her after the stars.

"You wanted me to have this name," Estrella said.

"And I made a mistake."

The word cut in like the slip of a needle.

Her mother drew her long fingers toward her mouth, covering

it. Not with the panic of saying something she did not mean. More like the regret of saying something she had never meant to speak aloud.

"You know why I did it," her mother said.

Of course Estrella knew. Her mother had hoped that a name that was not a flower could free her daughter from the blessings and curses of being a Nomeolvides woman.

"And look how well it worked," Estrella said.

From the stories her grandmother told, Estrella had been only two when she grasped handfuls of dirt and made pink starflowers. In the bath, she had splashed the water until borraja vines choked the drain.

And now, the starflowers on her bedroom ceiling must have been too much like tulips or Mexican sage, showing up without warning. Those blue petals were too close to the unexpected blooms that condemned girls to being called witches.

Standing here, with her mother who would not quite look at her, Estrella hated that ceiling of blue stars. And she hated her mother a little for what she'd named her.

She hated her name the way she'd never hated it before, now that it was hitched to that word. *Mistake*. It was like a new middle name.

"Estrella," her mother said. "I love what you are. And the mistake was mine, not yours."

Estrella flinched at the word again, wondering if she'd been mouthing it in a way her mother could see.

"Abuela warned you," Estrella said.

Her grandmother had told her mother; women before her had tried giving their daughters names that were not flowers. Azalea's great-grandmother had been named Luna and had spent her life drawing night-blooming moonflowers up from sandy earth, half of them as she sleepwalked across La Pradera. Three generations ago, a girl had been christened Maria, only to grow up with a gift for making Castilian roses, the kind la Virgen revealed to Juan Diego. A Nomeolvides woman named Alba had a gift for apricot trees; they flowered on La Pradera for forty years after her death.

And now Estrella, a girl whose flowers did not keep to where her hands put them. A girl whose mother wanted her to stay far from the boy she'd found in the gardens, because she feared their dreams and nightmares touching.

"Just tell me something," Estrella said. "Are you protecting me from him or him from me?"

"I just don't want you around him at night," her mother said. "I worry about whatever is in him calling to something in you. I don't want his dreams coming off on you. Stay away from boys who don't sleep."

A scream cut through the gardens. It had the far echoing sound of coming across the flower beds and paths. It broke into a sob, and as it broke it took the sky with it, ripping it in half like paper.

Estrella and her mother followed the sound. They each held hands to their throats to make sure they were not the ones making it.

They passed under the shadows of cypress trees.

Two figures showed against the green hillside.

Reid, taking slow steps back. Dalia, yelling at him, shoving her palms against his shoulders. He looked more startled than angry, like he thought Dalia was something feral he might provoke with any small movement.

"You did this," she said, her words shredding into screams. "This happened because you came here. She didn't want you here."

On the back of her tongue, Estrella found the bitter taste of blood and pollen, the taste of death for girls who strayed from La Pradera. The salt and bite would rise to each of their lips if Reid turned them off this land.

"You did this." Dalia threw her hands into Reid hard enough that he stumbled back. "This place was protecting her before you came here, and you ruined it."

Estrella ran at Dalia. She threw her arms around her cousin from behind, pulling her off Reid. Dalia cried out, but Estrella held on.

Dalia's scream collapsed, splintering into sobs. Estrella kept her hold, her grip keeping Dalia from sinking to her knees.

"What happened?" Estrella asked, grasping her cousin so tightly her mouth was against Dalia's hair.

Dalia sobbed harder, each cry rattling through her body so Estrella felt it.

"What happened?" Estrella asked, raising her voice to cut through Dalia's.

Dalia's words came broken. They rose between sobs a few at a time.

Estrella caught them and strung them together.

She's gone. She's just gone.

Dryness spread over Estrella's tongue. It felt like a stone in her mouth.

Bay.

Their love had taken Bay.

Dalia let a few words break from her lips, like she was surfacing between waves. How Bay had been there and then, in a whirl of wind, had disappeared.

She had seen it. Dalia had seen it happen.

Estrella had always thought this part of the curse was pure rumor, the stories about lovers disappearing right in front of them, even vanishing from their hands as they held them. They had all thought they could count on this, that they had been spared the sight of their lovers vanishing.

Instead, lovers were lost at night, a Nomeolvides woman waking with a gasp from a dream. She rose from the nightmare of losing her love, and, for one half-asleep moment, felt the relief of it having been a dream. Then the next moment came, when the dragging weight of her own heart made her realize it was true.

Or, as she knelt in the garden, her heart turned and felt as though it was cracking, a stone breaking open and showing the crystal inside, and she knew.

But Dalia. Dalia had witnessed the moment of losing Bay. She had seen her fading into the air.

With each string of words, Estrella shut her eyes harder. Even with so few words, Estrella could see it. This thing the Nomeolvides girls had all feared since the day they realized their childhood love had grown with them.

Bay was dust stripped from the ground. She was rain swept across a valley. She was a veil of sand shimmering gold and then dissolving.

In one moment she existed for them to touch, and then was nothing.

The wind threaded between Estrella's lips.

Bay could not be gone from here. She was as deeply rooted in La Pradera as the magnolia trees. She cast a shadow as strong as the tallest hedges.

There was no La Pradera without glimpses of Bay. Marjorie braiding her hair. Bay poking the back of her grandmother's chair with the button end of her épée, needling her into a hand of baccarat banque. Those satin trousers that made Bay look like a centuries-old portrait but that she wore so well other rich daughters had pairs made for themselves.

Now Bay had vanished the same as Calla's father, and Abuela Flor's lover, and the man who collected maps, and anyone who loved too deeply and stayed too long.

They had done this. The venom of their own hearts had collected like rain, and they had done this.

Estrella and Azalea had done it when they fought about who Bay thought was prettier, fraying the ribbons in each other's hair and leaving bruises on each other's shins. Azalea writing Bay's name in places it would lay against her bare skin had done this. Calla falling in love with the smell of yew wood and how close it was to the scent of Bay's hair had done this.

Gloria keeping that creased photo at the bottom of her drawer. Dalia swallowing two glasses of sparkling wine at a summer ball and then wrapping Bay's braid around her fingers and whispering against her neck.

Estrella thinking of kissing her every time the wind stirred up scent of lily magnolias, like lemons and worn linen. She imagined pressing her lips to Bay's so lightly the wind would find its way between them.

They had loved her in ways that streamed from their bodies as much as the flowers they grew. Estrella had loved her in the blue and white and pink of starflowers. Azalea had loved her in sherbet-bright blooms. Calla had loved her in straight-stemmed lilies, Dalia in countless cream petals, Gloria in bells that opened at first light.

They had each been a little bit in love with Bay Briar. And this had been such strong poison that their nighttime offerings could not temper it. The truth of it sank into Estrella with the heat of her cousin's back, the damp and blossom-sweet warmth of her wearing-off perfume, the sour salt smell of the tears glossing her cheeks.

Bay. They had, all five of them, killed Bay.

FOURTEEN

For the first nights, he heard them in their rooms. The Nomeolvides girls bit their pillows as though this would keep them from crying. He heard the rustle of pillowcases against sheets, the wet, rough noise caught in their throats.

Their mothers gathered on the worn sofas downstairs, running their thumbs over the rims of ceramic cups. From the way they shook their heads at their roselle tea, Fel thought that the mothers were grieving, too. They were grieving for Bay, who they'd all lost, though no one would say how she'd died.

But the mothers tilted their heads toward the ceiling; their daughters' sobs were coming through from the floor above. They were crying more for the breaking of their daughters' hearts than for the loss of Bay Briar.

Their own mothers, the Nomeolvides girls' grandmothers, sat outside on wooden benches, reading from their Bibles in soft voices and praying with their heads bowed to the grass. The sky clouded over. Rain beaded the leaves like drops of glass, and a spring wind left the air cold. But still, they read to one another from their Bibles, and they stayed.

Fel pulled wool blankets down from the linen cupboard and left them folded at their feet. But they did not take them, as though the penance of their own bodies might bless their granddaughters.

He searched for some thread of grief in Reid. Some halted breath. Some pause as he stepped onto the paths Bay had walked. But Reid had meant the things he had told Fel under the stares of painted men and women.

Reid and Bay did not belong to each other. He did not consider the loss of her as something that was his. He did not wear the dark colors the Nomeolvides family wore, the younger ones in purples and greens, the older ones in black and brown.

After a few days, Reid prodded them all into town and into a shop where Fel could not see walls. There were only dark suits and bright dresses and angled mirrors that reflected them back over and over.

Reid wanted them all measured. But the Nomeolvides grandmothers did not close their Bibles and prayer books. They did not give up their rosaries. They did not lift their eyes. They did not yield to the women trying to push them toward the mirrors. Their weathered hands held on to the beads and the leather covers. So the women at the shop had to work around the Bibles and prayer books and the red glint of the rosaries. They had to weave their measuring tapes over and beneath.

The Nomeolvides mothers tried to lift their daughters' chins. They tried to make them laugh, told them that maybe Reid would set a tablecloth on fire with a candlestick and have to leave La Pradera. Maybe he would set so many things on fire with so many candles that there would be no place in the world that would want him.

But their cheer sounded so dry and forced, Fel expected it to catch in their throats.

As the women at the shop turned and measured them, Estrella and Gloria stared out the windows, as though they might catch Bay passing by. Calla held her hands lightly cupped in front of her, like she was holding something that might fly from her palms if she drew her fingers apart. Azalea winked to the women in the shop, setting a fingernail to her teeth, tilting her head back with a silent laugh when her flirtation made them shiver.

Dalia kept her eyes on the corner point between the ceiling and two walls. As a measuring tape whipped across her waist, Fel saw she was holding her back teeth together, flinching at the touch of hands she did not know.

Fel looked away, feeling guilty for watching.

He tried to draw out anything he might know about the town's main street. But it seemed as far from his memory and as unfamiliar as the garden valley. Like all those flowers, it dizzied him. Everything seemed so defined, so bright, it felt sharp. The cobblestones looked as perfect as the brick of the enormous house. The coverings arching out from the storefronts were as green as La Pradera's lawns. The dresses in the window were as complicated as the flower-covered arches, frilled skirts puffing away from dress forms.

Everything here—even the white trims and the tints of the palest flowers in the window boxes—looked clear, the edges cutting. The far memory of where he had once come from, small and blurred, felt both duller and warmer. He felt its colors, not bright, but gray, brown, its most vivid shade the auburn of rust.

The contrast between this place and what little he remembered pressed cold against his skin. His fingers prickled with wanting to cross himself, to join in the grandmothers' prayers.

But the loss of Bay was not his, and this family was not his, and he had no place shoving his way into their blessings and whispers.

Coming back to the gardens, seeing the wild land that led to the scrolled iron gates, stirred something in him. It felt like a single dark point spinning between stars.

He brushed his fingers over the woody stalks and purple-spined flowers of milk thistle.

He had gathered these from the roadside, brought them back to the one who was taking care of him. He and the one who had taken care of him had peeled away the spines and eaten the stalks and hearts and leaves.

In spring, they had filled their arms with dandelion greens and snapped wild asparagus from their stems, sunrise turning the tips gold.

In fall, they had been so hungry they took their chances with wild mushrooms and feral grapes one color off from nightshade berries.

They had eaten the blue, star-shaped flowers Estrella drew up from the land.

He felt the tastes of all these things in his mouth, all seasons at once. His heart filled with the remembered joy of finding things that were safe to eat, and his stomach wavered with the memory of his fear and hunger when they had to eat things not knowing if they would make them sick.

He sealed this grief and wonder inside him, locked them behind a heavy door. He did not want them crowding the stone house. There was already so much grief and worry thickening the air.

That night, as the sun drifted down into the garden valley and the blue of the sky deepened, Estrella and her cousins crowded into Dalia's room. No lights on. Azalea and Gloria lay on the bed, Azalea's head resting on Gloria's stomach. Calla settled into a nest of pillows she'd thrown on the floor. Dalia sat on the windowsill, one bare foot dangling off, her eyes on the window like she was waiting for the stars to tell her something.

They had cried themselves out, all of them. Except Dalia, who Fel had seen outside, arms wrapped around herself against the chill. Dalia did not wail or sob. She faced the moon with her back and shoulders straight, her jaw held tight, and Fel wondered if this was a sign that maybe Dalia loved Bay a little harder.

Not more than the rest of them. Not deeper. Just harder. It had taken such sure root in her that when it pulled away it turned her up like the ground.

Estrella lay across a woven rug, her shoulders against the rough wool. A bar of light from the hall fell across her stomach and hips. It caught in the folds of her slip. Through the thin fabric, he could make out a softness in her stomach and thighs that he hadn't noticed through her dresses and skirts. Her breathing was so slight and shallow he had to stare to find its rhythm. Her eyes took in the ceiling, head tilted like she had never considered it from this angle.

They all shared so many features, the Nomeolvides girls. Maybe Estrella's hair fluffed out, neither curly nor straight, and Dalia's fell in coils, but they still looked more like sisters than cousins.

The same with the older women. They shared a similar half-curl to their silver and black hair. One might have six or seven inches on another, and a rounded face instead of a pointed chin, but they all seemed like photographs of one another, younger and older, shorter and taller, fuller and bonier.

The guilt of watching Estrella and her cousins crawled over the backs of Fel's hands. He passed their door.

The things he had remembered spun inside him, insisting he do something with them.

He did not know how to thank these women for feeding him and giving him a place to sleep and lending him clothes owned by men he had never met.

But he could do this.

No part of this house was his. But he had dried enough dishes and scrubbed enough pans that their kitchen was familiar country. They had sent him out to the garden for squash blossoms and oregano lace enough that his hands could pick leaves from the wooden box planters without him thinking.

He could only remember ever cooking one thing that he would be unashamed to serve these women; the thing he and the one who took care of him ate when they had money to buy food. And he could do it with the least costly things in their kitchen. He could cook for these brokenhearted women who had forgotten to feed themselves.

Fel remembered hands gesturing over a meat counter. Negotiating. The one who had taken care of him talked butchers into giving them the fat trimmed off good cuts of meat for a few pennies or for nothing. They rendered it into manteca, spiced it, and then poured it over stale bread, again bought with pennies.

Now Fel stood in the Nomeolvides kitchen, melting down manteca, dyeing it red with paprika and chili powder. He tore green herbs into pieces, letting them fall into the bright sauce.

For a minute, this was his family and his family's kitchen. The sage-colored walls and the deep orange of the tablecloth. The copper pots and cast iron pans.

This could be a place he could be unashamed to come through the door holding wild asparagus and dandelion greens.

He sliced day-old bread and spread it over a metal sheet. He brushed it with olive oil and garlic cloves and left it in the oven until the edges browned.

As he swirled the spoon through the wide copper pot, this family and this kitchen felt so much like his that he didn't worry about the paprika staining the wooden spoon. He stirred in bay and oregano leaves, and they sank into the manteca colorá. The stems gave off a low, bitter smell that made him remember the gold and orange of fall leaves.

He did not know if it was the bite and warmth of paprika in the air, or the noise of spoons against the copper pots, but he did not have to ask the women to come downstairs. They came, and they did not order him out of their kitchen. The grandmothers tied the extra herbs with twine. The mothers took down plates from the cabinets and set them out on the long wooden table.

Then the daughters came, barefoot and with their hair unbrushed, their grandmothers' handed-down sweaters over the slips they wore to bed.

Gloria put out water and wine. Calla let a cotton napkin flutter to each place setting. Azalea took handfuls of knives and forks from the drawers.

Fel almost told Azalea that this was nothing worth the glint of hammered nickel and copper, that he could not remember eating this with anything other than his hands. But he kept quiet.

Estrella stood in the kitchen doorway, her eyes looking red and soft, her lips parted with a kind of surprise that made her seem like she was reconsidering him. She wrapped the too-big sweater around her, the pale blue of her slip falling to her knees.

She held one hand to her chest like she was keeping her heart from breaking out of her. She looked at his paprika- and herb-stained fingers like this small thing had both wrecked and mended her.

That look, like he had overwhelmed her in a way that both broke her heart and held it inside her, was enough that he wanted to remember everything he had ever been and done. Even if it was marked by the scars crossing his back, he wanted to remember.

He wanted to sift through it all to find the things that would make her look at him like this.

The light of her watching left him, worry covering her face when she saw Dalia. She took Dalia by the shoulders and led her to the table.

Fel spooned the manteca colorá over the bread, softening the edges. He served the Nomeolvides women, grandmothers and mothers and daughters, hoping they would speak, talk to one another about anything, knowing they wouldn't. He sat down with them, and they ate. The paprika's spice slid over their tongues, the herbs coming up through the red enough that they still tasted green and alive.

FIFTEEN

The arrival of the slim-skirted woman shouldn't have worried them. They had seen women like her before, walking the paths in oyster-colored high heels, the points catching between flagstones.

But this one kept a leather folio in her arms. She made notes like an appraiser. She did not bother to introduce herself as Marjorie's friends always had. Without warning, the woman ordered the brick house be cleaned and stripped of its older drapes, ones fraying to threads because Bay had loved rubbing the cloth between her fingers. She hired decorators who spent hours deciding on the right fabric to drape the ballroom. She brought in winemakers who laid out bottles for Reid to consider.

"A family friend," Reid said. "She's doing me a favor."

This was his version of an apology for how the woman picked at every loose stone and stray vine.

The grandmothers cast their eyes toward Estrella and her cousins, each grandmother watching her own granddaughter, searching for five identical nods that would say, yes, they understood they had to obey.

They could grieve Bay. But they could not grieve her by defying this man who now held La Pradera and so held their lives.

We stay here or we die, Abuela Mimosa had reminded them the night before. *That means we obey whoever rules this land.*

From behind the trellises, they watched the woman. She waved a hand and told Reid they would need more flowers.

"We need so many we can cut all the ones for the arrangements without anyone noticing," she said. "I want everyone to drop dead when they see this place."

"You first," Azalea whispered, and for the first time in days the cousins had to hide their laughs behind cupped hands.

Bay had vanished into the air like salt into water, and the only attention Reid had was for the plans of some woman he would probably take up to his room.

Or his car.

That afternoon Estrella passed the carriage house, and a shriek of laughter came through the wooden doors. "Reid!" in a girl's voice, slipped between two full laughs.

Estrella edged toward the carriage house, setting her hands against its stone face. She was just tall enough to look into one of the glass panes that broke up the dark-stained barn doors.

Reid and the woman had stuffed themselves into his gleaming convertible. Not in the seats, but across them, lying on their sides. Reid kissed her hard enough that she backed against the dashboard, and she kissed him hard enough to press him against the seat. Estrella wondered how they weren't catching the gearshift in their backs.

Reid clutched a bottle of whiskey, label gleaming gold. His arm trailed out of the front seat.

Their kissing, the spilling-out of their limbs, brimmed with mischief but seemed emptied of passion.

They weren't in love.

They were just bored.

The woman's shoe stuck out of the front seat, the kind of simple but precise heel that cost more than anything Estrella owned. And this woman was wearing it not with Sunday clothes but with a faded dress, no bra.

That was the thing about people with so much money. They could throw on dirty clothes picked up from their bedroom floor and still seem finished. They could wear expensive shoes with cheap shifts and look as though they were setting the dress code.

And Reid. He was two or three drinks in. Estrella knew for sure when he accidentally hit the horn with his elbow and collapsed into laughter as deep and real as the girl's.

Estrella pushed herself off the barn door, calling Reid *pendejo* under her breath all the way back to the stone house. But the next afternoon, when she saw the woman crossing La Pradera in a different pair of shoes, pearl-colored this time, she felt a question twirling inside her like a curl of smoke.

How did that work? How did two people kiss and slide hands over each other's shoulders without the specter of a vanishing curse watching them from the corner?

The question clung to Estrella's skin, walking up and down her forearms with the lightness of a moth's feet.

It distracted her later, when she put her hands into the dirt, the current from her palms stirring buds from the earth. It even distracted from the things that distracted her the rest of the time. Her cousins' dahlias and morning glories, which looked so much like they were cut from silk her wonder over them never faded. The grandmothers' trees bursting into bloom so full they looked like whirls of cotton candy. Her mother's shape and shadow as she painted the wooden trellises in roses.

But that crawling feeling, the moth's weight of that question, drew her until she was sneaking back toward the carriage house the next afternoon.

Estrella stood on her toes, peering through the glass and looking for the woman's good shoes and Reid's creased shirt. If she were a little taller, like her mother or Gloria or Calla, she could have stayed on flat feet.

Her thought of Gloria and her mother drifted away on the wind, but Calla.

Calla.

Her thoughts of Calla stayed, blazing in front of her.

Reid and the woman had not thrown themselves into the car.

The butterscotch leather of the seats had been darkened with handfuls and more handfuls of wet earth. Green stalks rose thick and bright, cracking the upholstery. Long leaves sheltered the stems.

And capping each stalk was the curving bell of a calla lily. Some grew orange, blushed with red, some so burgundy they look wine-stained. Others were deep purple edged in cream.

But they were all the work of her youngest cousin's hands. Her youngest cousin, whose name had blessed her with a gift for growing perfect calla lilies.

It drew the breath out of Estrella's throat. It was stunning and bright as the sky catching fire at sunset.

And it had ruined Reid's beautiful car.

Estrella ran, catching Calla by the arm in a side garden.

The pressure of Estrella's fingers must have warned Calla. She turned, her expression guilty but unashamed.

Estrella caught her breath. "I don't want to jump to any unfair conclusions."

Calla smiled, an acknowledgment that if Bay had not vanished, if Dalia did not walk the halls at night like some lost spirit, if Reid was not laying his claim to La Pradera, she would have laughed.

Estrella let go of her arm. "Why?" She had meant to speak a whole question. *Why did you do it? Why would you risk yourself and all of us?* But her weak breath cut the question down to one word.

Calla checked over both their shoulders. When she saw no one near the hedges and rows of azalea bushes, a clenched-jaw rage came into her face. "He cornered Dalia. I saw him."

Estrella's breath turned sour in her throat. "What?"

"Nothing happened," Calla said. "I made sure of it. But he was trying to kiss her, and she was pushing him away, but she did it like she was flirting. She knows she can't make him mad, so that was all she could do."

"Then how did you make sure nothing happened?"

"I hid behind the bushes and I threw a rock," Calla said.

Estrella nodded. "Good."

Calla allowed a little pride into her face. "They thought it was a rabbit or a fox or something. It distracted him enough that she just said good night and left."

The perfumed sweetness of the roses and the lily magnolias filled Estrella. Most days, she liked it, the smell of these gardens so strong it seemed liquid. But now it made her forehead ache.

"Throw all the rocks you want," Estrella said. "But you can't do this. Do you know what he could do to us?"

Calla bit her lip. "It's not fair."

"I know," Estrella said.

To Marjorie Briar, Estrella and her cousins had been las haditas, garden fairies who promised rich men magic held in seeds and bulbs. Marjorie taught them to trick men with too much money in their pockets, to part them from the contents of their billfolds. And if they ever came back complaining that the bulbs did not take into flowers as grand as those on La Pradera, they convinced them the only answer was to buy more.

But Reid just wanted them to grow flowers that could be stuffed into vases. He wanted a ball not so the Nomeolvides women could sell their sewn burlap bags of iris bulbs and hydrangea seeds but so he could impress rich men. So he could work out how to wring enough money from La Pradera to pay his debt.

And Bay. Reid had taken the loss of Bay no harder than misplacing a fountain pen.

Reid's reign had seeded in all of them, for the first time, the idea of leaving. They wouldn't do it of course. They knew it could cost them their own lives and their mothers' broken hearts. But the thought was new, and enough to frighten Estrella as she lay in the dark at night. She dreamed of La Pradera striking her sick as soon as her nightgown hem crossed the property line.

"I promise you," Estrella said. "The minute we can get rid of him, we will."

"No," Calla said. "I mean"—she shook her head, shutting her eyes—"yes, I want that. But it's not that. It's his shirts."

"What about his shirts?"

"They're wrinkled," Calla said. Her lips pressed together tight, a guard against tears. "He wants our cousin, and he has all that money, and he can't even put on an ironed shirt."

A little piece of Estrella cracked. She loved Calla for how this small thing bothered her. She felt Calla's rage and frustration so sharply tears burned at the corners of her eyes.

"Listen to me," Estrella said. "We'll fix this."

"I don't want to," Calla said. "I want him to see it."

She could not let Reid come down on Calla for this. Not Calla, not brilliant, vindictive little Calla. She might have been taller than Estrella, but she was all thin limbs and round eyes. Sometimes, when Estrella was not close enough to have to look up at her, Calla still seemed ten.

"You're not taking the blame for this," Estrella said. "I am."

"No," Calla said. "I'm not letting you."

"You have to. Because you catch things before any of us do. We need you. Reid doesn't know how much you notice and I don't want him to. Let him keep underestimating you."

"But then what's he gonna do to you?" Calla asked.

"Don't worry about me," Estrella said. "Worry about Dalia. Take care of her."

"How?" Calla asked.

Estrella thought of Calla folding up her thin arms and legs behind a bush, making noises that sounded like the skittering of a deer or rabbit.

"Keep throwing rocks."

Estrella sifted through her thoughts for the way out of this, how to rub out any trace of what Calla had done.

The bottle of whiskey in Reid's hands, the gleam of the gold label, drifted back to her.

Estrella combed out her hair and put on her best dress, a blush-colored one she'd worn to a midsummer party last year. The bodice was sewn with ribbons and satin flowers. The straps, thick pink ribbons, fastened in bows at each shoulder. The skirt brushed her calves, and the memory of how Marjorie used to pick out their dresses with their mothers stung.

Liquor crates had been coming in for the ball, stacked high in an unused shed. Estrella stole bottle after bottle. Aged whiskey. Imported grappa. Champagne wrapped in pink foil. Absinthe the bartenders would serve by lighting sugar cubes in slotted spoons, the liquor burning blue green.

She slipped through the carriage house's side door, popped the bottles, and soaked the interior of the car. Grappa flooded the consoles and rained down over the calla lilies' leaves. Absinthe left the steering wheels stained and sticky. Scotch dampened the dark soil. Champagne filled the flutes of the calla lilies, foaming over the petaled rims.

She poured out liquor and wine onto the chrome and leather. The fragrance of sugared grapes and bitter wormwood filled the carriage house. The fumes made her body feel light.

From the last few bottles, she poured out enough to soak a few rags, and stuffed one in the neck of each. She held a lit match to a rag. The soaked cloth went up, and she threw it into the car. She lit the next, tossed it in, and again until they littered the inside.

On the way out, her foot kicked green glass. A half-empty champagne bottle she'd missed. She grabbed its throat before it toppled, and took it with her.

By the time the bottles blew, Estrella had climbed one of La Pradera's grass-covered hills. It gave her a view of the flash and the fire lighting the carriage house windows.

She sat on the grass, drinking straight from that bottle of champagne that probably cost more than Reid would ever pay her family. The windows in the carriage house doors showed ribbons of fire jumping up from the car.

In every flick of light, the fire swallowed any evidence of Calla and her lilies. The bells and stems caught and went up, disappearing into the flames.

It didn't take long for Reid to notice, and for men to arrive in their red trucks.

Fel appeared in a smoke-filled doorway.

He coughed into the bend of his elbow, his shirt grayed with smoke.

Panic prickled her. She hadn't seen him go in. She'd been so set on burning any evidence that Calla had touched the car, she hadn't thought about Fel, quiet and so unknown to them that he was unpredictable.

He spoke to the firemen, gesturing inside and telling them, Estrella guessed, that no one was in the carriage house.

Her heart settled and slowed. He was okay, this boy who cooked for her family when they could not cook for themselves, this boy who searched the thick gray of liquor-filled smoke to make sure they were not lost in it. His clothes and hair were smoke-dulled, and he was coughing to clear it from his lungs, but he was okay.

And Estrella had turned to ashes anything that could damn Calla.

There was nothing for Reid to do but stand, try to deaden the horror on his face, and look around at who was there to witness it.

The men threw open the barn doors, letting the bitter smoke billow out. They had the fire out with a few snowy arcs of the extinguishers. But it had done its damage. The car was ruined, and the carriage house would smell like smoke for weeks.

Reid's eyes moved in Estrella's direction. They missed her at first, passing over her.

When they snapped back, she knew he'd seen her.

His mouth stayed open. But even from this distance she could see the rage, the disbelief, boiling down into one expression.

She held his stare. She didn't want anyone else blamed for this. Not Calla. Not Fel. And for one reckless minute she wanted him to throw her out of the gardens. She didn't want any part of the little kingdom he meant to make out of La Pradera.

With the glow from the carriage house, and the warmth of the champagne spreading through her, there was nothing to fear in the whole world. He could kick her out if he wanted to. She'd die a legend. She'd be a story Dalia could pass on to the next Nomeolvides daughters.

Estrella would be the girl who went out in the light of all those flames.

She raised the bottle in Reid's direction, the pink foil label peeling under her fingers, and she swallowed the last of the champagne.

SIXTEEN

The woman who insisted Fel call her Abuela Lila told him that, between the flower beds, the blossoming trees, and the sunken garden, there were more petals in La Pradera than souls in the world. Everything here bloomed. The clouds of hydrangeas and lilacs. The arbors and trellises. The beds of lilies and hyacinths.

So when Fel had first seen the fire, he'd thought it was made of petals. He'd thought their flicker was the fast and sudden blooming of red and orange flowers.

But as he came closer, the flames resolved, looking more like liquid, like spilled molten iron, than petals.

The fire had seemed small until he went through the doors. The smoke had gathered hard and thick enough that it choked him. It stung with each breath but something about it felt familiar. Not comfortable, but known.

He felt the fire's warmth on his forearms as he checked the

smoke-filled room. But it wasn't until Reid came for Estrella that Fel understood she had set it.

By now, the firemen had gone. The smoke had risen toward the sky and faded. And La Pradera smelled so much like ash that it reminded him of fall, the burning of leaves.

Reid came to the stone house, where the grandmothers' staked vegetable plants and fluffy herbs seemed like chicks gathering around a hen.

Estrella knelt in the side yard, bringing up borraja petals in the shadows of tomato plants. Her cousins were brightening a sparse flower bed with pink and orange flowers. Fel had just softened it by running a tiller through the empty earth, and now he was doing the same with a cleared-out herb bed the grandmothers would replant. He pushed the tiller through the dirt, and the metal spurs glinted silver against the dark earth.

But Reid did not cross the break in the low garden wall or follow the path toward the front door. He did not enter the trembling gardens crowded with dark green leaves and trails of flowers.

He said Estrella's name with the solemn tone of a priest calling her to confession.

Estrella drew her hands out of the earth. She brushed her fingers first against each other and then against her skirt, leaving faint shadows on the pink fabric. And she followed him, her shoulders straight, drawing herself up to her full height so completely that for a minute she looked as tall as her mother. She interlaced her fingers in front of her, and that stoic look, like she was an accused witch going to her trial, thickened Fel's apprehension into worry.

That worry loosened his grip on the hand tiller. It urged him after her. But as she passed the low stone wall, she paused, letting Reid get a few more steps in front of her.

She turned back, so quickly Reid did not notice. She kissed her fingertips and blew air over her palms at her cousins. It made her look like she was starting off on a trip and would bring them all back glittering stories as souvenirs.

That gesture was for her cousins. She caught each of their eyes, and didn't seem to notice Fel standing with the tiller, the metal stars slowing until they were still. She had set a fire to tell Reid how little she wanted him here, and she had done it in a dress nice enough to wear to Easter service. A slip the pale blue of a robin's egg showed at the hem. Her lips shined a darkened shade of the same rose color as her dress.

Since she had found him in the valley made of flowers, his soul had searched after the muted colors of a life he could not remember. He had come from a world that was so gray and dulled he wondered if maybe *it* had been el Purgatorio, the place where he'd been meant to work out his sins. But it had been familiar, and he remembered enough good in it that he had wanted to go back. To find the things he had lost. To learn the name and features of the one who had taken care of him, negotiated for stale bread and unrendered manteca, given him the little wooden horse to keep in his pocket.

But now he wanted this. He wanted this painted world that

thrilled him even as it frightened him. He wanted to understand the language of women who laughed with tears dampening their cheeks, even if he would never speak it.

He wanted the color of this unknown life. He wanted to grow the kind of bright, fearless heart that lived in this girl.

SEVENTEEN

Estrella knew this room. She knew its antique chaises, its marble-bordered fireplace, its cut-crystal decanters of port and plum brandy that the fireplace lit up like gemstones.

When Marjorie had been alive, it was a room where guests gathered after parties, draping themselves on the damask and brocade. It was where Marjorie convinced men a few drinks deep that the best investment they could make was the tailor's shop or bookstore in town, or the theater that was a month from shutting down, or that they should put up the money to repave a cobblestone street in exchange for a plaque declaring the town's gratitude.

Good talk about your name is priceless, she urged, refilling their drinks, laughter at the corners of her mouth because she never cared what anyone said about her. Only what they said about Bay, and Estrella's family.

But daylight made this room seem sad, desolate. Like the way funeral flowers smelled flat and chalky after the mourners left.

Reid slipped the cuff links from his shirt and folded up the cuffs. Estrella flinched, wondering if he might hit her.

He set out two glasses and uncapped a crystal decanter.

"That wasn't just any car," he said, his tone factual, uninvolved. "It wasn't some new model off the lot."

Of course it wasn't. Estrella had seen enough nights of rich men's Morgans and Aston Martins crossing La Pradera's gates. They considered new cars garish, showy. Instead, they bought older ones, secondhand, limited editions that cost more than new cars.

"I don't know you," he said. "But I think I know enough to know you don't want your family to have to pay for your mistakes."

The words snaked down her back, cold as the drops off an ice cube.

"That sounded like a threat, didn't it?" he asked. "I didn't mean it that way."

His voice was open enough that she almost believed it.

"What I meant was I know a little bit about what a debt to your family feels like," he said.

She thought of the candelabra. The rare books, the antique piano, the irreplaceable art. All up in flames.

"You do, don't you?" she asked.

He gave her a pained smile. "So you've heard."

Without looking at the glasses, he poured amber alcohol that smelled as strong as nail polish remover.

"So Bay," Reid said, and the muscles in Estrella's shoulders clenched. "It's true, the rumors about all of you and disappearing."

It didn't sound like a question, so Estrella didn't answer it.

Bay was nothing to Reid. Reid was not Estrella and Azalea, folding Bay's laugh into their jewelry boxes like beaded hairpins. He was not Calla, sharing marzipan plums with Bay because they were the only ones who liked things that sweet. He was not Dalia and Gloria, their wrists smelling of orange blossom perfume as Bay kissed the back of their hands, the younger cousins imagining the brush of her lips just below their own knuckles.

"Doesn't that make you worry about your boyfriend?" Reid asked.

Who? She was so close to saying it out loud she had to bite her lip to keep the word from coming out. Then she remembered, the lie told about the boy she'd found in the sunken garden. She and her cousins had guarded the secret of his appearing as much for their mothers' and grandmothers' sake as for his. More.

"Fel," Estrella said. "His name is Fel."

She was cutting this off. Reid's questions held not concern but the curiosity of a tourist.

"Please don't ask Dalia about what happened," Estrella said. Dalia slept less than Fel did now. Estrella heard the hallway floor creaking under her steps at midnight. "Don't make her live through that again."

Reid held his hands up, a gesture of surrender.

If he meant to hide his smile, he gave it so little effort that it only flattened into a smirk. How charmed he must have considered himself. What golden luck he must have thought was his that even a family's legacy conspired to give him these gardens, free from Bay's objections. Of course he would think the whole glittering universe existed to spin anything he wanted out of stardust.

He was a man, and a rich one, and these together made him believe the planets and moons orbited around the single point of his desires.

"So you and your family," he said. "You make flowers."

Estrella's lungs eased at the subject change.

He knew the answer. Everyone did, as least as far as the rumors carried. They either loved the Nomeolvides women because Marjorie Briar had loved them, or they whispered behind their hands that they were all cursed witches, and that they were glad to see them keeping to these hills. They passed stories back and forth about how the women on the hill could grow flowers in the harshest winters, out of frozen ground or on trellises covered in hoarfrost or even out of icicles themselves.

Reid held out a second glass to her.

"I'm going to give you a chance to pay this back," he said. "Just you. Your family doesn't have to be involved."

She waved the glass away, but a ribbon of gratitude folded in her chest. This was the one human, yielding thing about Reid, his understanding of the burden children felt when they owed their families more than they could repay.

"You do want to stay here, don't you?" he asked. "All of you? You don't want to be las hijas del aire again do you?"

Even in his awful accent, the words stilled the air in Estrella's throat.

"Towns have long memories," Reid said. "If you know who to ask."

The back of Estrella's neck pinched with wondering how much this town remembered. Did they remember the Nomeol-vides women who took out apartments above the dress shops and antiques dealers, who set out wreaths made not of flow-ers but of lemons? Or the girls who found jobs as bookkeepers or cake decorators, who crossed the street rather than pass by the flower shop?

Estrella could imagine being one of those girls, hopeful and hiding, wanting homes where the only flowers were ones pat-terning the curtains. She could feel the heat and chill of their shame and their fear when hundreds of alliums or carnations were found crowding an employer's desk, or splitting open pallets of cake flour, or, worst of all, filling a child's crib. In every town before, these things had gotten the Nomeolvides women fired, or chased from their homes, or killed.

The world outside these gardens held two kinds of death, the vengeance of La Pradera, and the knives of a world that did not want them.

"If you want to stay, that's good news to me," Reid said. "Because I want you to."

The chill of La Pradera's hold prickled over Estrella's skin.

Don't go out there, La Pradera whispered. *Don't wander. Don't stray. For women like you, the world offers only death.*

Abuela Mimosa's words echoed through her. *We stay here, or we die.* If Reid or anyone else threw them off this land, Estrella had no faith La Pradera would show them mercy.

"What do you want, Reid?" Estrella asked.

"Not as much as you're worried I want," he said. "Just something for our guests at the ball. Do that, and we'll call all this forgiven. We'll pretend it never happened."

"What kind of something?" she asked.

"It'll be easy." He shook his head, like the thing was so minor it wasn't worth naming. "You could do it with your eyes closed."

EIGHTEEN

Each day, Reid gave Fel the tasks he wanted done. The bulbs in the lanterns looked dull, and Fel should check them. Lichen was dulling the stone on the fountains, and Fel should polish it away. The copper benches were growing a patina, and Fel should scrub them clean.

This last one he hated most. Fel knew the grandmothers liked the green on the copper, that they thought of it as the breath of some far sea.

Fel scoured rough cloths over the metal. When the green did not fade, he wondered if it was defying him. It was clinging to remind him he was rubbing away a thing loved by women who looked after him.

With sweat dampening his hair, he looked up and saw the grandmothers standing on the grass, handing him the salt, vinegar, flour, and olive oil.

"You'll need this," Abuela Mimosa told him. "It'll strip it, then you'll shine it."

He wanted to make apologies for the fact that he had no will in him except to do as he was told. So at night, with the sun down and Reid's tasks for him done, he did small things for the ground around the Nomeolvides house.

Light from the stone house spilled out, the upturned leaves catching it. The plots here weren't as thickly or brightly flowered as the garden valley or the courtyards, but they sat close to the house, crowding the windowsills with green, and they grew not only petals but things the women ate.

He pulled weeds from the herb window boxes. He braced young tomato plants to their stakes. He cleared dead ivy stickers from the stone, which Azalea told him was best done by burning them away with a lit match. He didn't believe her until Calla and two of the grandmothers nodded their agreement.

And his favorite, tilling the wood-bordered beds so they would be easy for the women to slide their hands into. The spinning points on the tiller looked so much like ornaments that at first he'd been sure they were a child's toy.

"What are you doing?" Estrella asked.

He turned toward her voice, the tiller spurs slowing.

She stood at the edge of the garden, the wind turning her hair to streamers. Her skirt blew around her knees like a river was pulling at it.

"They look like stars," he said, the tiller spurs slowing to a stop. The moon glinted off the metal.

"There's stars up there." Estrella tilted her hand toward the sky. "If you wanna look at them, just look at them."

"But these ones you can touch," Fel said.

She looked amused by him. He didn't mind. If she thought he was worth looking at, worth considering, he didn't mind.

"I'm glad you're back," he said. "Calla and Gloria thought he'd locked you in the attic. They were working on a way to break you out. I told them if you could find a matchbook you could do it yourself."

A surprised smile brightened her face. "Did you just make a joke, Fel?"

"I do sometimes," he said.

She sat on the low stone wall, her skirt fluffing up around her.

"What you made the other night," she said, pressing her fingertips together, and he understood how hard this question was for her to ask, this reference to a night when the Nomeolvides girls were too heartbroken to put on their shoes. "What's it called?"

He shut his eyes, feeling the sense of the name near him. He reached out for it, expecting it to flit away from him.

But it stayed.

"Molletes," he said. "They're called molletes."

"No, they're not," she said.

Her protest, and the laugh underneath it, made him open his eyes. He remembered so little, but he remembered this, the name for manteca dyed red with paprika and then poured over bread.

"What do you mean, 'no, they're not'?" he asked.

"My family makes molletes all the time. It's not that."

"Then what is it?"

"It's a bolillo you cut in half and then you put stuff on it."

He didn't even try not to smile. "Stuff?"

"I don't know," she said. She sounded a little frustrated, like she was trying to teach him a word that could not be translated. But she was smiling, too. "It depends what we have. But it's usually not red."

"That's what I know as molletes," he said.

She tore stray threads off the hem of her slip. Wisps of blue trailed off her fingertips.

"Was he hard on you?" he asked.

"Reid?" Estrella asked. "No."

"Did he hurt you?"

"Do I look hurt?" she asked.

"He just let you go?"

"Not quite. He wants a favor. He wants me to charm his rich friends at his little party. Show them how polite and sweet and entertaining we can be. I'll do it"—she lifted the corner of her skirt like she was curtsying—"and all will be forgiven."

"And you don't worry about him thinking you owe him something?" Fel asked.

"I'm not afraid of him. My mother always says the same thing about men like that. They're cotton candy. All puff and show, but throw water on them and they dissolve."

There was something brittle in how she moved and smiled.

If she kept trying this hard not to seem thrown by Reid, it would splinter her.

Fel grabbed on to something else he could get her talking about, words she'd said that he didn't know.

"What's cotton candy?" he asked. It sounded made up, or maybe it was the kind of cloth Estrella's skirt was sewn out of.

"You're kidding, right?" Estrella asked. "What are you, two hundred years old?"

If he'd been in el Purgatorio longer than he could imagine, maybe he was. "I don't know."

Estrella stood up from the wall. "Come on."

When she had found him in the valley made of flowers, he had known to let her lead him. The understanding that she was his way toward anything familiar felt woven into him. But now, a mirrored kind of understanding, that he should not follow her this time, had the same depth and shape.

"I don't think that's a good idea," he said.

"Why?" she asked.

"I heard your grandmothers talking." He had caught their whispers, their agreements that they must keep a close watch on Estrella and her cousins. "They said . . ." He stopped himself, struck with the fear that he might be speaking what wasn't his to tell.

"What?" Estrella asked.

He hesitated. Estrella had been the one to find him, but her family had been the ones to let him stay.

"They said they didn't want you going anywhere without their permission," he said.

"Their permission?" she asked. "Are they kidding? Gloria and Dalia and Azalea are grown women. Calla and I are close enough. And they want to treat us like children?"

"I don't know." He felt caught, wanting neither to agree with her family nor to turn on them. "They said they don't want you leaving. They said it could hurt you."

"They still think we're children. They think we don't know how this place works. But we know. We all know the stories."

"What stories?" he asked.

"If we try to leave La Pradera—I mean really try to leave, for good—the land hurts us," she said. "It wants to make us stay, so it hurts us when we try to leave. But that's if we try to run away. Not if we go down the road for cotton candy."

"But how would it know the difference?" he asked.

"How would what know the difference?"

"The land," he said. "How would it know if you're taking a walk or if you're trying to run away?"

"It knows," she said. "It just knows."

"How?"

Estrella took slow steps toward him. "I want you to listen to me very carefully, Fel." She came close enough that he had to pick between looking down at her and backing up. But her face was so serious, so intent, he could not move. "Never underestimate what the ground under your feet knows, what it can do.

What it can give you and what it can steal. It gave us a home when there was nowhere else we were safe. It defied every town that tried to make sure we'd be wandering forever."

This close, the air between them smelled like her, half the dry spice of the perfume she shared with her cousins, half the fruit soap that left a little of its sugar on her body.

"And then it defied what happened to you," she said, her voice low, more like a warning than a secret. "It brought you back from wherever you were before. It made you appear after you'd vanished."

He tried to remember disappearing. What it felt like. How it had happened. Whether it had hurt or just been a fading out of everything, even the sense of his own body.

It didn't feel right. It didn't feel like a story that was his. But she sounded so sure of it that on her tongue it became truth. It became his. He just couldn't remember it.

"Don't think for one second you can hide anything from this place," Estrella said. "No one ever has."

His guilt slid through him again. But he still didn't know what he'd done, so there was still no confessing it.

"I think it's my fault," he said.

"What is?" she asked.

"That your family's worried."

"That's not true."

"But they're worried about you," he said. "And I think that is my fault. Because I'm here."

"No." Estrella set her hand on his upper arm, like she could pull him back from what he was thinking. "They like you. Even Azalea likes you, and she doesn't like anyone."

He could see her trying to laugh at her own joke, to get him to laugh.

It didn't work on either of them.

"That's your cousins," he said. "I'm talking about your mothers and your grandmothers. They don't like how I just showed up."

"You know that's not true."

"Fine," he said. "Then your mother."

He felt the small breath of her putting a little more space between them. She dropped her hand away from him. Her face showed what she now realized, that Fel understood more than just the shared whispers of grandmothers. He caught the warnings of mothers to daughters, ones neither thought anyone else had heard.

"I don't think she wants me around you," he said.

"It's not like that," she said. "It's more that she doesn't want me around you."

"Isn't that the same thing?"

His own guilt threaded together with the thought of his scars, the memory searing across his skin.

"Your family," he said. "They've been good to me." They had been good to him even when they had seen his crimes written on his back. "I don't want to do anything they wouldn't like. Especially your mother."

Something in her eyes shifted, like the glint of a polished stone.

"You want to talk about my mother?" Estrella asked. "She thinks she understands everything. But she doesn't understand me."

There was both relief and disappointment in how fast Fel knew what she was talking about. She wasn't talking about this, the small stirring of night air between them. It was a thing he sometimes thought he'd imagined and that sometimes seemed real enough that he could see it growing feathers.

Estrella was talking about Bay. She was talking about her own heart, and how it loved in a way her mother would judge without turning it over and learning the shape of it.

"Today I solved a problem my mother knew nothing about," Estrella said. Her words twisted, each one sounding harder, like a knot tightening. "She still doesn't. I fixed it, and she had no idea. My mother, all our mothers, they think they're holding everything up, but we have it too. It's ours too. So forget what my mother thinks I should or shouldn't be doing because we're going and getting some damn cotton candy, okay?"

He backed up. Whatever cotton candy was, he was now afraid of it. But when she took his hand, he didn't dare resist.

Fel had seen the Nomeolvides girls away from La Pradera. He had seen them being measured for dresses in town, none of them falling ill or turning to dust. But now he wondered if their mothers and grandmothers being with them had been a kind of blessing, their presence protecting Estrella and her cousins. Now he and Estrella were slipping through the night without anyone's permission.

Estrella held on to his hand and guided him through the dark. She led him around fallen trees and over thick roots. She warned him about jagged rocks and ruts in the earth.

She had done this before. But he still shuddered wondering if, by letting her do this, he would lose her. La Pradera would grasp at this girl fleeing its borders. The grandmothers hadn't said anything about what the land did to girls who ran, so that left him imagining her heart giving out in her rib cage, or her fingers turning to petals even as she clasped his hands.

"Stop," she said.

He halted his steps.

"No," she said. The fingers of her other hand brushed his so that, for a second, both their hands were touching. "I mean stop worrying."

Now he wondered if she was a witch. He hadn't when she found him in the valley made of flowers, or when he saw her drawing petals up from the earth. But now he wondered about this girl, beautiful and smelling of wood betony and knowing things he did not want her to know. "How did you . . . ?"

"I can feel your heartbeat in your palms." She set her hands against each of his, and the feeling of her fingers in the dark made him quiet. "Stop worrying."

"You really believe the land will know?" he asked.

She dropped one of his hands and took tighter hold of the other. "I know it will."

She turned, and the flick of her hair was a wing spreading

through the dark. She pulled him through trees and across barren land and brush fields. The air around her had been vibrating, but now it slowed and stilled. When she spoke, it was with a laugh under her voice again.

"The back way to town," she said.

A little farther, and the dark opened into the spilling light of the town's streets. The storefront she led him to was all wooden barrels and glass jars. Jagged sticks of rock candy stood bright as La Pradera's flowers. Sugar pumpkins were capped with bright green stems. Hard candies dyed red with thin white stripes shone like marbles. None of it looked real. They seemed more like things to put under glass than to eat.

Estrella grabbed bags of spun sugar in the same pale pink and blue as her dress and slip. Off a wide wooden spool, she measured out a length of paper covered in neat rows of sugar dots—pink, yellow, and blue.

"Pick something out," she said. "Something you've never had before. We have to educate you."

The only thing he could look at without making himself dizzy was a small box of some kind of sugar molded in the shape of fruits, then painted. The colors were so much softer than the wrapped candies, and it drew toward him something he could not quite recognize. Something almost remembered.

"We're buying that too," Estrella said to the man at the counter, throwing her hand toward the box Fel was holding.

"We can't eat all this," Fel said, his unease worsened by the fact that he did not have money to give her.

"Oh, don't worry," Estrella said. "We'll have help. There's a saying in my family. The meaner the girl, the bigger the sweet tooth."

He thought of Azalea showing him how she made her favorite potatoes from those strange flakes that looked like snow. He remembered the sternest of the grandmothers putting him under the spray of warm water and telling him he was not lost, only misplaced.

"I don't think anyone in your family's mean," he said.

He felt her glance slide over him, picking up the worry he didn't want her to catch.

"It's not my money anyway," she said. "It's Reid's."

"You stole money from Reid?" he asked.

A hand fluttered to her chest. "I'm wounded that you think I'm a girl of such low moral character."

He drew back, worried he'd offended her. But then her smile glinted, first in her eyes before curving the corner of her mouth.

She was making fun of him. She liked making fun of him. Of how the colors of things shocked him. Of how his face always showed his wonder at the grandmothers turning tortillas over blue flames, fingers so close the fire almost touched them. Of how he did not understand the cousins running barefoot over wet grass when they all had shoes.

He didn't mind. It didn't bother him to be something Estrella batted at to see what he would do, like a cat at a feather. She was more curious than cruel.

"I might have told Reid we all needed more money to look pretty for his little party," Estrella said.

That let Fel laugh. "I don't think you said it like that."

"You're right. I was much more persuasive."

Her pride was so sure he could almost taste it on the air, like sugar mixed with the bite of chili powder. She was both shameless and soft, openhearted and vicious. He wondered how she remembered to be all these things at once, how there was any space left in her to lure flowers from the earth.

Estrella handed the man money. Fel didn't want to know where she'd hidden it, if she'd slipped it out of the band of her underwear or from between her breasts when both his and the cashier's backs were turned.

The man at the counter gave her back two paper bags. She thanked him and handed one to Fel.

"Let your education begin," she said.

Even through the paper, he could feel the soft fluff of the spun sugar, the thing she called cotton candy. It gave under his hands like gathered cloth.

He thought of how he would pass these things to the Nomeolvides women, grandmothers and mothers and daughters, like a bright communion.

At night, with Estrella, this town was all lights and water-slicked cobblestone. Lampposts lined the sidewalks. White lights wrapped the trees, making everything look covered in snow.

They passed a bulb-signed theater and a tall-windowed hotel.

A man's voice spilled out of the space between buildings. "You out here looking for a new boyfriend, Nancy?"

Fel heard the hard taunting in the man's voice.

The words struck Fel hard enough that for a second he thought the man was talking to him.

Fel looked down the brick-lined alley, the ground wet with runoff.

A boy who looked younger than Fel leaned against a wall, the brim of a dark felt hat shading his face. Suspenders showed against his pin-striped shirt. Two men stood across from him, trying to needle him into looking up.

The boy did not speak.

"Hey," the other man said, and kicked at the wall close to the boy's knee. "You're too good to talk to us, Nancy?"

Nancy. That one word, said as an insult not a name, made others rush back to Fel.

Uphill gardener.

Molly.

Backgammon player.

Fel's thoughts caught on each of those words, and the memory, the cutting pain of how he'd heard them thrown at someone he loved.

His body acted for him. He threw the man who'd kicked at the boy up against the damp brick. Then he was hitting him, and when the other man went at him he hit him next.

He was hitting them because a long time ago, in the gray world he had lived in, he had heard someone he loved called these kinds of names and he had been too small to do anything. The memory of the rage and the helpless feeling, the sense that he had been too young to stop it, charged his hands.

The one who took care of him. The one who kept them both from freezing or starving. He had been a man who liked men, and so everyone felt it was their right to judge him, to call him names.

His brother.

Fel had had an older brother. The man he had hunted mushrooms with, picked dandelion greens with, the man who had bargained for manteca and day-old bread, this man had been his brother.

He knew this. He knew this the way he knew the weight of the wooden horses. And because he could not weep for this true thing, not here, it fed the rage in his hands. He could not defend his brother from the words, from the names *Nancy* and *Molly*.

But he could quiet these men. If he could not protect his brother, he could protect the boy in this alley. He could hit these men hard enough that fine cuts split open the backs of his hands.

Estrella dug her fingers into Fel's upper arm, pulling on him, yelling at him to stop.

The boy cut between them all, trying to block the men from hitting Fel or Estrella.

"Hey," another unknown voice sliced through the air. "What's the problem here?"

They all broke away from one another, turning toward the mouth of the alley.

A man stood at the edge, wearing the fine suit and bearing of someone who worked for the hotel and could throw anyone out of it. Or out of the alley next to it.

He wasn't looking at the men, or Fel, or even Estrella.

He was looking at the boy. But not with the hard-jawed judgment of deciding he'd been the start of the trouble. He was looking at the boy with the deference he might give a wealthy man.

The boy stepped back, holding out his hands. "Everyone's okay here, right?"

Fel still didn't recognize the boy. Not his shape. Not his face, still shadowed by his hat brim.

But that voice stilled Fel. He knew it, even though it was lower now, dropped with effort. That voice was the only one he had heard at the long wooden table that was not the similar, braiding sounds of the Nomeolvides women.

"Nobody's hurt here," the boy said. "We're all gonna go home, okay?" He patted the air with flat palms, calming them all.

The men backed toward the street, stunned either by the fine-suited man or the unexpected power of a boy they had thought nothing of.

The suited man followed them, nodding at the boy as he left the mouth of the alley. The boy nodded back, the last sign Fel needed that they knew each other.

The men's shadows faded, Fel's knuckles sore and throbbing.

Estrella's fingers shielded her mouth, her gasp so soft it sounded like a breath in. Fel wondered if she was short enough to see the boy's face, or if that same voice had caught her.

Estrella and the boy in the felt hat passed a startled look between them, like they were two mirrors reflecting it back over and over.

The boy's hair was darker, shorter. But Fel recognized the features.

"Bay," Estrella said.

Bay shook her head, jaw held tight. "Not here."

"Fine." Estrella went around to the other side of the building.

They followed her. Of course they followed her, Fel because he had learned to follow the Nomeolvides women when they told him to, and Bay out of a worry so heavy it struck Fel like hot air.

The brick sill of a first-floor window gave Estrella enough height to pull on a rusted fire escape ladder. Her steps rattled the metal frame as she climbed to the first landing.

She stared down at both of them with a look partway between invitation and threat. "Then how about up here?"

NINETEEN

Estrella tore open a bag of cotton candy. She would wait
until Bay started talking. She twirled off a piece of spun
sugar, and then handed the cotton candy to Fel. She hoped
he'd join her, both of them giving off the sense that they had all
night. They would stay until the silence wore Bay down.

Fel did the same thing she'd done, pulling away a scrap, and
then passed it to Bay. He looked at the fluff sticking to his fingers.
He seemed unsure if it was candy or fabric, and for a minute she
wondered if he saw it like she had the first time her mother bought
it for her, like blush-colored clouds whirled onto a paper cone.

Most of the time, Fel's wonder made her protective. It made
her slow and careful with him. But now it frustrated her. Right
now, everything frustrated her.

"You eat it, Fel," she said. "You just put it in your mouth."

He did it, his eyes on her as he swallowed it. That startled
look made her a little guilty, but she caught the glint of some-

thing else. His interest maybe. His amusement at her getting this worked up over spun sugar.

Bay tore off a piece of cotton candy but didn't eat it. She set the bag between the three of them, the puff leaning to one side on the rusted landing.

Bay. Alive. Hair dyed auburn, cut short, the longest pieces now free from her hat and brushing her cheekbones. Bay had forgone her satin coats in favor of slacks and collared shirts that made her the same as a hundred men.

Whatever thrill Estrella felt to see her turned damp and heavy. She should have thrown her arms around her, shrieked with the joy of knowing her heart and her cousins' hearts had not killed her.

But the only words in her were bitter.

"Nice haircut," she said.

"Thank you." Bay took off her hat and ran a hand through her cropped hair. "I miss the braid a little, to tell you the truth. This keeps getting in my face. But I don't miss being called Miss Briar, I'll tell you that."

A faint laugh turned in Estrella's throat, but she didn't let it become sound. In all the time Estrella had watched her, Bay had never been bothered either by being called a girl or a boy. But that word, *Miss*, engraved on invitations or written in calligraphy on envelopes, had made Bay shudder. To Bay, *Miss* spoke of what the rest of the Briars would expect her to be. A proper young woman in neutral, pearled pumps, diamond drop earrings, a knee-length lace dress.

The kind of woman everyone except Marjorie expected her to be.

"Which part?" Estrella asked. "Just the *miss* or the *Briar*, too?"

"Both," Bay said.

"What do we call you?" Fel asked.

It was such a genuine question, his voice so open, that it made Estrella cross her arms just to remind Bay she was not forgiven.

"On the street, don't call me anything." Bay's eyes flashed from the fire escape landing to the wet ground below. "Down there, you don't know me. But right now, up here, call me Bay. I'm the same girl."

The word *girl* prickled against the back of Estrella's neck, her skin hot with the rush of being near Bay. This version of Bay had abandoned her French braid. She wore the understated colors of men's clothes. She was beautiful either way, and it was a sharp, stinging reminder of what Estrella and her cousins all shared.

"You're not the same," Estrella said. "You let us think you were dead. The Bay I knew would never do that."

"I know," Bay said. "But I had reasons, Estrella. I would never do this to your family if I didn't have a good reason."

"Everyone is mourning you," Estrella said. "Do you understand that?"

"I'm sorry," Bay said, her head down, voice low, looking so guilty that Estrella almost declared her forgiven. "But this is important. I can't explain it right now, but I have to do this."

"What's important enough to let everyone think you're dead?"

"It doesn't matter."

"You did this for something that doesn't matter?"

The cotton candy bag listed a little further. Fel righted it, but it leaned again. And that small defeat, the forlorn puff in a crumpled bag, seemed to open Bay.

Bay sighed, and then she spoke. She told them how she had known Reid wanted more than he was saying. How he had reminded her that she was no Briar heir, and that it was only by Reid's gracious generosity that he let Bay stay. How he had tried to threaten her with the fate of the Nomeolvides women, how with the twist of the right rumor, they would be hunted as witches.

How about you help me, or I force them off this land and they die?

Estrella shivered, wondering how much Reid knew about La Pradera's hold on them, if he had heard any stories of runaway girls coughing up pollen until the breath left them.

"But La Pradera is yours," Estrella said, hoping Bay would refute everything Calla had said. The problem with Marjorie's will. The mistakes the lawyers had made. The words—*fee tail, devise*—that Estrella still did not understand. "Marjorie left it to you."

"It's not that simple," Bay said. "But I'm not giving up. That's why I'm here. I needed Reid to stop watching me."

"What will you do while he's not watching you?" Fel asked.

Bay offered her surest smile. "Gather ammunition."

Estrella scooted a little closer. "What do you have?"

"Nothing," she said.

Before Estrella's shoulders slumped, Bay held up a hand.

"I'm working on it," she said. "The Briars have secrets. Everybody does."

"You know Reid's, don't you?" Estrella asked.

Bay shook her head. "Not big enough. I need more. And I'll find it."

Estrella watched the flickering of Bay's eyes, even brighter with her hair dyed dark. Next to Fel, with his skin the color of wet brush, his eyes as deep brown as the rusted fire escape's metal, Bay's face looked even paler, her freckles as delicate as spilled cinnamon. They were both a kind of family to her, one she and her cousins had grown up next to, the other found in her family's garden and taken into their home like a lost son.

She did not know what to do with them now, the boy she feared for the beautiful and frightening things he might mean, and the love she and her cousins shared. Even though Bay had told all these lies, even though her mother warned her that Fel was a boy who did not sleep, that protectiveness still lit up inside her, for both of them.

"How has no one recognized you by now?" Estrella almost whispered it. "People here knew Marjorie. And they know you."

"I'm out of my Bay Briar costume," Bay said, gesturing to her haircut, her suspenders, her plain polished shoes, the hat she'd set on the landing. "You'd be amazed how no one looks past that. Most of the time, people don't look past what they think they know."

Estrella studied Bay.

People so often knew each other by the ways they were not the same. It was why Estrella and her cousins, with their skin in close though not matching shades of brown, all looked alike to La Pradera's guests. It was why no one recognized this dark-haired stranger as a Briar. Without her pale French braid, her flourishing gestures, her outfits that were a few ruched seams away from belonging in Marie Antoinette's court, Bay was skimmed over as some unremarkable young man.

"Why take the risk?" Estrella asked. "You could go anywhere."

"I've got to pay for everything somehow." Her eyes flicked to the hotel windows. "The easiest way is to stay here."

"How?" Estrella asked.

Bay's smile held a wince. "You do know why Marjorie's father was exiled to La Pradera, don't you?"

Estrella shook her head. That was one story Marjorie had never told, how she and her father had come to live in the place Briar failures were sent. If the grandmothers knew, and Estrella was sure they did, they never let it slip. At least not in front of her and her cousins.

"Gambling debt," Bay said. "Why do you think my grandmother taught me all those card games?"

"So you could run up your own gambling debt?" Estrella asked.

"No," Bay said. "So I'd have what she called *a moderate relationship* with gambling. She wanted me to take hold of it instead of it getting me one day like it got her father. It's the same reason she taught me the right way to drink a glass of wine when I was sixteen, so I wouldn't be a drunk when I was forty."

Estrella remembered the rising laughs from Marjorie's guests when young Bay beat them at cards. All of them roared over the felt table and the winning hand so much they didn't mind losing their money to eight-, or ten-, or thirteen-year-old Bay.

"You're gambling to cover your room every night?" Estrella asked.

"It's not gambling if you know you'll win," Bay said, and now she couldn't help her grin.

Estrella cringed.

"I'm not playing like everyone else," Bay said. "They're not even my chips. I'm there to drive up the bets. That's what I do. Every table I'm at is a high-stakes table when I'm done with it. None of the men down there want to get shown up by a kid, so they all raise until I fold. And you should see how satisfied they are when I do. Even if they lose, they feel like they've won. The house makes more, and the dealers give me a cut at the end of the night."

"And the dealers don't know who you are?" Estrella asked.

"They didn't even recognize me until I started talking about my grandmother," Bay said. "But sure, of course they do now. I know them the same way my grandmother knew their fathers."

It was so perfect Estrella couldn't help laughing.

But the shimmer of her own laugh wore off, tarnished by remembering every awful moment since Bay had gone.

"How could you risk us like this?" Estrella asked. "With you gone, did you even think what would happen if Reid threw us off the land?"

"He would never do that in a million years and you know it."

Estrella's lips stilled, the truth leaving no room for her objections.

Reid wanted to turn La Pradera into a place that made so much money, he could buy his way back from the damage done with a lit candelabra.

Without the Nomeolvides women, the gardens would go feral, flowers withering or overgrowing their beds. Even under the most devoted hands Reid could hire, the gardens would be a weak imitation of what the Nomeolvides women had made them, and he would have to pay more to keep it up than the gardens would ever make him.

"And you know me," Bay said. "I wouldn't let that happen."

"I thought I knew you," Estrella said. "But you used us." She didn't understand how awful it was until she said it. Bay had taken the legacy of disappearing loves to lay out her path away from La Pradera.

And Dalia. Sobbing, screaming Dalia. Whatever trick of the light Bay had used to convince Dalia she was turning to air and sky had worked so well, Dalia carried the memory up and down the halls at night. Each night, Estrella woke up in the bed she was sharing with Dalia to find her cousin's side cold. Every few minutes, Dalia's shadow broke the seam of light at the bottom of the door.

"You used Dalia," Estrella said. "How did you even make her believe that?"

Bay may have had the hard-jawed resolve, the faked arrogance, to drive up bets at the card tables. But she didn't have the blank expression to hide what she knew. Her guilt was so pained and clear even Fel caught it. He turned to Estrella, waiting for her to understand.

"Dalia," Estrella said, the idea so new she laughed as she said the name. "Dalia knows."

"Don't blame her," Bay said. "I begged her to help me."

"We all would have helped you," Estrella said. "All you had to do was ask."

"I didn't want you all to have to lie," Bay said.

Even though Estrella believed it, she found the heart of why Bay had asked Dalia. It was clear in the perfect contrast between the neat, pale braid Bay had worn for years, and Dalia's hair, loose and half-curly. It was in Dalia's cruel laugh and kind hands. It was in the forbidden lingerie showing at her neckline in ribbons of purple or deep red.

Estrella wanted to say Dalia's name just to check again, just to see the slight hope in Bay's face, the soft lift of her eyebrows, the parting of her lips.

The bond held tight between Estrella and her cousins had not just been their adoration of Bay. It had been that Bay seemed to love none of them back, or at least that she loved each of them only a little, and all the same.

But Bay was in love with Dalia.

Bay still hadn't eaten the scrap of cotton candy. It was dissolving on her fingers, turning to wet, pink sugar.

Voices filled the alley below, and the warm, bitter smell of cigar smoke rose up through the grated landing. Bay eyed the space underneath them, not afraid but anxious, as though these might be men she'd spurred on at the card tables.

"I promise you," Bay said, putting her hat back on, "as soon as I get what I need to keep you and your family safe, I will come back."

Estrella didn't need that promise. Of course Bay would come back. Bay would come back not just to the place Marjorie had made her own. Not just to the Nomeolvides women who had brought Bay back to life after Marjorie's death.

She would come back for the Nomeolvides girl she loved.

Bay nodded a farewell greeting at Fel, then set her hand in Estrella's hair and kissed her on the forehead.

In the moment of Bay's lips touching her hairline, Estrella expected the same flutter as when she'd kissed Bay years ago, her heart like a cabbage moth's wings. But this was a kiss Bay might give her own cousin, and it landed on Estrella's skin as dull as an ache.

Bay climbed up three more flights of the fire escape and then disappeared onto the roof.

Estrella leaned against a stretch of brick and shut her eyes, the feeling of Bay's mouth left on her forehead. Estrella had never felt more like Bay's little sister. Dalia was her beautiful cousin, fire-eyed and straight-backed, her hair sweeping behind her like a cape, and Estrella was still more girl than woman.

When she opened her eyes, Fel was holding out the little box of marzipan fruit to her.

She shook her head and gave him as much of a smile as she had. She felt how forced it must have looked on her closed lips. But she didn't want to hold a soft round of marzipan on her tongue.

She wanted to rip things apart with her teeth.

TWENTY

The main street ended. The space between lampposts grew. The last ones led Fel and Estrella to a green-flanked road.

Estrella was eating tiny rounds of sugar off a strip of paper, scraping them off with her teeth. When he'd seen the bright rows—candy buttons, she'd called them—he would not have thought this kind of rage could be brought to eating them.

He tried not to stare, both so she would not feel strange and so she would not think they had to talk. He was grateful for the quiet.

The understanding that he'd had a brother let in the first sliver of light. Then, the scent of the sugar fruit Estrella had bought him opened that crack, wide enough that the light from the moon and the stars flooded it.

He and his brother had lived somewhere else before coming

to the gray world. No matter how he grasped at it, he still could not remember the shape of the gray world, but now he remembered so much else.

The smell of the painted fruit, the sweetness of the sugar and drunk bitter scent of the almonds, it made him remember things shared on holidays when he and his brother were children. The perfume of rosewater. The spice of anise. The carmín that dyed rock candy, and how his brother loved telling him that the red came from crushed insects.

These memories took root, turning to rows of uncountable trees. They became the orchard Fel had once run through. They bloomed into almond and cherry blossoms, fluffy as the cotton candy Estrella had set in his palms. They splintered into the thin leaves of olive trees.

All these things pressed into him, and his heart felt as though it might give and break like a bone.

The sound of ripping paper drew his eyes to the girl walking next to him.

She bit off a candy button so hard she took a scrap of white with it.

"You're eating paper," he said. "Do you know you're eating paper?"

She swallowed and looked at him. He still wanted the distraction of her. But speaking had been a mistake. He saw in her face that she took it as an invitation to ask questions.

"What happened back there?" she asked.

He could say these words. They were true, and if he did not

speak them when he had the chance maybe they would stop being true.

"I had a brother," he said.

She tilted her head, waiting for the rest.

"A brother who liked men," he said.

"Liked men as in . . ."

"As in the way you and your cousins like Bay."

Her eyes widened. She tried hiding it with a few blinks.

"It's hard not to notice," he said.

"And that doesn't bother you?" Estrella asked. "You don't think we're all damned?"

He felt like he should say yes. He felt as though this was another test, and the angels would strike him down on this road if he gave the wrong answer.

But lying was just as much of a sin. There was nothing to tell her but the truth.

"No," he said. "I don't believe that."

He didn't believe anything that his brother was could be wrong. Even if he could not remember his brother's name, or his face, or anything more than his hands, he knew those were hands that had cared for him. Hands that were smart, and even more callused than Fel's, and that made so little into enough to live on.

And now Fel remembered those hands on another man's back, fingers slipping under his suspenders. The warmth of Fel's slight shame covered him, like this was something he might have seen when he wasn't supposed to.

"Maybe if my brother hadn't loved like that I'd believe something else," Fel said, and with saying this came the deeper breath of confessing something. "But I don't think it's anyone else's to judge."

Estrella laughed softly. "You're not from a hundred years ago."

That deeper breath turned to a worn-out sigh. "I don't know." He shut his eyes, still walking. "I remember where I lived when I was little."

That was the place where he'd learned to pick dandelion greens, heaping them into esparto grass baskets. A world and a whole life before he and his brother had gone to the gray world, where sometimes those same dandelion greens were all they could find to eat. When he was small, the sharp, bitter taste of the greens had been the taste of early spring to him, not the taste of being hungry.

"What do you remember?" Estrella asked.

He opened his eyes. "The trees raining petals. When they were in bloom and the winds came. Just all those petals. A whole snow of them." He remembered those trees planted in wide, deep beds, each a little higher than the one before, so the snow thickened as it fell. "All that pink and white snowing down over everything."

Estrella bit her lip, like she was trying not to smile. Her fingers softened the edge of the candy dot paper. The colors of the buttons had stained the pads of her fingers.

He knew she was imagining it. She couldn't not. The air

glimmering with confetti. Those petals, tiny and round. Weightless.

Beneath the memory of the falling blossoms, small flowers grew in the shadows of wide trees. A stalk that held petals the color of Estrella's skin. The brown of blossoms matched her, the paler undersides of the petals like the paler undersides of her hands and feet.

But this was something he didn't know how to tell her.

They left the lampposts behind. He couldn't find the moon. In the dark, there was just the taste of almonds and sugar on his tongue, and the shape of Estrella against the grasses and trees.

Their fingers at their sides brushed.

"Sorry," he said, drawing his hand back.

She held on. Her grasp stung his hand, sore from hitting the men in the brick alley, but he didn't move. That brush of their fingers was a door cracked open, and she was widening the space, not letting it fall shut.

She stopped. She looked at him. And the feeling that her stare would not land, would not settle on his eyes or his mouth was so strong he felt it on his skin.

He knew what this was. She couldn't have Bay, so she wanted whatever else was in reach. She had everything that had happened tonight knocking around in her, all that spite toward Bay and toward Dalia, and Fel was the ground she could bury it in.

She had found him in the valley made of flowers. Her family had looked after him. It wasn't his place to ask her, *please, please don't do this.* To tell her he felt for her what she would never feel for him, not when she'd given her heart to someone who was beautiful in braided hair and the bright colors of citrus fruits, and beautiful in men's trousers and suspenders. There was no fighting that. He didn't want to.

And he didn't want to be what she played with in the meantime, not like this.

Estrella let go. She took her hand back with such sudden force that Fel opened his mouth to say he was sorry, again.

But then that hand was on the back of his neck. She caught his mouth as he opened it, ready to apologize, and her lips kept him from speaking. The dye and sugar of the candy buttons cut through the almond taste on his tongue.

For a second, her mouth shoved him back far and fast enough that he could barely hold on to something else remembered. It was slick and cold as an algae-covered stone, but he got a solid grasp on it, the last time someone had kissed him, in the gray world.

That time, another boy, assuming Fel was the same as his brother, had kissed him. How little Fel liked it had seemed like a failing. He did not like boys, at least not this one, he had thought with such collapsing disappointment. How could any difference in himself from his brother be good? He wanted to be his brother, smart and kind and unafraid to ask for what he wanted. If sliding his hands under another boy's suspenders would make him more like his brother, he wanted that too.

The other boy had laughed at him, pushed him away. He told him how awful he was at it, how much worse he was than his brother. And that had seemed like another of Fel's failings.

But this, Estrella kissing him, this brought him back to a time before the gray world, when there had been color, and he and his brother had lived in sunlight softened by olive trees. When he closed his eyes and kissed her back, Estrella brought him to the colors of a place he could almost touch.

With her mouth on his, the world was snow. Not ice. Not winter. The snow of countless almond and cherry blossoms, the storm of white and pink they had both thought of at the same moment.

This girl who had found him had turned him into an ember, glowing at the end of a candlewick. She could either pinch him out into nothing or light him into a flare.

But the feeling of a truth he did not know, awful and unnamed, hung wide and close as the clouds. And he could not stop wondering if this was the shadow of the thing he had done, the reason God had taken his memories. The reason he had his own crimes etched onto his back. This was the weight of his own sin, and he could not even remember it enough to confess it.

He could not give Estrella what she deserved, someone clean and true.

He broke the touch of their mouths, hard enough that he stumbled back.

A thread of cold air cut between them.

The white of her eyes shone in the dark. He couldn't tell if that startled look, the flicker of her irises moving, was from what she'd done or because he'd stopped her.

Before his fingers could find her hand in the dark, she was running off the road and toward the trees.

He called her name. But she kept running, until the night and the tall grasses swallowed her.

The pads of her fingers had left the dye of candy buttons on his shirt and his hands. He touched his neck, and it came off on his fingers. The blue and yellow and pink were his proof she had touched him.

TWENTY-ONE

Estrella stood in the hall, the first time she could remember pausing in front of Dalia's door.

The cousins all entered one another's rooms without knocking. They never apologized if one walked in on another half-naked, or drying her hair, or scrubbing salt and baking soda over the red stains on their underwear at the same time every month. When Fel started sleeping in Estrella's room, she had tied a green ribbon around the doorknob, a reminder to her cousins that she wasn't in there, and not to walk in on this skittish boy changing his clothes or sweating through a nightmare.

But opening this door felt like holding her lungs still to go underwater.

At the sound of the hinges, Dalia looked up, pausing mid-stitch. She was sewing a fabric leaf back onto a nightgown. Calla's.

Estrella had always recognized Dalia as beautiful in the way all her cousins were beautiful. But now, Estrella saw the woman Bay loved. Her black hair and dark eyes warmed against the fire colors she wore, the softened oranges and peaches, the butter yellows and chili reds. Her eyelashes were lush and curling as the center petals on her cream dinner plate dahlias.

But that lie. It spun and whirled and pulled Estrella down.

"You know, we had a great-great-aunt who wanted to be an actress," Estrella said.

Dalia set down the nightgown, tucking the threaded needle into the gathered fabric. "Estrella."

"Abuela Flor told me about her. She used to play in the chorus in the theater in town sometimes." Estrella let the bitterness thicken in her voice. "If she was as good an actress as you, she could've been the star of every show."

Dalia's eyes shut. "Estrella."

From her dress pocket, Estrella pulled a bag of strawberry vanilla drops, Dalia's favorite. She threw them at her cousin.

Dalia caught the bag against her chest. She looked up from the sugar-sanded red and cream.

"I held you," Estrella said, her back teeth set so hard the words sounded choked. "My heart broke when yours broke."

She had thrown her arms around Dalia as she screamed and cried into the air. She had blinked at the ceiling in the half-empty bed, worrying about her cousin who slept even less than the boy down the hall.

But Estrella knew now. It hadn't been grief keeping Dalia awake.

It had been the unfamiliar guilt of keeping a secret from her cousins.

Estrella shut the door behind her.

"You're a liar," she said, startled at how level the words came.

"Bay had to get out from under Reid and you know it," Dalia said. "The best way to do that was for everyone to think she was gone. If you had a better idea, I'd love to hear it."

"I don't blame you for what you did. I blame you for keeping it from me. From all of us."

"It was safer for everyone. I did this for us."

"You did this for you," Estrella said. "Because you wanted to be the only one she was still alive to. You wanted her to be yours."

"That is not true." Dalia got to her feet. "And even if I did, so what? We have to answer to each other for everything?"

"We don't lie to each other. We don't keep things from each other."

"Oh, we don't?" Dalia asked. "So you just forgot to tell us you were planning on torching Reid's car?"

Estrella shoved her anger down. She tried to dull the whispering voice reminding her that she and Calla had kept their own secrets.

"You don't know anything about that," Estrella said.

"Because you didn't tell me, or any of us. And you didn't tell us what you did to make Reid forget about it. Are you in bed with him now?"

"That's disgusting."

"I mean what are you doing for him?" Dalia said. "What does he want from you?"

"A good show for his friends," Estrella said. "That's all."

"What does that mean?" Dalia asked. "Are you his date now?"

"He just wants me to show his friends how we grow flowers. It's nothing."

"I don't like this," Dalia said. "You're not a sideshow. He has no right to ask you for that."

"A few flowers for a whole car?" Estrella asked. "That's the best deal we'll ever get from someone like him. Leave it alone. If it was something you needed to know, I would have told you. And if you'd asked me earlier, I would have told you then. I didn't lie to you. We're not supposed to lie to each other."

"We give each other reasons to," Dalia said.

"What does that mean?"

"Remember Gloria and that boy at Marjorie's costume ball? We ate them alive. And Azalea with that girl's lipstick on her dress? We acted like she was cheating on us."

"We did not."

Dalia set a harsh glare on her, a visible reminder of the cousins' silent judgment. They laughed over Azalea flirting with pearl-wearing women just to provoke them, or Calla's joking pronouncement that the first boy at church to grow a mustache would win her heart. But when they saw anything true and deep in each other, they turned their backs. When they caught a dreaming smile or a halting nervousness across the ballroom, their disapproval stamped out any ember of new love.

Their family's curse had made them cold toward each other.

They had held together on everything but this. They did not want to see one another mourn vanished lovers like so many of their mothers and grandmothers and great-grandmothers had. They had all worried over the same thing, and it had made them harsher than the sternest of their grandmothers.

"We were protecting each other." Estrella took a step forward, breaking the light of the bedside lamp.

"We didn't protect each other from loving Bay."

"Because we thought loving Bay was safe."

"Only because you thought she'd never want any of us," Dalia said, her voice raising to a yell before she tamped it down into a whisper.

The words went into Estrella deep and fast.

Their mothers did not notice the other moments that made color bloom in their daughters' cheeks. How Azalea flirted with girls in ruffled dresses. How the thing that first made Estrella fall a little in love with boys or girls was so often their hands, whether they were showing at the edge of a shirt cuff or a lace sleeve. How Gloria blushed when she caught the eye of women in sleek gowns, women who wore their hair in low, smooth chignons and who preferred gray or black or navy. And how she shared her laughter, her true, fluttering laugh, with boys who could more easily be called pretty than handsome.

Estrella and her cousins had grown up admiring girls and boys in the splintered light of chandeliers. They fell a little bit in love with women and with men at Marjorie's summer parties and winter balls. None of them had seemed safe the way loving Bay had seemed safe. Bay, the one they'd grown up alongside but who was never close enough for them to hold on to. She was the yellow fleck of a planet in the night sky, too far to grasp, but shining and easy to find, appearing in the dark so reliably they could almost believe she was theirs.

Estrella and her cousins blessed one another's love for Bay not only because they shared it but because they considered it impossible.

"Why can't we love who we want to love?" Dalia asked. "I love Bay. Gloria's too scared to fall in love with anyone, and so is Azalea. She'll kill you if you say that to her, but it's true and she knows it. She flirts because it's safe. Calla's young enough that maybe if we all stop being so knotted up about this she doesn't have to be too. And you"—Dalia looked at the door behind Estrella—"you care about him. And you're terrified about what that could mean."

"Because what if he disappears again?" This time Estrella was almost yelling before she choked her words to a whisper.

Azalea's first guess made as much sense as any after. This was a boy a Nomeolvides woman had once loved to vanishing, and now, generations later, the gardens had given him back. In him, her family found hope for their own lovers reappearing. But Estrella and her cousins worried that if they did not care for this boy, then the wrath of not only La Pradera but whatever great-great-grandmother had loved him would pelt all of them like hail.

Estrella could not be the second girl in this family to love Fel into vanishing. She had kissed him, eyes shut, her thoughts turning to blossoms streaming over terrace gardens. He had been the one to pull away, and it left her skin so hot that she could not look at him.

Dalia's eyes opened a little wider. Not surprise. Sympathy so deep it was almost pity.

"If we love them, we lose them," Estrella said.

"Sometimes," Dalia said.

"If we love them for long enough and they stay long enough, we always lose them."

The only lovers who did not vanish were ones who did not stay. The ones who left or who were made to leave were the ones who lived. Sometimes the men's superstitions drove them from La Pradera. Sometimes Nomeolvides women's hearts shrank from their own desire until one morning they told their lovers *Please go*, coolly as if it was the first night they spent together. And sometimes, in rare, blessed instances, both halves of a couple grew tired of each other at once.

The ones who stayed, the ones so taken with their own love that they decided to risk what they considered old wives' tales, were the ones they lost.

A sickening question came back to Estrella, the wondering about which of her relatives might have once loved Fel.

"He's someone else's," Estrella said.

"What does that mean?" Dalia asked.

"You heard what Azalea said the day we found him. He belonged to someone else. I don't want to be a girl who steals my great-great-grandmother's boyfriend."

"You don't know that," Dalia said.

"What other way do we explain it?" Estrella asked. "You believe the fairy tale our grandmothers tell us? That the gardens wanted to give us a brother and give them a son?"

"So you want to go on loving Bay because Bay is the safe choice?" Dalia asked.

"Bay? The safe choice?" A bitter laugh built in Estrella's throat. Maybe they had thought Bay was safe in some ways, but not this way, not in the sharp language of their family. "What do you think our mothers would say if any of us tried to be with her? If we hadn't all stalemated each other by loving her at the same time? They've only let this go on because she can't get us pregnant. Try kissing Bay in front of them, see what they say. See what they say when it's out in the open."

Dalia's flinch was so deep Estrella felt her own body mirroring it.

"Oh," Estrella said.

Bay wanted Dalia. Dalia wanted her in a way that ran deeper than the love passed back and forth between five cousins.

And they had acted on it, a dark-haired girl kissing a pale, freckled one.

"You're with her," Estrella said.

"That's not the point."

"But you are."

"I love her," Dalia said, the words quiet, given through the small space between her lips.

"We all loved her."

"She thinks the Briars don't want her because there's something wrong with her," Dalia said. "She thinks it's the same reason her mother left her with Marjorie. Did you even know that?"

The center of Estrella's heart pinched, a hard knot for Bay. But the instinct to defend herself washed over it, so before she could stop herself she said, "What does that have to do with anything?"

"We never bothered to know her," Dalia said.

"She didn't want to talk about her mother. Or the Briars. She told us that."

"No, she didn't talk about them because we didn't give her space to. We let her tell us she didn't want to talk about any of it and we left it at that, because we didn't really want to hear about it."

"Why would we want to make her talk about it?" Estrella asked. "Why would we make her want to talk about anything that hurts her?"

"Because that's what people need sometimes." For a few words, Dalia yelled, before drawing her voice back down. "And if you love them, you let them. You wait until they're ready. You give them the room to talk about it. But we didn't. We didn't want to see that there was pain in her. We just wanted what she was to us. How she entertained us. We wanted her charm, not her broken places. We didn't want to see that there was anything broken in her."

"That's supposed to impress me?" Estrella asked. "That you think she's broken."

"Everyone's broken. The only difference is how."

Without wanting to, Estrella breathed in Dalia's words. They stung like winter air.

"I love her for who she is, not who she was to all of us," Dalia said. "We thought everything about her was some costume, some kind of show, but she is a person. She doesn't exist for us to look at. She wasn't just there so we could admire her. She's her own person. We never left any room for that. And that's my fault as much as yours, or Gloria's, or Azalea's, or Calla's. We all did it. I did it. We made her ours, and we didn't leave any space for her to decide for herself. We gave her no room to be anything other than what we made her."

Each word clung to Estrella's skin like wet leaves, the stems scratching and prickling.

Dalia was right. The cousins had diminished Bay, reduced her to what she was to them. Even tonight, Estrella had done it. She had contrasted the satin trousers and French braid with the suspenders and felt hat. She had never considered the possibility that both were fully Bay, or that maybe neither was, or that both were but so were other possibilities Estrella and her cousins could not guess, because Bay had yet to live them.

"We acted like she was ours," Dalia said. "And she was never ours."

Estrella shook her head, not because this was untrue, because it was a truth wider than Dalia realized. Nothing was theirs. Not this house. Not their dresses, bought on Marjorie's account at the shop in town.

Not La Pradera. It was always its own, vicious and protective.

The only thing that was theirs was the legacy passed down to them, the fear that they would ruin anyone they loved. And now came this new guilt, breaking through like starflowers between forget-me-not vines. Estrella hadn't known Bay. Maybe none of them had. And if Dalia was right, and Estrella hadn't learned Bay in all this time, how could she ever know the odd boy La Pradera had given them?

"She never belonged to any of us," Dalia said. "She was always her own and we never let her be her own."

All of it rushed through Estrella. La Pradera in the hands of a Briar who had not lived here, had not grown to love this land and these gardens. Bay dying to all of them and then coming back to life. The lies Dalia had told, the tears she had forced, to both kill Bay and save her.

Fel's mouth on Estrella's.

The way he kissed her was soft, like he was asking permission, but his lips were almost as rough as his fingertips.

Her mother had been wrong. Men like Reid were not cotton candy. It was girls with hearts that could not be kept from falling in love, and anyone unlucky enough to be loved by them.

They all dissolved like spun sugar in water.

Estrella let everything awful and true shove her out of the room.

Dalia called after her, her name said like she was a child to be reasoned with.

But Estrella let all those things chase her down the stairs, out of the stone house, through the gardens where dahlias and calla lilies rose up around her like a flowering forest.

The lawns and paths flew under her feet, but still, she ran, until the gardens thinned and the land passed from tended to wild.

When she was small, Estrella worried that the mere act of crossing La Pradera's borders would kill her. When Gloria and Dalia had first lured their younger cousins out at night, the younger ones had winced at the act of setting their feet against the main road without their mothers' blessing.

But in the years after, Estrella understood the hold La Pradera had on her and her family. It was intricate, and complicated. They could sneak into town to buy the deep brown and cognac-colored ribbons their grandmothers thought young girls should not wear. They just couldn't run.

They couldn't leave La Pradera with the intention of leaving for good. Like the distance between the rustle of soft wind and the warning of a coming storm, La Pradera sensed the difference between daughters sneaking out at night and girls fleeing its hold.

The land always knew.

Estrella didn't care. She was breaking free of this before it wore her into dust. It could kill her if it wanted. By the time it took hold of her, she would be too far for it to drag her back.

Her mother, in refusing to name her for a flower, had thought she was doing her a kindness. Named Rosa herself, her mother had grown up believing she was nothing but black magic petals and secret garden roses, and had not wanted the same for her daughter.

Her mother had even hoped that by giving her a name that was not a flower, she would free her from the weight of the Nomeolvides gift and curse, and the hold of La Pradera.

Estrella would never know.

Unless she ran.

The sky rushed by above her, like the night was water sweeping the stars along its current. The wild grass rose to her ankles and then to her knees by the time she had to stop. Each breath turned wet and rasping.

She swallowed hard, but the trees in the distance blurred like the reflection on a stirred lake. Coughing rose up in her. It drew a line of pain from her collarbone to her sternum.

Her lungs forced a hard cough up through her throat, and she didn't have the air to fight. She had to work for each breath, and the effort seared into her. Her rib cage was something hot, lit.

Even in that moment of her eyes and throat stinging, she felt it, La Pradera grabbing her, fast and certain and vindictive.

As long as she stayed, it would protect her, giving her a place safe from the taunts and threats that came with her family being considered witches.

But it knew she was running, and it wanted her to understand it knew.

She doubled over. Coughing wrenched a spray of blood from her throat. It left flecks of red on her hands, a bitter taste on her tongue. The force of her next cough made her gasp for air, and the spray of blood dotted her skirt.

It didn't feel wet.

It felt like powder. Like ground cayenne, except more bitter than spiced.

The stars showed her the stains.

She brushed her fingers over the spots. The color smudged, leaving powdery trails on the fabric and her fingers.

Not just blood.

Pollen. Gold- and rust-colored pollen, like from the anthers of a lily.

She swallowed, and tasted it. On the back of her tongue, it felt chalky, and a kind of sweet that reminded her less of sugar and more of the medicine her grandmother gave her in winter.

The bitter taste of pollen rose in her throat again. She waited for it to clear. It didn't. The coughing felt like the force of her own palm pressing into her chest. But her hands were not on her chest. That feeling of weight came from inside her, her lungs pulling in on themselves.

The gardens wanted to keep her so badly they were killing her. They had their hands around her so tightly they were choking the life out of her.

Her lungs fought to breathe, but now she felt the weight of

the gardens pressing into her. A million flowers, a thousand branches, the wide spread of the sunken garden.

The pollen coated her throat and the back of her tongue. It burned through her chest and made her eyes water. The trees and sky looked like paint running. Whatever fight she had left was so deep inside her it grew cold and could not reach the surface.

Her own breathing turned on her. Her throat and the wet surfaces inside her lungs grew hot and tight. She was the snow globe that had once rested on Gloria's desk. Half the water had evaporated out, so the little white pieces of snow scratched the glass and the carved trees.

She fell to her hands and knees, lungs pinching and tensing. The salt of her own blood stung her throat. Her lungs could not take the full breaths the rest of her body wanted so badly her veins vibrated.

Under the night breeze, she heard La Pradera whispering her name, telling her that if she had a heart set on leaving and never coming back, it would kill her.

She would not leave the gardens alive. They would let loose their rage over her ungrateful heart, for letting them shelter her and then fleeing them. It would strike her down for abandoning the land her family had made their home.

And it would punish her family for what it was, women who loved their lovers out of existence. They had brought the curse of their hearts and blood onto this land, and for that La Pradera would forgive them. Unless they ran.

She collapsed onto her side, the sky filling her vision. The dark drifted down over her like a sheet.

Her name had not saved her.

Estrella's mother had hoped. If she named a girl for things held in the sky, how could she be tied to anywhere on this earth? But her mother had not freed her from their family's legacy.

She had just given it the shape of stars.

TWENTY-TWO

He left her alone, keeping his distance from the door she shared with Dalia.

He dreamed of the wooden horses, of tiny bursts of fire swallowing them. Wisps of green showed under each small flame. When he looked closer he saw that it was not fire, but red starflowers. They grew between the horse figurines. Petals brushed their painted flanks. The blooms, gold at the center but edged in bright red, looked like a fire's embers. They were lit wood chips, live and glowing.

He woke up with his hands already throwing the sheet aside. He blinked to clear the salt of his own sweat, dried on his eyelashes.

Floorboards creaked in the hall, the give of old wood under footsteps. Not her. He could almost tell her walk from each of her cousins'. The rhythm of their feet on the worn wood was like their voices, similar but with enough difference between them to tell apart.

He still slept in his pants, an instinct that felt like a habit, though he didn't know why. Now he pulled on his shirt and opened the door.

Dalia paused, not quite putting her weight down with her next step.

They spoke at the same time, Dalia whispering, "She's with you, isn't she?" in the same moment Fel asked, "She's not with you?"

So Estrella was still out there, hiding under the star-salted sky. She hid from Dalia because of the lies she'd told, and Fel because he had been too stupid and afraid to let her kiss him, and her cousins because she could not lie to them.

All the things he'd imagined as Estrella led him through the dark. The fear of her hands breaking into petals. The worry that her heart might forget it was the thing keeping her alive. All that he could not help imagining, because the older Nomeolvides women would not say what became of girls who ran.

What if, now, the land didn't know what Estrella was so sure it would? Or worse, what if she was one of the running-away girls, and the gardens could feel it in the distant echo of her steps?

He went for the stairs, and Dalia's voice brushed his back. "Fel," she said, as loudly as she could without breaking a whisper. It sounded half like a question, and half like a warning.

"If she comes back, don't let her leave," he said over his shoulder.

"You really think she'll listen to me?" Dalia asked.

Fel turned around. He read in Dalia's face the way she was

unfolding tonight like a crumpled piece of paper, imagining all the awful things Estrella thought.

"She loves you," Fel said. "No matter how angry she is now, she loves you. You know that."

Outside the stone house, the air smelled like winter-bare branches, as though the leaves and flowers had all left at once. Fel wondered if Estrella's path off La Pradera would light up like the trailing glow of stars, so the land could always find her.

But beyond the garden lamps, there was no light. There was no sign or star leading to her. So he followed the same pathless route she'd led him on, the back way toward town. He waded through grass that brushed his shins and felt thick as water. It was the kind of grass he remembered from being very young, thin green stalks tufted with gold.

He expected to find her sitting with her back against a tree, maybe tearing another row of sugar buttons off the rolled paper in her pocket.

Instead, he found a break in the grass where her body weighted it down.

Under the rustling of the bristles, he heard the soft, choked sound of her breathing.

With slow steps, he came closer, so he wouldn't startle her.

Her hair and her skirt fanned out in the grass, the fluffy stalks lapping at her skin. Her elbows seemed bent in a way more from letting herself fall into the grass than from lying down. Her hands almost touched her hair, fingers curled in on themselves.

From the sound, and her stare up toward the sky, he thought

she might be crying. The fluttering of her rib cage under her dress matched the staggered, caught breaths between sobs. He'd seen it on her and her cousins, their breathing frayed from so much crying.

But her cheeks did not shine with tears. Her lips were not pale with dry salt.

Her dress and her hands were dotted with red.

Her family's worry hadn't just grown out of nightmares.

The things that had sent him out into the dark were true.

He knelt next to her, guiding her arms to him and telling her to hold on to him. He swallowed hard enough to choke the panic out of his voice.

She turned away from him and coughed into her hair. He winced at the sound of it tearing her throat.

"Hold on to me," he said again. He didn't know if she had heard him, but then she did. She held on to him. So hard he felt her jagged nails, the ones her grandmother was always telling her to file, slipping under the collar of his shirt. They dragged it aside and cut into his shoulder.

He gave her a weak laugh. "You're good at that."

He liked the slight pain of it. It reminded him that he was not losing her in the dark.

With each step closer to La Pradera, her breathing deepened and evened. Her body felt less fevered, her rib cage less like hot metal wrapped in her dress.

"It won't let us go," she whispered, her words faint as the rushing sound of the trees.

"It's very beautiful here," he said, just to keep talking to her, to keep her talking. "Maybe that's why it wants to keep you. Because you make it beautiful."

But he could not make the truth sound kind, or safe. Speaking it only made it worse. It made the Nomeolvides women children of these gardens. The land was a vengeful mother who loved them only as long as they did not run from her. If they did, it drew cords of breath from their lungs until they could not run.

She did not thank him, and for this he was grateful even to the God who had left him with so many questions. Fel had never known how to thank Estrella for finding him in the valley made of flowers. He'd tried, but any words he thought of putting together felt worse than saying nothing. They were a single prayer candle in a dark church, doing little more than showing how every other corner lay unlit.

When he got back to her family's house, back to the bed she'd grown up in, her breathing was so quiet he thought she'd fallen asleep. But just as he turned away from her, he felt the brush of her fingers on his shoulder.

"I did that to you?" she asked, her words weakened into a whisper.

He looked over his shoulder. Her nails had cut into his skin, tiny half-moons of blood staining the back of his shirt. It mirrored the blood from her mouth that flecked the front.

"I don't mind," he said.

His pride in that blood opened enough space for a story his

brother had told him. Fel could not remember his brother's name but he remembered his voice, low and sure. The stories on his tongue. And this one he told over and over, whenever one of them got cut badly enough to leave a stain on their shirts they could not rub out with salt and cold water.

Their grandmother had heard the story from a horse breeder. She had told it to Fel's brother, and Fel's brother had told it to him a hundred times. Now Fel let the story onto his own tongue. He spoke it as he remembered it, as though his brother was el Espíritu Santo, the Holy Ghost giving him the words. It lit inside him, bright as a Pentecost flame.

"Red-shouldered horses," Fel said, echoing his brother's voice, "they have flecks of red in their coats. It's so thick on their shoulders it looks like a wound, like spilled blood. But that red shoulder is a mark of the spirit within the horse. It means the horse is brave."

The story taught Fel to wear his own wounds like a bloody-shouldered horse. It did not matter to his brother whether they were wide gashes they had to close with cheap liquor and sewing needles, or small as the half-moons of Estrella's fingernails.

Or wounds thrown across his back that healed into trails of scarring.

That which looked to others like injury was, to them, a thing of pride.

Fel waited for Estrella to fall back asleep, lured into dreaming not by his voice but his brother's, his way of telling stories that sounded even more like magic for being true.

Her hands, reckless and sure as her voice was weak, found him in the dark. She knelt on the bed to meet his height standing. She pulled off his shirt. Her fingers were so fast he didn't think to stop her until he was naked from the waist up and shivering under the possibility that she could see his back in the dark.

He felt the heat of her breath on the back of his neck and thought she might bite him, tear open the same place her nails had cut into him. Make him even more of a bloody-shouldered horse than she had with her fingers. He was sure of it when her lips touched his shoulder blade. Not like she was trying to smooth over somewhere he was hurt. Like she wanted to know the taste of him.

He flinched away, and Estrella's hands fell from him.

His hands grabbed for his shirt, but he left it, lowering his head to the dark floorboards.

He deserved this, standing before her and letting her see the record of what he had done but could not remember.

"What happened?" she asked.

He shook his head, to tell her he didn't know.

"Does it hurt?" she asked.

He shook his head, this time to tell her no, not anymore. But the pain was written so deeply into his body that some mornings he woke up sure his back was bleeding, worried that he was staining sheets that belonged to this family.

He could remember each stroke coming down on him so sharply he could not think of it without his shoulders tensing. Whenever he forgot, he dreamed of it. With each one, he had felt like he was sinking deeper into a fever, and he was surer that the lash coming down on him was made of lightning. It was fast as those rushes of blazing white in the sky, but hot enough to spark brush fields into wildfires. It was a cord of heat, searing him open.

His body remembered how the scars had come to be his. But he could not remember why.

Estrella put her palm on his jawline, her thumb across his cheek. She turned his mouth to hers. He felt the wavering breath in her body, an echo of what La Pradera had done to her. The way she kissed him was soft, almost hesitant.

Her lips held the sweet and bitter taste like a dull spice. Like the pollen that sometimes brushed his lips when the grand-mothers told him to drink the perfume of La Pradera's flowers, really take it in, so the petals touched his face.

He liked her kissing him like this, her mouth light on his. But he worried about what it meant, her hesitating with him when she seemed so sure about everything else.

"You don't need to be careful with me," he said, their lips brushing as he spoke the words.

She pulled away enough to look at him. "What?"

He tried to think of another way of explaining it, that she didn't need to treat him like something fragile. The scars that marked him had not made him more breakable than he was before.

They'd just left him with nightmares. They shoved their way in when there was so much else he wanted to remember instead.

So he said it again. "You don't have to be careful with me."

The light off Estrella's eyes showed her considering.

He wanted her to draw the air from his lungs. He wanted to give her the breath in him so she would forget how La Pradera had choked hers from her body.

He felt her taking this understanding into her.

She kissed him hard enough that he could not tell it from her biting him. This was not something she was doing out of pity for him, and he let himself fall under the relief of this. Her touch was strong and certain as a storm, her fingers like the shock of hail and hard rain, her breath a cold current against his back.

And when she was done with him, when she was through wrecking him, he slept. He dreamed that the ceiling was turning to blue borraja. A whole sky of it spread out above them, each bloom both a star and a scrap of darkness. It rained over them, like the cherry blossoms drifting through the far corners of his memory. Their hands on each other made them each part their lips, so they caught the petals on their tongues like snow.

And he slept. He slept in the way God and his own soul had not let him sleep since he first opened his eyes in the garden.

TWENTY-THREE

Fel's skin grew warmer as he slept. Estrella's veins had felt coiled, taut as cords, but the heat off his body made them give. The muscle around her lungs eased. She set her palms against his back. The contours of his scars crossed her hands, his skin as warm as the ground late in the afternoon. She wondered if it was his dreams that did this, blazing inside him like embers.

She traced her fingers along his scars. They branched over his back. He looked like ground that had been tilled too hard, rock that had been storm-weathered.

He had seemed so much more like some unnamed saint than a boy she could ever touch. He had seemed unknowable because she had assumed there was nothing more to know than his nightmares and the praying reverence he shared with the grandmothers.

But there were broken places in him, too.

She saw him carrying the shame of this, his grasping at re-membering what had happened. She wanted to tell him she felt nothing about these scars but hate for whoever had given them to him. The time he had once been alive, the time signaled by the clothes she'd found him in, was one Estrella thought of as a world that would punish boys like him for small, easy things. If he'd been on the crew of a ship, he could've gotten them from talking back.

But she didn't know how to tell him this without sounding like she was calling the time he'd lived in backward. So instead she kissed the line of each one she could find in the dark, the veins of scarring smooth under her lips.

Light spilled onto the windowsill. It crawled across the ceil-ing, casting a veil of gold over the starflowers she thought she'd imagined the night before. The deep blue of the borraja light-ened and warmed, the vines glowing like they were made of sun.

Estrella slipped out of this bed she had grown up in and down the hall, as though she could pretend she had nothing to do with the meadow covering the rafters. She acted as if it was not hers, or at least no more hers than his.

Dalia's dress for Reid's ball hung from the curtain rod, the skirt brushing the floor. Dawn filled the window, and the color of the dress lit up coral. The skirt, streaked with brushstrokes of black, looked like a wild poppy.

Estrella slid into bed next to Dalia.

She could hate Dalia when they were both awake. But asleep, she was the same Dalia who'd smuggled them the dark lingerie and deep perfume their mothers thought they were too young for. She was the Dalia who'd convinced rich men to buy their grandmothers gifts, whispering that if they gave las brujas viejas offerings they would bring luck back to their own estates. The Dalia who had the same craving for saladitos, her mother's salted plums dusted with anise and chili, every month when she bled.

Estrella combed her fingers through her cousin's hair, kissing her temple like she was a favorite doll.

Dalia groaned softly. "You're welcome."

"For what?" Estrella whispered.

"Lying for you," Dalia said, still half-asleep. "She'll wring your neck like a chicken, remember?"

Estrella tried not to laugh. Either Dalia had been listening in, or her mother had tossed the threat around like confetti.

The sun rose past the window, and the hallway outside turned to chiffon and satin. Yellow and pink trailed out of her cousins' hands. Lilac and green hung from curtain rods.

Estrella took in perfumed air in slow, even breaths. La Pradera's sudden hold, its pulling her back, had left her tired and dragging.

Dalia brushed color onto her cheeks while she was still lying in bed. She outlined her eyes in the blue of dark water. Then she pulled Estrella out of bed, shoving her dress at her.

Estrella gave in to knowing she would not tell. She would not break open Dalia's secrets and Bay's, not even for her other cousins.

"I don't want to do this," Estrella said.

"None of us do." Dalia put lipstick on her, a pink-red that stood bright near the blue of her dress. "But now you know what happens to any of us if Reid throws us out, so we have to." Dalia brushed a stray eyelash off Estrella's cheek. "Just do what he asked and be done. Trust me, you don't want to owe him anything."

"No," Estrella said. "I didn't mean that." She looked toward the door. "I mean I don't want to lie to them."

Dalia fastened the last hook-and-eye clasp on her dress. "Then don't say anything."

Estrella clipped on the necklace that had once belonged to her father's mother. Estrella had never met either one of them, her father or his mother, but she knew he had given Rosa Nomeolvides this necklace. Years later, long after he had left both her and La Pradera, Estrella's mother had caught her holding it as gently as a feather.

Her mother had said she could keep it, shrugging as though loaning a hairpin.

There were two kinds of Nomeolvides hearts, ones broken by the vanishings, and ones who counted themselves lucky to have seen the back of their lovers as they left.

Estrella and her cousins climbed the stone steps to the ballroom. The air glittered with white lights. The sound of string instruments—violins, a cello, a harp—wafted out the French doors.

All five cousins halted at the threshold.

Marjorie's balls had always turned La Pradera into a land as beautiful and magical as a fairy tale. The acres of flower beds, the swirls of hedges, the gardens dense with colorful bulbs all seemed like a kingdom that held an infinite number of enchanting stories. In the roses, visitors saw as many possibilities for love as there were petals on the blossoms. They looked into the fountains like they held a thousand wishes. The first bloom of closed hyacinths looked like painted Easter eggs hidden in the green.

But now there were no children in their Sunday clothes, spinning under the flowering trees. No mothers in straight black dresses, because the dresses they wore to funerals were the nicest ones they owned. No young men wearing the oddest suits they could find at the secondhand shops, and their girlfriends who'd sewn their own tulle skirts.

Instead of a party sprinkled with rich men and their wives, this was all rich men and their wives. They gleamed like the mirrored hallways flanking the ballroom.

The men had kept to crisp black and white, the women all polished color. A rich man's daughter wore a skirt that looked like the endless ruffles of a white peony. A woman Estrella's mother's age stood in a column of satin striped like a rare orchid. A laughing wife had on a yellow-and-red skirt with curled edges like tulip petals.

"What *is* all this?" Azalea asked.

The cousins turned to her, wondering if they had all spoken the same words.

The music, the lights, the smell of lavender and sugared liqueur. Those wisps of Marjorie's parties were here, making the rest seem even odder, close but off. It had that same not-quite-right feeling of dreams, the kind where Calla's and Azalea's rooms were swapped, or her mother had green eyes, or Gloria's grandmother had vines for hair.

All those diamond earrings were too hard against the pink and white lily magnolias. The green of emerald rings looked cold against the jacarandas' leaves. The pins on the men's silk ties did not belong with the mimosa and lilac trees, with their flowers like soft candies.

"Let's get this over with." Calla charged into the ballroom. She passed under the swaths of bright silk draping the ceiling, pinned at the corners of the room and then gathered at the chandelier.

Estrella passed a boy who stood out more because of his stance than his clothes, or his hair, or even how his skin was the same brown as her grandmother's. He did not stand straight and tall like the men in their black-and-white clothes.

He watched the polished floor like he was looking for the ground underneath it.

She did not register him as Fel until she caught his reflection in a gilt-framed mirror. He wore the black pants, dark green shirt, and black vest Reid had decided would make him blend in with the guests without being mistaken for one.

The feeling of touching him came back to her. She tried to stop the memory from spinning forward, but it got away from her, like the wind taking a spray of leaves.

His fingers brushed hers, an echo of the night before. It was so slight she couldn't tell if he'd done it on purpose.

This time, he did not apologize.

He leaned down to her, his mouth so close to her ear she could feel the warmth on her neck.

"Don't do that again," he said.

She tilted her head so he had to look at her. His breath and hers met, heating the space between their lips.

"Don't do what again?" She let the challenge sharpen her voice.

Until now, she had protected him like he was as young as Calla and only half as smart. She had handled him more carefully than her grandmother and her cousins' grandmothers. But men could not tell her family what to do. Not the ones in town who asked Azalea didn't she know how pretty she was, or who told Gloria to smile for them. Not the wealthy men they tricked into buying seeds and bulbs as though they were made of gold. Not even this boy who might mean so many things that they both loved him and feared him.

Estrella could demand his silence about the things Bay had told them on the fire escape. She could threaten him into staying quiet about what only he and Dalia knew, that she had tried to run, and La Pradera had taken rough hold of her for it. She could leave him in the paling blue before dawn.

Men and boys had no claim on their secrets or their bodies. La Pradera was a world in which women did not listen to men just because they were men.

But in making him look at her, she saw it, how the hard shine on his eyes was not the force of him trying to rule her.

It was fear. Worry flickered over his eyes like light.

"Don't run," he said. "If that's what the gardens do if you run, then don't run."

The feeling of holding on to him, her unfiled nails cutting into his shoulder, rose from last night. They turned from dreams to things real enough that they lived in her fingers, true as the possibility of flowers.

"I'll look for you," he said. "And your family will look for you. But don't make them see you like that. They love you and it will break them."

The certainty in his voice buckled, and she heard the words he left in silence. How her lips had been stained red with pollen and her own blood.

"Please," he said.

She felt his stare on her skin. It was a ribbon of water, tracing along each bead of her necklace. It was such bright contrast to the heat of his fingertips that she looked away first.

Letting her gaze fall gave Reid the chance to catch her eyes. He stood outside the French doors and nodded to her, and her stomach tightened even more than it had under the cinch of the dress.

Her repayment for the torched car.

She held to the possibility that Bay would get together enough Briar secrets to drive him off the land. But until she did, Estrella had to bring Reid the weighted-down obedience of a girl mourning Bay.

"Young lady." Reid's voice rushed through the doors and into the ballroom, loud enough that everyone turned their faces toward him.

He had warned her he would do this, call her something other than her name.

But the words sounded too old for Reid's voice. *Young lady.* Those were words for men twice his age.

Estrella had thought she had gotten so much for so little, Reid forgiving his car turned to ash for nothing but a demure smile and a few flowers. Now, though, with Reid calling her by something other than her name, this seemed strange, wrong, like he had crossed the threshold of her room. She hadn't expected it to feel like a kind of invasion.

Reid stretched a hand into the sugar- and champagne-scented air, and she understood. He had wanted to give himself the air of a showman or circus ringleader. The words matched the gesture of his arm, his pale wrist showing at the sleeve of his fine suit as he swept his hand from the doors toward an open lawn.

"Come here," Reid said, more voices going quiet with each word, "and make me an ocean."

This was how she would pay him back. How she would make Reid forget any thoughts of forcing them off La Pradera. He would demand something so impossible it drew gasps from the rich men and women whose steps brought up the smell of lemon and wax and shoe polish. When Reid had first told her what he wanted, it had sounded so easy and small. But now he summoned her with words he might call any of her cousins.

This way, he could put them all on display at once.

TWENTY-FOUR

Young lady?

Had Reid really said that? Like he was Estrella's mother, correcting her posture or saying her skirt was too short?

The music had faded and stopped so suddenly Fel wondered if the violinists and cello players had thought the words were as ridiculous as he had. Then he realized Reid had nodded at them to still their bows.

The start of a laugh vibrated in Fel's chest.

Estrella grabbed the back of his arm and pinched him. Hard. Under the small shock of pain, he wondered if this was what it would be like to be part of this family. It was such a gesture between brother and sister that he felt almost ashamed of setting his hands on the small of her back the night before.

It felt like a kind of betrayal, an impossibility, to both want her and want her family.

She pinched him harder.

"No wonder our grandmothers keep trying to feed you," she whispered.

"What?" he asked, matching her volume. "Why?"

"You're hard to pinch," she said.

"Then why are you pinching me?"

"Because I need you to be quiet," she said, both their voices becoming taut whispers.

"Then why didn't you just tell me to be quiet?"

Reid gestured to the grass in front of him, not forbidding, not yet. But with the widening eyes of impatience.

Estrella let go of Fel. She descended the few stone steps, the light from inside clinging to her skirt and turning it the same searing blue as the sky reflected in water. Clear glass beads winked near the hem. A strand of yellow ones crossed her hair.

She walked with the stares of all these men and women on her. Her cousins watched, but she did not find them over her shoulder. She did not kiss her hand and blow air over her fingertips. She kept her path straight through the open doors.

Outside, the fountain glowed like there was a small sun under the water. Candles floated between water lilies. The trees' boughs and branches reached out and intertwined.

The breezes swept petals into the air. Estrella crossed beneath the canopy of purple and white and pink.

Make me an ocean. Reid didn't look drunk. He didn't stagger. His words did not blur together. But that strange command made Fel wonder if he had a flask in his inner pocket, already halfway down.

A few guests whispered to one another, Reid's order holding them in the same wondering place. How could a girl make an ocean?

Estrella knelt alongside a tall hedge. The blue of her skirt, light on the dark grass, filled with air and then settled. Reid's shadow darkened the hem. She lowered her eyes, and slid her hands into the dirt. Fel could almost see the current from her palms stirring buds out of the earth.

The horror drifting off her family was a silent language Fel understood. Her mother—he found her in her pale yellow dress—watched, knowing she could not stop this. But her fingers were laced in front of her, and Fel understood that if Reid touched her, Estrella's mother would scratch his neck open.

Fel would help. One worried nod from any Nomeolvides mother or grandmother, and Fel would shove Reid against the fountain like the stone was a brick alley, and Reid was a man calling a boy *Nancy, Molly*, anything cruel and unanswerable.

Estrella tipped her chin up, as though she felt these thoughts. Her gaze found him, and her look was almost a glare.

He read the warning in her face.

Don't you dare.

Do not intervene.

If you try, you will make this worse for me.

If you try, I will make you regret it.

She slid her hands deeper into the ground. She held it

until it sprouted borraja. They were blue flames catching and spreading.

Fel shuddered between rage at Reid and wanting to protect this girl and the things she grew. He had held these petals on his tongue. He had opened his eyes to them covering the ceiling of her room. When they fell, he had caught them between his hands and her back, her shoulder, her hip.

And now Reid was turning them into a show.

Estrella gripped the soil, stirring new growth. Her palms cradled handfuls of ground until the next stems rustled the leaves. Green pushed up through the dark blue. Buds dotted the curled stems, turning paler green, then white, then lilac-colored. They grew and fattened, darkening from purple into blue. Then each fluttered open, five tiny petals around a yellow center. Their blue was the same as the after-sunset sky.

Forget-me-nots. Estrella drew her hands through the borraja and grass, bringing up her family's name. She freckled the leaf-covered ground with blue and violet. Forget-me-nots clustered between the borraja. The dark and lighter blue mixed together, giving the shades of a sea. The borraja and the forget-me-nots became one sheet of blue. They crawled along the grass like spilled water.

With fists clenched around the soil, Estrella made vine after vine of forget-me-nots, the curling green bursting with lilac buds and then blue flowers.

She knifed her hands into the soil. Forget-me-nots and borraja crowded the ground, blooms rustling among leaves. She drove her hands down, telling the earth this was what it would give her. Petals like coins of sky. The purple of buds so soft it looked watercolored. Borraja that looked like brushstrokes of night.

She had nothing left. She was forcing it.

The men and women gasped and laughed their delight. This girl whose name they did not care to know had done it. She had grown a blue sea in the middle of La Pradera. The little ocean of borraja and forget-me-not filled in full and bright. The bed opened up as round and wide as a pond. She kept her hands in the earth for so long, and the blue flowers grew in so thick that the bed looked like wind-flicked water.

They applauded like she was an attraction, a fascination.

Reid offered his hand, and Estrella took it. She knew, like her family knew, that these were the men who would advise Reid what to do with these strange, perfect gardens. If she defied them, offended them, they would tell him to level it and sell the land.

She let him help her to her feet. She curtsied when he gestured at her, like a performer at a carnival.

Reid's joy made him look half his age. He took this as a triumph, his show starting off the night, the guests leaning into one another and wondering if all the brown-skinned girls were as entertaining. He glowed with the satisfaction of seeing how festive Estrella's trick had made them. When the music started again, they paired together and spun across the gleaming floor inside. Some swept out onto the flat stones around the fountain.

Estrella brushed off her dress. She looked as wrung out as when he'd found her in the grass.

A flash of her ankle, and he remembered the story she'd told him. Something about red shoes. How her family had to make these flowers because they couldn't help letting their gifts stream from their hands, but how forcing it hurt.

Always, the Nomeolvides women looked like they were giving the ground flowers willingly, doing what their fingers would ache to do if they didn't give them the chance. But they made a row or small bed at a time. They wore themselves out so they slept, dreaming of new gardens.

They did not work themselves into this, how Estrella shivered even though the air had not yet grown cold.

No stranger would have noticed. To them, there was only the sea of flowers. But Fel knew her, and her half-closed eyes were a sign not that she was demure but that she was tired. The way she tipped her head toward the flowers was not shyness, but the will going out of her.

Reid had already been pulled aside by an interested couple, so Fel took his place in the hedge's shadow.

"You didn't have to do what he told you," Fel said.

She shook her head, eyes on the ground between them.

But when she spoke, she lifted her face and held his gaze. "Don't try to save me from things you don't understand."

There was no anger in her words, not even warning. Just advice wrung out of her.

They had both stopped at the edge of the courtyard. A few guests looked up from their conversations, taking sips of their drinks to hide it. Dancing couples inclined their heads to catch glimpses of the girl who had grown a small sea.

"And now people are staring," she said. "So thank you."

He held out his hand. "Then let's do something about it."

She shook her head, but her smile was there, enough to let him catch it.

"Do you know how?" she asked.

"Not at all." He set a palm on her back before they got swept into the rush of all those skirts.

She dug her hand into his shoulder, shifting them so they didn't crash into another couple.

Estrella looked him over.

"You clean up well," she said.

"Thanks," he said. "So do you."

She was kind enough to smile at the joke. The Nomeolvides women would always be beautiful, and he would always be hard to look at. He saw it in the grandmothers' faces, how even now that he was filling out his clothes a little better they still stared at him more with pity than pride.

The wind picked up, bringing a rain of blossoms. The moon and the garden lights blinked off the bronze wire and yellow beads in Estrella's hair.

She turned her head toward the lit-up fountain. Streams of glowing water fell from the stone.

"Bay always loved this," she said. "She always had some fantastic outfit. Satin. Pants of course."

"She's not dead," he said under his breath.

"But she's not here."

Fel put pressure on her back with his palm, moving her so she wouldn't collide with a woman in a cream dress.

Estrella laughed. When she laughed, she was the girl eating candy buttons off paper, one color at a time. She was the girl who'd turned his face to hers, her mouth finding his in the dark.

Her eyes landed on the small ocean, the wide span of borraja and forget-me-nots. The men and women stood over it, bending close to look but afraid to touch it, as though it might be hot.

He felt her fingers worrying on his shoulder.

"Look at me," Fel said.

Her eyes moved back to him.

He got a firmer grip on her right hand, and her left stilled on his shoulder.

She knew what to do with him. She could hate him, or she could tear his shirt off his body and bare his back, and he would let her. But her own flowers were turning on her.

"Don't look at it," he said. "Look at me."

She did, her stare all focus and intent.

A flare of heat rushed through him, and then a second, like one flash of sheet lightning following another. This was the spell of Estrella Nomeolvides. Not the flowers grown by her fingers. But the way she lured him toward things that made him feel as though his life before was knowable, even if only in glimpses. She showed him this world, the bright colors and green, the spiced powders and raw sugar, and in this world he found narrow paths to ones he had known before.

He tried to keep space between his left hand and her right, hoping she wouldn't feel how hot his palm had turned, but she kept her hold. He kept his right hand still on her back, her dress low enough that only three of his fingers lay against the fabric. His thumb and forefinger were on her bare skin.

He took his right hand off her, and readjusted his hold, his hand now closer to her waist. All his fingers on her dress.

They stumbled into a pair of Reid's guests.

"Sorry," Fel said, both to them and to Estrella.

The other couple widened their distance from them.

"You're awful at this," Estrella said.

"Thank you," Fel said.

"No, I mean it, you're terrible."

This was not the deep, steady pulse of music he almost remembered. It was not the hard rhythm of boots on the dusty earth beneath olive trees. This was music as airy as the flowering branches, and he didn't know what to do with it.

"Here." Estrella grabbed his shoulder harder. "I'm leading."

The force of her hands pulled them closer. The front of her dress brushed his shirt. A loose piece of her hair trailed across his neck.

Fel lost the feeling of the flat stones under him. The blur of every color pulled back. The thread of flower nectar in the air dulled. There was just Estrella, with the blue of her skirt whirling around her.

She didn't let him keep still. She pulled on him, and they stayed in the current of dresses and suits.

"How do you know how to do this?" he asked.

"My cousins and I have been waltzing around our rooms together since we were four." She gripped his hand. "I was the tallest girl for a couple of years, so I was the boy."

"How long did that last?" he asked.

"It didn't. Thanks for reminding me." She pinched him again, other arm this time.

Her skirt fanned out, showing the cloth underneath. With each filmy piece closer to her skin, the blue got a little lighter. The one against her legs was almost the shade of the slip he'd seen at the hem of her pink dress.

He lifted his eyes.

Instead of losing his gaze in the crowded courtyard, it landed on faces he knew.

Estrella caught his worry. "What?"

He turned her like it was part of their dance, so she would see:

Dalia laughing so hard she threw her head back, lightly shoving Reid's shoulder.

Gloria, Azalea, and Calla all watching, the oldest cousin looking like she was trying to talk the younger ones out of strangling Reid with his own starched collar.

TWENTY-FIVE

"I will cut out his heart" was the first thing Estrella got close enough to hear. Calla.

Then, "And I'll make him eat it"—Azalea.

Then, Gloria, saying, "No, you won't. Now stop it. Both of you."

The three of them stood, watching Dalia's fingers play at Reid's collar and at the curled white rose pinned to his jacket.

Gloria's hand landed on Calla's arm, stilling her.

Calla shook her head. "She's lost her mind."

"No," Azalea said, her gaze on Dalia and Reid so unmoving Estrella wondered how they didn't feel it on their necks. "It's Bay."

Estrella stopped, just close enough for the blue of her skirt to skim the lilac hem of Gloria's.

"She misses Bay," Azalea said. "And he's the closest Briar she has."

Gloria shook her head. "She's too smart for that. She's up to something."

"Like what?" Calla asked.

Gloria shrugged. "Stealing his wallet?"

"Slitting his throat in his sleep?" Azalea said under her breath. "She might have competition, though."

Azalea cast her eyes on Estrella, the first indication any of them had noticed her skirt brushing against theirs.

"You're not some puppy he can train to do tricks," Azalea said.

"Azalea," Calla said. She threw Estrella a fast but apologizing look.

Reid's request had seemed so small until Estrella had to do it, all those eyes fixed on her. Not just the guests', but her mother's. She could tell that her mother would have been disappointed, angry even, if she hadn't been afraid for Estrella. That fear had been like the green tarnish on copper, hiding the color underneath.

"I can't believe you let him do that to you," Azalea said.

"You and Fel both." Estrella could argue this down with Azalea on any other night. She had her own shame over this. She didn't need her cousins to give her more. They weren't the ones who'd heard Reid speak the words *las hijas del aire*. "Now what are you three doing?"

Azalea touched the air in front of her, pointing one polished fingernail to the scene of their cousin and the man they wanted off La Pradera.

"We're not doing anything until we talk to her," Gloria said.

"Then let's go talk to her." Azalea crossed the courtyard.

"Azalea," Estrella whisper-called after her.

Azalea would break Dalia open like a chocolate orange. Estrella had seen her banging them on the kitchen counter at Christmastime, the only one of the five of them who could make the segments fall apart with one sure whack.

The three of them went after Azalea, skirts fluffing out with each step.

Azalea tapped Reid once on the shoulder.

"Could we steal her for a minute?" she asked.

She shoved Dalia toward the hedge.

"Girl things," Azalea added over her shoulder.

"Girl things?" Calla whispered, leaning into Azalea. "He's gonna think we're all . . ."

"Let him," Gloria said. "Nothing else in the world makes a man like that more afraid than five girls on their periods."

Before Reid could catch Calla's gritted teeth, Fel appeared at the edge of their ring of skirts, mumbling something about a guest being allergic to silver-dollar leaves, which the florists had slipped into every arrangement.

"Then pull the eucalyptus out of the vases," Reid said.

Estrella inclined forward, ready to tell Reid that Fel wasn't his to order around.

Calla reached out, her hand slapping Estrella's forearm. Not in a way meant to hurt, but to stop her. Calla looked at her, flicking a glance toward Fel.

Estrella watched him, caught how he made his face a little blanker than usual.

He was baiting Reid. He was distracting him. Calla had understood this when Estrella hadn't.

Estrella knew Fel's touch, the taste of his mouth, the warmth of his bare back. But the small, feathered thing living in her rib cage had made her miss details about him. It had made her miss certain signs that he was not just sad and lost and kind but also smart, and always watching.

That feathered thing made her know him in a way her cousins did not, but they knew him in a way she'd failed to.

Fel stayed, asking Reid increasingly stupid questions—*But what do I do with it once I pull it out? How do I know how many arrangements there are? What if I miss one?*—until Reid gave the air a heavy sigh and led him toward the ballroom.

Azalea watched Fel trail after Reid. Pride made her tilt her head, like he was her little brother, nine or ten and just now learning how to go up against the will of other boys.

She patted Calla on the back. "We taught him well, didn't we?" She shared one sisterly sigh with Calla, and then turned her eyes back to Dalia.

Behind her cousins' backs, Estrella gave Dalia her own apologetic look, one of *I couldn't stop them.* Dalia's widened eyes and pressed-together lips answered back *You could have tried a little harder.*

But Estrella knew even Dalia didn't believe that. One cousin could never stop three. Not even Gloria, with her cloud of authority that seemed to be passed down to eldest women in their family like a string of coral beads. Not even Azalea, with sheer momentum on her side as she rushed toward whatever she had decided. Not even Calla, with her logic they only halfway followed so that before they knew it, she had talked them into something they thought they'd decided against.

No one of them could take on two or three or all four of the others.

Azalea took Dalia's arm, her fingers pinching into her skin.

"Are you drunk?" Azalea asked. "He's the enemy."

"The closer I get to him, the more we know, the more we have to fight back with," Dalia said, keeping her voice below the music.

Azalea and Calla rushed Dalia toward the high wall of a hedge, their skirts sweeping her into the inner curve. Gloria and Estrella followed, their dresses dragging the scent of grass after them.

"So all that giggling, that's just part of your plan?" Azalea asked.

"Azalea," Dalia said. Estrella could see her trying to keep her voice steady. "You have no idea what you're talking about."

Estrella almost reached out, wanting her fingers on Dalia's arm to be a warning. This was how Azalea always trapped them.

"Then tell me," Azalea said.

Estrella let her hand fall. Azalea had caught Dalia like a

bramble snagging the corner of her dress. The insult. The prov-
ocation. Then Azalea's invitation to correct her.

Dalia shut her eyes, and Estrella's heart shivered like it wore
a coat of hoarfrost. Ice crystals scattered and fell away.

Dalia led them beyond the hedge wall, the courtyard's music
and voices muffled by leaves.

"Bay didn't disappear," Dalia said.

"Dalia," Gloria said. Sympathy spread through her voice, as
though Dalia were letting herself fall into some dream where
their family's curse did not live.

"I helped her disappear," Dalia said. "She had to get away
from Reid so she could find a way out from under him and this
mess with the will."

"But . . ." Calla paused. "You saw her . . ." She stopped, lips
parted, realizing. "Oh."

The air felt braided with threads of warmer and cooler air,
the three of them sinking into the truth Estrella already knew.

Dalia had lied. Bay had asked her to. And all this blazed
through them, the sting like a shared wound.

Bay was not gone from them. It was a joy that would have
bloomed into a thousand each of the flowers they'd been named
for, if those other truths hadn't dulled it.

They had all thought Bay had loved them, or not loved
them, the same. But Bay had shared the trick of her death with
only one of them.

Azalea tensed, her collarbone looking sharper. "You know,
you could really make it on the stage if you wanted."

"Don't." Dalia threw a glance toward Estrella. "I've already heard that speech from her."

Azalea's head whipped toward Estrella. "You knew?"

Estrella lifted her eyes to glare at Dalia, a look of *thanks a lot*.

"I told her not to tell anyone," Dalia said.

"And anyone means us," Gloria said. The way she put no questioning in her voice gave the words a bitter edge.

"It was bad enough she had to lie for Bay, and for me," Dalia said. "I didn't want all five of us to have to."

"We all would've lied for her," Calla said. "And for you. But we don't lie to each other."

"Except they do." Azalea set her hand on Calla's shoulder. "Come on. If they're too good for us, we can leave."

"Don't you ever get tired of this?" Dalia asked.

Azalea looked back at her. "Of what?"

Dalia closed the space between them so she could keep her voice low. "All five of us acting like we're one person?"

For once, Estrella couldn't guess what Azalea or the rest of her cousins were thinking. Their faces didn't show her. Estrella was left wondering if they, too, struggled for full breaths in the tight space of being one in five, one more generation of Nomeolvides girls. Guests never learned their names. At balls, Marjorie's business acquaintances mixed them up, Azalea with Estrella even though they looked the least alike, Calla with Gloria even though they were years apart, for no other reason than that they were both tall.

In Azalea's flinch, Estrella thought she might have caught it, the sting of her realizing Dalia was right. But then it was gone, replaced by Azalea asking, "So you're better than we are now?"

"Azalea," Gloria said. "Just listen to her."

"There's nothing to listen to," Azalea said. She looked at Dalia. "You're a liar"—then at Estrella—"you're her little apprentice liar"—she circled back to Gloria and Calla—"and if you don't realize that, you're both as stupid as they think you are."

"Stop." Gloria held out her hands, one toward Dalia and Estrella, one toward Azalea and Calla. Her eyes crawled back to Dalia. "Do you swear she's alive?"

"Jazmín, Verónica, Mirasol, Luna, y Amapola," Dalia said, listing all five names of their deceased great-grandmothers. It was an oath between them, as solemn and sacred as crossing themselves and naming the Father, the Son, and the Holy Ghost.

Gloria held a breath between her lips, letting it drain with a sound like wind through the blossoming branches. "Then we thank God and La Pradera for it."

Azalea's eyes slid over to her. "That's it?" she asked. "You don't care that she lied to us."

"Of course I care," Gloria said. "But what I care about more is that what we were afraid happened didn't happen."

"We only thought it happened because she pretended it did." Azalea's eyes snapped back to Dalia. "We really need to make sure you get some kind of award for that performance."

"What do you want more?" Gloria leaned into Azalea. "To rip her apart right now, or to make sure we keep Bay safe?"

Azalea tensed, caught between her own conviction that she had been wronged, that all of them had, and the raw truth Gloria put in front of her.

Gloria kept looking at her, her expression urging her on. *So? Which is it?*

Azalea tilted her head back, her shoulders falling with one slow breath out. "Fine."

This was how, on Gloria's insistence, they all took the hundreds of stone steps down to the sunken garden. They did as Gloria said, giving La Pradera the offerings that showed their gratitude for not taking this woman they all loved.

Gloria and Estrella took out their earrings and tossed them into the curling vines. Calla brought her favorite book of fairy tales and buried it among the rocks and ivy. Dalia crushed dulce de cacahuate estilo mazapán between her fingers and sprinkled it over the earth like fairy dust, peeling the candy rounds of sugar and crushed peanuts from their rose-printed wax paper.

Azalea kept her eyes on Dalia. "We're not okay."

Dalia gave a small nod, accepting the hard edge of Azalea's grudge like a knife offered blade-out. "I know."

Azalea slid the thin bangles off her wrists, throwing a glance at Estrella and then back at Dalia. "And you dragged her into this."

"I didn't mean to," Dalia said.

Azalea tossed the bangles into the pond. "I don't care what you meant."

They watched the bracelets, the gold glowing like rings of light as they sank.

"Do you ever wonder if this is a sin?" Calla whispered to Estrella.

Estrella was lifting her skirt, ripping away the crinoline layer that was her favorite shade of blue. "Why would it be?"

"Because we're supposed to be giving our offerings to God, aren't we?" Calla asked.

"You really think God hears us down here?" Dalia cut in, doing the same with her dress, pulling away the layer that was the softest shade of coral.

"We're Nomeolvides girls." Azalea threw the last of her bracelets into the water. "I don't think God hears us at all."

The glow from the band billowed out like rippling water. Estrella and Dalia lay their skirts on the pond, and they twirled and sank down like veils of light.

La Pradera was their god. Her family could pray. They could read their Bibles. But the bright colors and the night voices of this place scared off any saints and angels. What God would listen to the prayers of girls whose hearts were poison?

The wind picked up, blowing a spray of water into Estrella's face. She shut her eyes, let it brush over her cheeks. She remembered the fever La Pradera had settled over her when she ran, the swelling sense that still things were moving. The feeling that the darkness outside was ink or an ocean. Wondering if the wind was shivering all the flowers in the world as much as it seemed to be.

La Pradera held them. It took the men and the women they loved, and if they ever tried to leave, it took them, too.

The rage of the three cousins still hung in the air, like the bitter tang of smoke. But this, they did together. This—their love for Bay, their understanding that La Pradera's power was the only match for the curse of their blood—made them more sisters than cousins.

Above them, the well-suited men and gown-wearing women danced, drunk on champagne and lavender liqueur. But down here, with the sunken garden's walls rising up around them, the slopes covered in green, this was their world. The floor was thick with every flower the Nomeolvides women grew. Low garden lamps gave the ground enough light to show its color. Cypress trees cast their silhouettes against the walls. Blossoming branches patterned the walkways in flowered shadows.

The cousins streamed toward the stone staircases.

"Are you coming?" Calla asked.

"Soon," Estrella said. "I'll be right there."

Dalia and Azalea paused before the first step.

"Azalea," Dalia said.

But Azalea rushed up the stairs in front of her, ignoring her.

"Just give her time," Estrella heard Gloria whisper. "She'll come around."

Estrella stayed. She stood before the pond, the water still enough to mirror the moon.

The air here smelled like wild sage and blue shale. Soft waves of meadow cordgrass and pink muhly grass, things that sprouted wild in the wet ground, grew in the willows' shade. The feathery stalks looked like clouds of fairy floss when dry, and pink rock candy when they got wet.

Estrella crouched near the water. Her dress fluffed up behind her. Flower beds fringed the banks. The ends of willow fronds floated on the water.

Forty feet down to the bottom. The lowest point of the sunken garden.

Estrella shut her eyes and asked La Pradera not to break her and her cousins apart. They could last through a hundred fights about who'd borrowed whose yellow shoes, but they could not fight like this, cold and silent and mistrusting.

She asked these gardens why they had given her family Fel, a boy so kindhearted that he carried guilt none of them could name but all of them could see on his frame like a weight. She asked what La Pradera wanted her and her family to do with him. She asked it to let him out from under his own nightmares, to save him from being a boy who did not sleep.

She asked it to help him get back all he did not remember.

Estrella traced her fingers along her necklace. The one thread of romance her mother allowed was the story of its colors. The tumbled-stone beads, as round as pearls and as big as shell peas, were the colors of a rare bird from the Atacama Desert. Bronze and lilac. Cobalt and violet. Their feathers were bright bursts on the silver land. It was proof of Estrella's own blood, worn on her neck.

Estrella had loved it like it itself was a desert bird, bright and flickering.

She grabbed the necklace, all she had of her father's family, half her blood. And she pulled until the strands snapped.

The beads, the blue and green and bronze, flew and scattered. They broke the surface of the pond like raindrops.

Trails of light slid through the pond. They grew brighter and dimmer as they moved into shallower and then deeper water. When they stayed still for a second, they were points of light. When they moved, they were comet trails. They skittered and broke through the surface. One spun away from the water like a firefly. One flew, mirroring the path of the one in the pond.

Another splashed up and joined the one in the air. Still another stayed underwater, lighting up the pond and the willow streamers.

Some stayed. Some flew out and clustered on the meadow cordgrass and muhly grass, lighting up the pink fluff. They looked like fireflies or tiny stars.

"Estrella?"

She thought the voice was an echo of his voice from earlier, the gardens throwing it back at her.

But she turned, and he stood there, the pond casting bands of bowing light over him.

"Fel?" she asked.

He stepped out from the willow's shadow.

Later, she would tell herself he'd kissed her first. She would remember that. He'd started this. Maybe she wrapped her fingers around the back of his neck and pulled him toward her, but he'd still started this.

She kissed him hard enough to realize it wasn't just the air but Fel that tasted like wild sage and smelled like blue shale. The insistence and faltering of kissing him had its own rhythm. It was the alternation of which of them wanted it more and which of them thought they should stop. They passed the two back and forth so one of them was always pulling away while the other drew closer.

The feeling that she should stop collected in her.

If she thought she could ever love him, she shouldn't let his mouth near hers. If there was anything in her that wanted him, she shouldn't learn the pattern of his breathing when he kissed her.

If she wanted his body not to vanish, she could not put her hands on him.

This was the heart of being a Nomeolvides girl. The more she loved a boy, the more reasons there were not to touch him.

The price of knowing he would be there for her to touch was her not touching him.

She knew this, even as he set his hands on the waist of her dress, slid his tongue between her lips, even as she dug her fingers into his hair. And with the moon veiling the clouds, with the garden lanterns and the little stars her necklace had turned to as their only light, it was almost as though, for those few seconds, La Pradera could not see them.

But around them, the ground was whispering, the grass and flower beds giving up strange things Estrella could not name.

TWENTY-SIX

Indigo milk caps. As they grew from the grass, they took root in Fel's memory.

He knew them. They spread through the garden valley in fairy rings big enough that, even with the sweep of Estrella's skirt, they could both fit inside. The mushrooms stood pale and bright against the dark earth and grass.

Estrella breathed in, and he could hear the wonder in that breath, like she'd never seen mushrooms that color. On land her own family made beautiful, she must have thought there was nothing to find, no unfamiliar magic.

She knelt down, and the back of her skirt trailed across a fairy ring. The garden lamps slipped gold light into the folds of fabric.

"What are these?" she asked.

"Mushrooms," he said, letting a laugh into his words. What did she think they were?

She hesitated to touch them, hovering her fingers a little above the caps. "They're blue."

He crouched near her. The mushroom caps were pale purple, but he lifted the margin to show the dark gills underneath, a storm blue tinged with violet.

He remembered finding these with his brother, how the wonder of it never dulled. Each morning he forgot the deep blue, and each night he found it again.

But it wasn't just the thought of his brother spinning back toward him.

His family.

He'd had a whole family. The shape of it was rising toward him like kelp breaking loose from a seabed and floating to the surface.

He'd had a mother. With hair the color of a cork tree's outer bark, and with hands as soft as lily petals. She and her sisters used to hunt these mushrooms in the forests, finding their pale caps at the bases of white pines and oaks. Her grandmother sold them in the markets. They had to be sold quickly because within a day the blue turned dark green, and the rich families sending their cooks to buy food would not pay as much for green mushrooms as for blue.

Estrella stroked her fingers over the caps. She lifted the margin to look at the gills herself, dark as blue amethyst.

Fel put his hand on hers, the memory of his fingers moving them. He snapped the stem, and blue paint spread over their palms.

Wonder made her laugh light as a breath. She cracked one of the stems, let the milk bleed onto her fingers, and pressed a dot onto Fel's nose.

He laughed. "Hey."

She ran her thumb over his left eyebrow.

He snapped another stem, and the blue trickled into his palm.

She scrambled to the other side of a cypress tree, her laugh as soft as the brush of leaves.

He came after her. He ran his hands through her hair and streaked it blue. She ducked out from under his hold and hid behind a tree in bloom.

"Give up yet?" she asked around the tree.

She had her back against the other side. All he could see was her profile, the sweep of her hair on her shoulder, the edge of her skirt.

"Never." He found her and painted comet trails on her cheeks.

She smudged bands of blue amethyst on his hands and forearms, staining his skin indigo. When they needed more paint, they cracked another stem, and the color seeped onto their fingers. The milk in his hair brushed onto his forehead. The whites of his fingernails were blue sickle moons.

He reached for her cheek. Without meaning to, his fingers grazed her mouth. A slick of milk rested on the inner curve of her lip.

He came a little closer, pinning her against the tree not with his hands but with the small distance between his body and hers. Blue shone wet on her eyelashes. She blinked, and they left wisps of paint on her cheek.

The warmth under his palm registered. He'd set his hand against her waist, and his fingers left darker blue stains on the blue fabric.

"Sorry," he said.

"Don't be." She put her hand to the side of his face.

The gesture felt as dangerous as it was small, a calling back of him kissing her in the dark.

Then he felt the mushroom milk on her palm. She'd painted half his cheek.

He set his hand on hers. "You did that on purpose."

A smile curved one side of her mouth. She dropped her hand, her palm dyed indigo.

A rush of blue sped past the corner of his vision.

He turned, looking for it. Another fairy ring maybe. Or the moon lightening the sky between trees.

At first, he saw nothing. Then, far off in the aspens, he found it, a horse as deep indigo as the mushrooms' gills. A colt, small and young but strong, a carved horse figurine come to life.

"Fel?" Estrella called.

He startled at how far away she sounded.

She was no longer under his hands. He staggered toward the blue horse. He set his palms against the trunks of flowering trees, steadying himself.

The horse flicked its mane, a lighter blue like the mushrooms' caps. Then it galloped off, the dark taking it.

"Fel?" Estrella said.

But her voice didn't find him. One word echoed across the night, dyed indigo, until it settled on his lips.

"Caballuco," he said, like the name of someone he'd just recognized.

"What?" she asked.

He shut his eyes, and saw the carved horses together. Green, yellow, white, purple, orange, red. And two he remembered that were not on Estrella's shelf. One pure black as her hair, the other indigo, deep as the mushroom's gills.

That color opened him, and there was more rushing back to him than his hands could hold.

He remembered his brother smelling like hay from being around horses. How he brought the faint sun scent and tang of it home on his clothes. How Fel got it on him, too, the few times his brother talked his way into bringing his younger brother with him to see a criollo stallion or a red-shouldered mare.

Fel's brother had taught him the names of horse colors like they were another language. Palomino and dark bay. Blue roan and red roan. Dun and dapple gray. His brother had taught him the secret meanings of the names. How could *flea-bitten gray* mean anything good, Fel had wondered until his brother taught him it meant a white horse freckled auburn.

His brother, who had seen Fel come home with a bruise on his temple, had never offered pity or scorn. Instead, he had taught Fel one thing: how to tell, from watching how other men walked and laughed, whether an unbroken stare would provoke them or scare them off.

His brother, who had made Fel believe that the brown of his skin was a thing to wear with pride. They would never be pale men, never fair like the drying husk of a white onion, and for this, they should be proud. Their blood held the history of their family.

A family. Fel had a family, and they were all this brown his brother told him to take pride in. His brother marked their family by the colors of horses, the brown of a bayo rodado or bayo encerado. If anyone else had compared Fel to an animal, it would have stung as an insult. But the hills of his brother's dreams were crowded with horses, so there was no better compliment.

Estrella took hold of his arm, saying his name.

He looked at her.

There were so many colors of her. Her hair as dark as a grulla colt's mane. The deep gold in her skin. Her eyes as brown as his brother's favorite Andalusian horses.

Fel could not remember the awful things he had done, the sins that had made God strip his memories from him, giving them back only in small pieces.

But this girl. She had led him through these gardens. She had given him back everything good. She made him more than the things he had done that were written onto his back.

Her heart had a stronger pull than all of it. And the beauty and force of her pulled him down to his knees like she was some beautiful, terrifying angel.

Under his shins, the grass gave off its clean, damp scent. He put his hands on the small of her back, the blue of her skirt billowing and settling. He let his cheek rest against her stomach, and through the fabric of her dress, he kissed her hip, a place she'd let him touch in the dark.

He braced for her to pull him to his feet and ask what he was doing. But she set one hand in his hair, and the other on the back of his neck. His tears came without sound, so when he saw the darker blue stains on her dress, they surprised him. He tried pulling away.

But she kept her hands on him. Her fingers met on the back of his neck.

This dark garden valley, glowing with veins of light from the pond, spreading rings of blue mushrooms, gave him back more of his family than his heart could hold.

He'd had a mother who sometimes deferred and other times defied. When she made torrijas every Holy Week, she added honey and spice and olive oil as her own mother had taught her. But when her mother insisted she should not let her sons near horses, not after her great-grandfather had died being thrown from one, she'd ignored her.

He'd had aunts who told him that he should plant wood betony around where he slept. The stalks of purple blossoms would scare ghosts wandering from graveyards and witches from his threshold.

He'd had a grandfather who'd worked as a cork harvester, and then bought enough land for a whole grove of wild olive trees, passing them down to Fel's father.

The thought of the olive trees broke into a million green leaves, each knife-thin, and Fel caught the blunt pain of remembering what had happened to them.

A cold winter. A bad frost coating the leaves like sugar.

It had killed the trees. And with that memory came his half-formed understanding of why he and his brother had had to leave the place where they'd been born.

There was no money. With the trees frozen and dead, there was not enough to eat and there was not enough work. So their mother and father had sent them across a wide sea.

Even if he crossed that sea again, his family was gone. All of them. Fel knew that. He had felt the Nomeolvides girls trying to guard him from this, but he heard their whispers, their guesses about how he had appeared from a hundred years ago, and he knew that any family he had, he had lost.

But they were still his. They had risen from the broken-down, half-remembered places, and they were his again.

His brother was still here. The flapping of bird's wings were his whisper. The dark of the pond's surface was the color of his favorite wooden caballuco, the paint on the winged horse soft and chipping. The crush of grass under Fel's feet were hushed as his brother's steps, always quiet even over rocky ground.

Fel was everyone he had lost, and the land he had left behind. He was the almond trees ringing his grandmother's village. He was the roan and silver grullo horses whose coloring had enthralled his brother. He was a cork oak, stripped bare every ten years.

For so long, he had caught these things only in worn threads, like remembering scraps of a dream, how trying to remember that dream only made it drift further away.

Now all of this streamed into him so fast that he had to do something with it so it did not crush his heart into dust.

Estrella pulled him up from his knees. She kissed him so slowly it felt more like a blessing than a sign that she wanted him. He accepted it.

He picked blue mushrooms from their rings. He brought them to the Nomeolvides kitchen so he could cook them with lemon and green herbs and chili. He would do this how he'd seen his mother do it, the way she and her sisters had made them for one another and for their brothers when they were lovesick.

He did the only thing he knew how to do for these women who had become his family. He cooked for them. The indigo of the dirt-shadowed mushrooms brightened as he brushed them clean. They heated into teal, bright as the feathers on the bee-eating birds his grandmother kept as pets.

As Estrella handed him cut lemons and set out ceramic bowls, he gave in to a memory that felt like a thing torn out of him.

Fel and his brother making a cake for their father's birthday, covering it with hundreds of borraja petals they'd picked and washed. The petals were the deep blue of the sky; their edges seemed dipped in purple.

First they stuck the petals to the icing one at a time, then by handfuls. They opened their palms and rained blue over the cake. By the time they ran out of borraja, the cake looked less like a cake and more like a sea creature from a fisherman's stories, with scales made of sky and water. When their father and mother saw it, they could barely stop laughing long enough to taste it.

Fel would make that same cake for these women. The same way, so that maybe they would laugh. He would make what he knew for when loss wore them down, and for when there was so much joy between them the air in this house smelled like lilacs. When they could not sleep, he wanted to stand at the stove with the grandmothers, frying leche frita, and set out glasses of anís or tigernut orxata. When the March thaw came, he wanted to cook them estafado de pollo, stirring purple potatoes into the red sauce and shelling spring peas from their waxed pods. When they were heartbroken, he wanted to pour them the blackthorn and hard liquor bite of patxaran.

That night, Estrella asked him about the word. *Caballuco.*

"There's a story," Fel said, speaking into the dark between them. "About dragonflies. How they're really little horses that come from the devil. That they're the souls of those who've sinned and that you can tell their sin by their color."

His voice sounded like a thing outside him. It was buzzing near him like the dragonflies that screamed through the air, hovering around saints' day bonfires. They were flashes of iridescent blue above the embers.

Fel pulled down the purple caballuco from the shelf, and set it in Estrella's hands. "But my brother, he thought the story was a lie. That those dragonflies were horses that missed running. Not sinners. They just missed being horses. So they fly now."

"Your brother?" Estrella asked. "The one . . ."

"Yes, the one who liked men," Fel said, laughing softly. "He's the one who taught me anything I know about horses. He knew a lot more than I do."

When a shallow sleep took Fel under, he dreamed of indigo caballucos. Their teeth. Their blue-lavender manes. Their song that was both laugh and warning.

He woke to her fingers on his forehead.

"Fel," she said.

He sat up, blinking away those last flashes of the caballucos, their backs sprouting wings. His fingers found the blue stains on her skin, turning teal.

"Do you remember how you got here?" she asked.

He knew what she was asking. He had heard her family talking enough to know now. She thought he'd disappeared because, sometimes, those they loved vanished. She was asking if he remembered vanishing. His heart vibrated with so much hope he could not help taking this question as a sign that he was one of them, those they loved.

"No," he said. He said it without sadness, because however he had died to the gray world and the soft, olive-leafed world before that, he was in this world now. Estrella's.

This was the place he was coming back to life.

TWENTY-SEVEN

S he woke him in the hours before dawn. He still smelled like the pond in the sunken garden, all willow water and meadow cordgrass. La Pradera left its scent on anyone it touched. But the earth smelled different on this boy than it did on her own fingers. On him, it was deeper, like fall.

They had left the mushrooms on the stove, grandmothers and mothers and cousins spooning them from the copper pot as they came home. The air in the house still smelled like lemon and spice.

Now both mothers and grandmothers slept, their dreams heavy with worry and perfume. The guests were gone from Reid's party, Reid was sleeping it off in the Briar house, and La Pradera was theirs again.

Estrella led Fel out into the gardens, where the two of them and her cousins passed around alegría candy, the puffed amaranth and honey smell warming the chilled air. They got into the extra crates left over from the ball, opening bottles of rose cordial and lemon liqueur.

Fel was both an odd visitor she wanted to watch and an uncertain boy she wanted to guide through the thorn-sharp world of the gardens. She wanted to show him where he could step without falling into the snares and traps of this place.

She wanted to see La Pradera the way he did, find the wonder in the tiller spurs like they were silver stars.

Calla ordered him to stay still like he was a younger brother, not a boy with three or four years on her. She tied to his wrist a scrap of cloth, brushed with glowing paint, the same as they tied on one another after every ball and summer party.

"It's so we don't lose each other," Calla said.

"Here." Azalea handed Fel a bottle. "Unless you're not legal."

"You don't want to play that with me." He took a swallow without flinching and handed it back to her. "You'll be under the table before dawn."

Azalea took a drink twice as long as his, trying to hide her wince. "Try me."

For that second, they seemed a little bit happy. In the town down the hill, they had their shared love, alive and not vanished. For right now, Gloria, Azalea, and Calla put aside their anger toward Dalia and Estrella. Estrella had heard Azalea say to Dalia, "If anything happens to her, I'm holding you responsible," but after that, Azalea seemed to let it fall.

In that forgiveness, even if it was just for tonight, Estrella could even shrug away making that ocean of blue petals.

She had turned her family into a show. In doing what Reid asked, she had made them all more objects of fascination than women. The fact that there were reasons she had to, the truth that Reid could throw them off La Pradera whenever he wanted, didn't soften what she'd had to do. The logic didn't wear down the edges.

But for right now, she could put this away, sure as locking it inside her jewelry box.

Bay was alive, and in her being alive was the possibility for everything so ordinary it was luminous. Azalea tossing her head to clear her hair from her face. Dalia stealing the lower corner of a darkening window and checking the lipstick she'd borrowed from her mother's dresser. Gloria and Calla wiping their mouths on the backs of their hands, hoping the hard candies they shared hadn't turned their lips purple.

Tonight, they were the same girls who snuck out of their windows and ran into town on summer nights, first buying swirled sticks of candy and then lace-trimmed camisoles they didn't want their mothers to know about. Except for these small things, the world outside La Pradera's did not call to them. They knew what was waiting. A world that thought their gifts were magic within estate gardens but witchcraft on wild land. Towns that called them murderers for loving farmers' sons and ministers' daughters into nothingness.

Gloria stood next to Estrella, both of them watching Calla fasten the knot on the back of Fel's wrist.

"Are you worried?" Gloria asked.

"About?" Estrella asked.

"That he was someone else's," Gloria said. Her voice was open, not accusing.

"Yes."

Estrella wanted to reach into Fel and find every scrap of remembrance that might tell her who he had belonged to, which of their great-great-grandmothers. Was she the kind to forgive? Or would she be jealous even from the grave, striking down both Estrella and the boy she herself had once loved?

Fel looked seventeen, eighteen at the most, caught in the age he was when he vanished, the age he had been when that love burned so fast and bright he disappeared.

"Do something for me?" Gloria said.

Estrella looked at her.

"Don't love him too hard," she said.

Estrella put her hands against her dress, one spread over the other, like this was where Gloria's words had gone in.

Don't love him until he is nothing.

Don't let your heart kill him.

Estrella felt her lips part and stay parted, until all she could say was, "Gloria."

"Please," Gloria said. "Azalea and Calla, they love him. They've gotten attached. And not the way we got attached to Bay. Worse. They love him like he's their blood. Maybe you've been too distracted with Dalia and Bay to notice."

"That's not fair."

"I don't want anything bad to happen to him," Gloria said. "First Bay walks out on us and now Reid's made us a circus act. They can't take anything else. It'll destroy them."

"I care about them too."

"I know."

"And I care about him."

"That's what I'm worried about," Gloria said. "There's a difference. You want him. They want their mothers to adopt him."

"Whose fault is that?" Estrella asked. "You're the one who told us to treat him like a brother."

"What did you want us to do?" Gloria's voice grew fiercer even as she lowered it. "We gave La Pradera our jewelry and it gave us a person. I didn't want to test that."

Estrella's eyelashes felt hot, the corners of her eyes prickling. "What do you want from me?"

"I want you to wake up," Gloria said. "All of us, our hearts for women and for men. You know what that means?"

"More ways to lose them?" Estrella asked.

"Our hearts or the ones we love?" Gloria asked.

"Both."

The word came out bitter. Estrella let it. This was what their mothers would say if she and her cousins ever told them the things they folded inside their hearts. *Twice as many paths to trouble,* their mothers would whisper. As though their daughters loving men and women meant they wanted all of them in the world. There was no way to tell their mothers the truth and make them believe it, that hearts that loved boys and girls were no more reckless or easily won than any other heart. They loved who they loved. They broke how they broke. And the way it happened depended less on what was under their lovers' clothes and more on what was wrapped inside their spirits. What secret halls and trapdoors their souls held, and what each one hid and guarded.

Estrella's heart and her cousins' hearts, the way they were as likely to fall in love with women as with men, was a language the five of them shared. But they did not know how to teach it to their mothers and grandmothers. All their mothers and grandmothers could do was listen and decide for themselves what it sounded like.

Estrella had fallen in love twice. They had been different not because once was with a woman and once was with a boy, but because once was with Bay and once was with Fel.

"There's nothing wrong with who we love," Estrella whispered. "What's wrong is what's always been wrong. We're Nomeolvides girls."

Letting Bay go, accepting that Bay loved Dalia in a way she did not love the rest of them, had not lessened the poison in Estrella's blood. She was still a girl born from generations of broken hearts. That was the dangerous thing. Not that she and her cousins all spoke the language of loving boys and girls, but that they all shared the legacy of losing them.

"And we thought we'd be the ones to get out of this," Gloria said. "We thought we were so much smarter than our mothers."

Estrella settled into the feeling of the six of them, her and her four cousins and this boy. For that minute, she didn't think of kissing him. She thought only of keeping him. If keeping him meant thinking of him as a brother and nothing else, she could do it.

A breeze brought the thread of perfume off Gloria's skin.

Not hers. Not the clean orchid scent, and not any scent familiar in the stone house.

Estrella touched her cousin's neck, like she could trace her fingers over the place where another woman's perfume had rubbed off on her skin.

"Who is she?" Estrella asked.

She tried to keep her voice soft, flat. She just wanted to know.

There were so many parts of themselves they never let one another see.

Gloria's eyes glinted like the beads sewn into her dress.

"I never ask for a name," she said. "It's easier that way."

TWENTY-EIGHT

"Luminous paint," Calla told him, explaining the scraps of cloth glowing blue green in the dark. "They're how we find each other."

Lamps lit up patches of different-color flowers. Bulbs set near the ground made the trees glow from underneath. But they were flickering off. And that glowing blue green would mark them until first light licked at the dark sky.

Calla finished the knot. She offered her arm to Gloria, who tied a band onto Calla's small wrist. The gesture was so intimate, a thing done between cousins who were more like sisters, that it stung.

Watching them, the careful motions of Gloria's fingers, put a ringing in Fel's brain, like the echo from a thunderstorm.

He knew this. Not just the scene of two Nomeolvides girls caring for each other.

He knew this work of siblings marking each other.

Fel shut his eyes, and saw his brother's hands tying a scrap of cloth onto his shirt. On that scrap, his brother had written a name.

The first three letters Fel knew. They had been pinned to his shirt when Estrella found him. *Fel.*

But the longer he shut his eyes, the more letters showed themselves, like glowing paint appearing in the dark.

Fel.

Felipe.

And then a name he could not make out.

He heard his brother arguing with the men who had told them what to do.

You can't have two last names, the foreman yelled at them.

They're not two last names, Fel's brother said. *It's our father's name and our mother's name.*

Well, pick one, the man said.

Fel's brother said he would not choose between their mother's name and their father's. So he had told the man they would use their second name—*Felipe*, a family name; they both had the same one—as their last name.

This was how they had marked themselves in the gray world, where the threat of death was so close it hovered like a low ceiling. They wore their names always tied onto their clothes, last name first, then first name, so that if they died they could be known.

Fel's brother had not wanted this. Wearing this tag, and switching their names—last name, first name—had seemed like an admission they were already dead. But the other men had talked him into it.

You think the foremen keep track of us? Fel remembered these words, the rhythm of a man's accent. *You think you matter any more to them just because you came up from slate picker? And your brother*—at this, he'd tilted his head toward Fel—*to them he's always gonna be a breaker boy. We all are. They give us our dollar a week and then they forget about us.*

You wear this, another man said. Fel remembered he had hair as black as Fel's, but fine and straight, hair that looked neat even after a day's work. He knew little English and no Spanish, but he had met Fel's eyes with his own, the brown so deep it felt cool. *For your family.*

Without our names pinned on us—a third man this time, another unknown accent, a hangman's laugh—*our mothers'll never know if we're in the ground or the gambling halls.*

Now Fel opened his eyes, finding no light but the moon and the glowing bands the Nomeolvides girls tied onto one another's wrists.

The gardens were full of not just one caballuco, but a hundred, in as many colors as La Pradera's flowers. They rushed through the trees in reds and oranges and greens. They sprouted dragonfly's wings, enormous and sheer. They flew above the highest boughs. Their golds and purples streaked the dark. They screamed across the stars.

The caballucos had become too big for his hands. He could not hold them. They stood bright and fearless. The tans and browns of Fel's body and clothes could never match their gold and green.

He and his brother had carried those carved wooden horses in their pockets, a charm against their fate. They had thought the caballucos would keep them from death. No harm could come to them as long they carried them.

But this had been a fairy tale. The same as how his brother had talked of buying land, how both he and Fel would decide whether their first horses would be grullos or palominos. But his brother had never had his land. He never taught Fel all the names for the colors of horses. He never told Fel another trick for staying out of fights he never wanted into in the first place.

Because Fel had lost him as much as he'd lost himself.

Fel's own stupidity bit at him. He had never wondered how the caballucos had turned up in these gardens. How they had come to gather in a tiny, colorful herd on Estrella's shelf.

They were here, because this was where Fel and his brother had died. The caballucos were a sign of death, but Fel had turned his face away, refusing to see it.

The caballucos had been the only bright color in the gray world, the world that had once stood in the same place as these gardens. The gray world was not flowers but rock and rust. It was Fel and his brother sleeping outside in their clothes, dust sticking to them so hard it felt like part of their skin. It was getting rich men in town drunk enough to win money off them, not for fun but so he and his brother could pay to get broken bones set.

The gray world was the truth of this place. La Pradera was the lie. Everything Estrella and her cousins had given him was lies. Their family's legacy was fairy tales. What to them was the color of raw gold dust was to him the shade of a dun horse, or the color of a quarry they had made into a garden.

Fel wished the caballucos could grow to the size of real horses. He wished they would gallop across these grounds and break through the walls of the stone house. Their brays and the buzzing of their wings would scare every Nomeolvides woman into telling the truth.

He thought he heard Estrella saying his name, but he couldn't hear. The caballucos laughed their laughs that were half-horse and half-human. Their color was the milk from a thousand indigo mushrooms, pouring everywhere, dyeing the night air.

They were laughing at him because he had believed he had life and breath of his own.

He had believed they were things he could hold in his hands.

The sounds he had forgotten rushed at him. The crumbling and collapsing of rock. Men calling out in fear or warning. Rubble crashing down, folding them all into its wave like it was night falling.

This was why he could not remember his brother's name, or face. It hurt too much to remember him, because he had lost him in the gray world.

"Fel." Estrella's hands slid onto him.

The feeling of her touch, this girl with one palm on his

back and the brush of fingers on his forearm, broke him into pieces. He was made of wood and paint, a caballuco figurine, splintering.

She'd found every crack he'd shown. Like his dreams of the caballucos disappearing between floorboards, she'd slid her fingers into those open places.

He wrenched away from her. This girl had been part of the family who turned a graveyard into a garden. They had hidden and covered over the truth of his brother's death and his own.

To anyone but his own brother, he had been nothing but an underaged miner. He was an immigrant whose name no one cared to learn. He wore his own name on his shirt because he was not worth listing on a role sheet.

Fel looked at Estrella, still in that blue dress, the sky color bright against the night. Her skirt traced a wide arc behind her. A few drowsy fireflies hovered their tiny bulbs near the glowing bracelet on her wrist.

"You lied to me," he said.

His mouth still felt warm from hers, the night air cold against his lips.

"What?" she asked.

"You hid this," Fel said. "All of you. You took the truth and you turned it into flowers."

When she blinked, the indigo of the milk mushrooms showed on her eyelashes. "Fel."

She reached out for him. Her fingers struck his forearm.

He drew back. She grabbed him, one hand landing on his upper arm, the other on his side. Her touch, the first from her he hadn't wanted, shocked through him.

His breath pulled in on itself. In one half-second, there was less air in him than he needed.

"This is what your family does?" he asked. "You take all this blood and death and you make gardens out of it?"

"Fel," she said. "I don't know what . . ."

He held up a hand.

"No," he said. "Stay away from me."

His steps crushed the grass, and it let off a scent like leaves and citrus.

Estrella was a girl drawn in blue and brown and gold, and he wanted to hide his face from her.

She could have her gardens and her family and the lies she spoke as a first language.

He had been cared for and watched and taken into this family, and they had all covered over the thing that had killed him and his brother and so many others.

"I loved you," he said.

He tried to throw it all away. Estrella spreading blue paint on his skin. The pond giving off light like it was full of stars. The caballucos screaming through the dark. Estrella and him cooking the indigo mushrooms until they turned teal.

"Fel," Estrella said, coming toward him. Her stricken face broke through the dark. She cut through that blur of stars and memory.

Gloria set a hand on Estrella's shoulder. "Let him go."

It was the one thing he could still be grateful for, the oldest Nomeolvides girl stopping the girl he had loved from following him.

La Pradera turned to a beautiful, terrifying fairy tale. Trees in bloom and bushes covered in color grew from the earth. Thick stripes of flowers banded the ground. Roses and vines dripped from wooden frames. Branches drooped so heavy with blossoms they should have broken.

The gardens were a whirl of petals. The stone and brick walkways were winding paths that led nowhere but back onto themselves. The flowers stood so bright and full they looked like frightening magic, their heads nodding in the wind so they seemed like they were watching him.

He had one decision left to him. There was a little of his own life still in his hands.

Fel crossed the gardens. Water lilies sat still in the fountains. A broken champagne glass had left shards over the flagstones.

Stone steps led to the still-open French doors, strewn with flowers and lost bracelets and curls of lemon peel. Wind puffed up the curtains, airing out the smells of cologne and liquor. The traces of women's perfume faded, giving way to the nectar and petal scent of the blossoming trees outside.

Inside, the ball had been left behind in scraps. Shoes had been cast off. Half-full glasses sat abandoned. Flowers, taken from arrangements to be tucked into hair or pinned to lapels, had been discarded. Lost beads and buttons freckled the floor and tables.

All the guests had gone. Reid had probably passed out somewhere.

Fel would wake him up.

He now understood why Reid's touch had felt as uncomfortable as hands wrenching his wrists. Why he had shuddered away when Reid set a hand on his back.

Reid would answer for the things his family had done, and then covered over.

Fel looked for him on the first floor, then the second, stopping at the room Reid had claimed as his study.

Reid was not there, not passed out on the desk or on the leather-covered chairs.

Light from the hall showed the desk, messy with letters.

The paper looked so heavy, so woven, that Fel could not help picking up the leaves.

He sifted through them, the handwriting of rich men declaring that they wanted their own estates to have grounds like La Pradera.

One referred to how his wife would love to have a rose garden like the one here, screened in by wooden lattices.

Another mentioned the wide flowered valley, calling it a sunken garden.

A third included a last line that Reid should stay in touch *when you start sending them out.*

Sending them out. Like the Nomeolvides women were

books. Like they were things to be possessed, given away and returned.

This was why Reid had wanted so badly to impress them, why he'd made Estrella perform in front of them.

He wanted to interest everyone watching.

Estrella had thought Reid just wanted a favor.

She had no idea he had turned her into an advertisement.

Fel backed away from the dark-polished desk.

The Nomeolvides women had worried over what Reid might do with La Pradera. He'd heard their worried whispers that princesses would start saying their vows in the courtyard of blooming trees. Presidents' sons would hold their eighteenth birthday parties here just because girls would love the flowers. They'd worried that Reid would take the enchantment of this place and turn it into a spectacle.

But Reid planned to send the Nomeolvides women to other estates. He would order them to wealthy family's houses, where their skirts would skim unfamiliar ground and they would press their hands into dirt they'd never touched. Men they did not know would tell them where to grow crowns of spring buds.

Reid could send them out to every rich man who wanted them, and always call them back to La Pradera. They could never get free from him, because this place held them. Running from Reid meant running from this place that held their lives. If the ground sensed them fleeing, it would strike them down.

Fel's lungs tensed as he thought of Estrella, her hard, gasping breaths, the pollen and blood on her sleeves. He wondered if Reid sending them out would bring the same wrath down on them, and his chest grew tighter, like a cramped muscle. He worried the same thing he'd worried when Estrella led him through the dark.

Would the land know? Would it understand that these women didn't want to leave it, that it was only on Reid's orders?

Another question spun through him, a worse one.

If Reid made them draw up flowers on someone else's ground, would La Pradera grow jealous and vengeful? Would it hate them for sliding their fingers into different earth, and kill them for it?

"What are you doing?" a voice came from the doorway.

Reid still looked a little drunk, blurred around the edges. But when he saw the papers in Fel's hands, the air around him crackled like the sky before a lightning storm.

Fel's best chance was playing startled, lost. He dropped the letters. He held his hands out in from of him, showing his palms, proving he wasn't trying to pocket anything on the way out.

But when Reid came forward, when he grabbed him, it choked the words out of Fel.

He knew better than to speak. He knew the way to survive rich men was to seem harmless and stupid. Reid would give him some rough lecture about touching things that weren't his. Maybe he'd strike him. Then he'd shove him out of the room.

But Fel could not keep his lips still.

"They're not your property," Fel said, spitting the words out. "None of us are."

"You're going to mind your own business," Reid said, his voice low, reasoning. "You're going to walk away."

"Did you even think about what this could do to them?" Fel asked. "Leaving could kill them."

"You've seen them in town," Reid said. "Did it kill them? Try thinking next time you talk."

"This is different," Fel said. "You know that."

Reid tightened his grip. "And you don't know anything."

"I know you can't do this. They won't let you. I won't let you."

He tensed for Reid to hit him.

Reid got behind him, setting his forearm against Fel's throat.

"Say it." Reid set his arm harder against Fel's neck. "Say you don't know anything."

The pressure against his throat built until he felt it in his forehead. It raked through his hair.

"Just say it," Reid told him, "and we can be done here."

Fel kicked back at him, catching him in the shin hard enough that Reid stumbled. Reid came at him again, and Fel drove his hand into Reid's jaw, hard enough that he felt the backs of his own knuckles splitting.

The Briars had already decided the loss of him and his brother were no more remarkable than misplaced slips of paper.

Whatever the Nomeolvides women had done, he would not let Reid do this to them.

Fel would give the grandmothers the truths he had found on those heavy pieces of linen parchment.

He grabbed the sheets he'd let fall. He took them down the stairs, the inside of his rib cage hot with these things he needed to tell.

Reid caught up with him. He threw him down in the lightless gardens, hitting him so his chest clenched and he gasped to breathe.

The papers fluttered from his hands. He hit back, catching Reid in the stomach and the side. But for every strike, Reid returned a harder one. Every blow darkened the edges of his vision like an old photograph.

Fel kicked at him again. But the edges of him were going numb. His eyelids. His fingertips.

Gasping at his next breath paled the sky and made it seem close, like the moon was a chandelier in the center of a room.

Fel tried wrenching out from under Reid's hold. He was losing the feeling of his own body. He shut his eyes, trying to get a full breath. Through the blunt pressure of Reid's fists, only thin threads of air made it down to his lungs.

There was more will and rage in him than his body could use. It vibrated out of him. The flowering trees all arced toward a center point in the sky like the asterisk in a star marble.

Fel tried bucking out of Reid's grip. Reid twisted his arm, sending a rope of pain up to his shoulder.

Reid forced him back down, and Fel landed against the earth.

Blue petals brushed his skin. His hands found borraja. Forget-me-nots grazed his neck.

Estrella's ocean. Her sea of flickering blue.

The petals crushed under him. But beneath their soft blue, the earth didn't harden into solid ground against his back.

The earth gave.

Fel bucked again, throwing a shoulder up toward the sky. If he could move fast enough, just once, he could break Reid's hold.

But the earth was pulling him, taking him. It was folding him into its dark ground.

It stirred. In the flashes of opening his eyes, Fel caught the ground whirling and spinning around him. It moved in currents. It shifted like wide ribbons of water, glinting like the moon and sun off a river. A storm, but it did not rise. It stayed low on the ground. He could hear its faint thunder, how it tunneled deeper underground.

He tensed against Reid's grasp.

With the last will he had in him, he reached up toward the light.

But then the ground spoke.

Don't fight, it whispered, not in La Pradera's voice but in his brother's. *I've got you. I'm not letting you go.*

He felt it in his own body, as though his skin was turning to shale.

Waves of earth tumbled over Fel. The current broke over his

body, weighing him down. The rivers of ground folded him into their countless grains.

The storm bound him and covered him. It took the blood on his knuckles and the glowing band on his wrist. It held him so close it was teaching his body to become the ground. A ribbon of earth, thick and heavy, slid over his eyes, so he could not have seen even if he could open them.

The current shifted again. He sank as fast as if he'd plunged into water. He fell into his brother's voice, telling him he would take him into the earth to save him. *I have you. You're okay.*

Then he was nothing but ground.

TWENTY-NINE

He knew.

You took the truth and you made it into flowers.

He had felt the pull of her heart on his, the dangerous force of a Nomeolvides girl falling in love, and he had hated her for it. Worse, because the same blood that crafted this land into flower beds, the blood that made a jagged ravine into a sunken garden, was death to their lovers.

That was the only way she made sense of it, him turning on her as fast as the wink of a firefly. And now, hours later, she woke up screaming, feeling like her heart was crumbling to ash in her rib cage.

She was the same as so many Nomeolvides women before her, feeling the loss of their loves like their hearts were rounds of coal, glowing hot and then burning out so fast they felt cold. It was the way they knew. Their lost loves took a little of their own hearts with them, and they felt it tearing away.

Estrella was a spirit outside her body, outside the chiffon shell of the dress she'd fallen asleep in. The darker blue stains, the evidence of his touch, felt damning.

Dalia held Estrella like she was having a nightmare.

"It's okay," she whispered. "It's okay."

But the center of Estrella turned to a worn-out peony, falling to a hundred petals.

She had loved him to his death.

She broke from Dalia's hold.

She found his things as they'd been.

The shoes he'd cast aside for one night in favor of the polished ones Reid had told him to wear. The undone laces stared up at her, a reminder that if he'd left, he would've put his plain shoes back on.

And the different-color figurines, a herd of winged wooden horses crossing a shelf. These he would have taken with him no matter how fast he'd left. But they were here, colors bright, paint cool from how long it had been since the warmth of his fingers had touched them.

He hadn't run from La Pradera.

If he was gone, this was hers. His vanishing was hers.

It didn't matter that he'd gotten enough sense to run from her. Her teeth had already been in him. Pulling away had just dragged them through him deeper, hurting him worse.

She took this understanding into her. It spread through her as she held those painted wooden horses in her hands, these things he never would've left behind.

Her cousins crowded around her, telling her they'd look for him, he had probably just gotten lost. He would come back.

But she knew. The turning at the center of her, that feeling of embers going dark, told her. It flared and stung, and then she was screaming into her hands. She screamed into the horses' small bright bodies, into their rounded wings, because her heart was too dry and wrung out to let her cry.

They screamed back to her. They spilled onto her skirt, catching in the folds like her dress was a small, bright sky. Held in their colors and screams was the low thread of Fel's voice, slipping from her like the beads of her necklace sliding underwater.

She had killed him. She had been the second Nomeolvides girl to love him out of existence.

In this family, broken hearts were passed down like lockets. And Estrella had been enough a fool to think she could refuse the one meant for her simply by not opening her hands.

She had loved him until there was nothing left of him.

Her cousins found her down here, kneeling on the floorboards. Their mothers recognized her screaming. Their grandmothers nodded from the hall, a shared sadness and understanding across their faces.

Sorrow was a family heirloom, written into their blood like ink on a will.

The words that had been waiting in Estrella's mouth needled her. If she did not let them off her tongue they would cut her, so she opened her mouth and let them go, those sharp, glinting things.

"I am poison," Estrella said, the last word raising her voice a little louder, like an anthem.

Poison.

THIRTY

He was not alone here in the dark.

Fel reached out toward a voice that sounded a little like his own but deeper. Surer. Certain as a call across water. Fel remembered that voice. He had carried it with him.

We're gonna raise horses one day, you and me.

His brother.

They were two brothers again, a man and a boy. The boy knew the man's dream of working with Andalusian horses, held close even here. He tasted the burnt sugar of the figs his brother loved when they could find them growing wild. He felt the blood and calluses made on their hands, their fingers turning rough alongside each other's.

Fel hovered in the same living and not-living space he had come from before Estrella found him. But there was enough of him that he and his brother could pass back and forth memories of a world their mother and father had sent them away from.

Cutting wild asparagus with their father's knives.

Slipping the lacy shells of red macis from between nutmeg seeds and their fruit.

How their grandmother left behind not just her recipes for pomegranate-orange-blossom water and pickled lemons, but her sadness that one day Fel and his brother would have to leave the place they had been born.

Adán. The name spun through what was left of Fel.

His brother's name had been Adán.

Adán had saved him, pulling him back into the ground when Fel thought Reid might kill him. Adán had drawn him back into the dark and the rush of voices.

It wasn't just them. There were others down here.

They were the bodies and spirits taken into the ground. These voices carried the scent and color of where the land had pulled them into its earth. Flowering branches or bare boughs depending on the season. The perfume of roses at midnight or lilies at dawn. The tiny leaves and thread-thin stems of cut hedges. A slope of jacaranda and magnolia.

But Fel had not been taken by these vengeful gardens. Not like they had.

He was one of the first men dead. He had gone into this ground long before Nomeolvides hands ever touched it. The truth he had died to and come back from went deeper than their fingers could reach.

These were voices that brought with them the heavier smells of iron and limestone. They carried metal and salt from both earth and blood. This was the bitter growth of a story untold, kept underground.

Fel and Adán and the other men left here had been forgotten. The bodies of named men, men who had died with them but who were more likely to be missed, had been unearthed from the dirt and rock. But no one searched for Fel and Adán and the forgotten men. The foremen found the bodies of men they considered worth looking for, and left the rest.

Fel and Adán and those left here were the unnamed, the unaccounted for, the unlawful. They were the ones who carried forged papers. They ones left off role sheets because they were not worth the trouble to write down.

They were the ones sent into the bed depths so thick with dust they could barely see. It burned their lungs, and at night they coughed it onto their mats along with sprays of blood.

They were the ones lying about their ages, and the foremen knew it. But because they needed men who could be paid little, they handed them scrapers and picks, shovels and wheelbarrows.

The Briars wanted the deposit fast, the foremen told them. So they sent Fel and Adán and other unnamed men into stretches of the mine floor jagged with faults and slips and fractures.

If there was going to be a fall, the foremen said, they'd have warning. They'd get them out fast enough.

Fel and Adán believed them because they had to. Because they were brown-skinned men who could find no other work, and if they did not believe the foremen, they would go back to starving.

But there had been a fall, an endless river of rock and earth rushing down toward them, and it had killed them. Then it had been lied about, made into gardens. The Nomeolvides women had no idea that the ravine they made into a valley of flowers had been a quarry.

And a graveyard. The Nomeolvides women had planted flowers in places men had died.

Armed with the blur of half remembering, he had hated Estrella, hated all of them for it. But none of them had known. He understood that now, the things he had not realized finding him in the dark.

They had been complicit in covering this over, and they had no idea.

The land had become vicious, and hungry. It did not care that the Nomeolvides women did not know. It held them responsible for turning death into gardens. It demanded their tears sown into its ground like seeds. It drew their lovers into hills and hollows. It took from the women who spent their lives kneeling in this earth.

They covered the death of so many men, the fall that had happened here, all blood and rock and dust. They had silenced the land with arbors and flowering trees. They had hidden its story with countless bright petals. And La Pradera made them pay for it. It took any man they loved. In making this land beautiful, the Nomeolvides women had also made it ravenous. Wrathful.

Bloodthirsty.

This land had seen so much death that by the time the

Nomeolvides women spread their petals over it, it had grown a taste for it.

What still existed of Fel wrung out with all the things his brother would have taught him. How to keep the flint shell of his heart from cracking before he was ready. That being forbidden a thing would only make him want it more, but sometimes it was easier not to want something if he knew he could never have it.

It was the possibility, the potential in a laugh or the brush of fingers, that could leave them in pieces. It had etched on Fel's rib cage the memory of light on a girl's skin, her ankle wearing thin cords of gold and moon silver.

The earth should have given Fel the sense that he couldn't breathe, like the ground falling over him so long ago. But down here, he had no body to be crushed, no breath to be taken, no blood to be lost.

All that was left were his dreams of indigo horses, turning teal beneath the sun's heat.

A girl setting her lips against his forehead as he slept.

The wild flicker of her skirt, like petals scattering.

This was a thing he'd learned: that setting his hand on a girl's back, and that girl letting his hand stay, led to fairy rings, and ponds full of stars.

Even in its first faint traces, love could alter a landscape. It wrote unimagined stories and made the most beautiful, forbidding places.

Love grew such strange things.

THIRTY-ONE

Her mother did not try to hold her as she cried into the sheets Fel had slept in. Her mother did not try to stroke her hair or shush her with a soft voice. Instead, she soaked a cloth in rosewater and with rough, quick strokes she cleared the trails of salt and the indigo dried on Estrella's cheeks. She handed Estrella a small cup and told her to swallow it down. The alcohol burned the back of her throat, then left the taste of anise and honey.

The sting of the liquor faded, and Estrella fell into the open well of sleep.

"Luisa," her mother said from the doorway.

Estrella sat up, half-asleep, wondering if, for a moment, her mother had forgotten her name.

"The one I loved most wasn't your father," her mother said, her shape a silhouette in the hall's light. "We loved each other the way friends do, your father and I. But I loved someone else in a very different way. Her name was Luisa."

To another daughter, it might have stung, the revelation that her father was some lesser love to her mother.

But this one name shimmered with the possibility that her mother understood the hearts of Estrella and her cousins.

And right now it kept Estrella breathing.

"What happened to her?" she asked.

"I sent her away," her mother said. Even in the dark Estrella could make out the hardening of her face, bracing against the memory. She looked washed clean of excess color, her lips pale against the brown of her face and her deep eyes. "I told her I didn't love her."

Estrella sank back onto the bed. "I should've sent him away."

"Where?" her mother asked. "This was the only home he had."

Estrella's eyes fell shut, and she breathed in the air through the window and the soft breath of her mother whispering, "Sleep."

This was what turned Nomeolvides girls into women. Not their first times bleeding between their legs, but the first time their hearts broke. Estrella could feel hers inside her rib cage, a bird trapped in an attic.

She still wore her blue dress, limp and creased. The stains from the mushroom milk had turned a deep green. She slept in the bed that still smelled like him, the salt of his sweat and the scent of leaves in the gardens. She dreamed of setting her mouth against him, kissing the places where pale scars crossed his back like he was a map. She dreamed of the heat that lived just under his skin. And when she dreamed of him, she woke to starflowers spreading across the ceiling. The vines unfurled, wrapping around rafters and trailing down to the curtain rods. The purple blooms opened and showed their five blue petals.

She didn't care who saw them. She didn't care if they reminded her mother or her grandmother of girls driven from their houses for being witches. Estrella was more dangerous than any bruja. She had killed the boy she'd brought back. And this was a thing worse than loving him into disappearing in the first place.

She opened herself to her family's worry. She hoped it would sharpen into scorn, because that was what she deserved. Not their concern. Not their sense that she should be looked after. Their contempt. Their blame.

Estrella deserved the name her mother had given her. She deserved how it made those blue flowers unpredictable, waiting at the edges of her dreams. She deserved the way it kept her a little distance from her cousins, making her a lesser Nomeolvides girl.

Later, her cousins filled the room, carrying haircombs, a clean dress, glasses of water, cups of tea. They came with hands ready to lead her into the shower and spin her into something living.

"We have to tell her," Estrella said.

Her cousins stilled. She had said so little since shutting herself in this room that now her voice caught them.

"What?" Gloria asked.

"Bay." Estrella slid to the edge of the bed, her feet brushing the floor. "We have to tell her to get away from us."

"Why?" Calla and Azalea asked, a half second off from each other.

Estrella stood, the floor cool under her feet. "So we don't kill her."

As her cousins traded glances, the feeling of standing filled Estrella. The sense of her own weight and will came back into her body.

She could not save Fel. Nomeolvides girls had been the death of him twice. But she and her cousins could warn the girl they had grown up loving.

"We have to tell her to get away from us before we kill her," Estrella said.

"No," Dalia said. "We're not telling her to do anything. We're giving her time to do what she needs to do."

"You convinced us all that we lost her," Estrella said. "Do you really want to know what that felt like for us? Do you want it to happen for real so you can know?" The force of her own voice shocked through her. "Is that a chance you'll take with her?"

"This was her home," Azalea said. "Where do you want her to go?"

"Anywhere," Estrella said. "Away from us. Away from Reid."

"We are not Reid," Dalia said.

"We're worse," Estrella said, "because she thinks we're safe."

Dalia's flinch was so deep Estrella felt it.

"Our love is her death," Estrella said, "and you know it."

Dalia looked like she'd fallen into water, floating and weightless, like she'd lost the feeling of standing on this floor they'd all worn with years' worth of steps.

"If we don't want to lose her," Estrella said, "we have to let her go."

When Dalia nodded, it was slow, like she was answering through a dream. That nod, the giving in of her heart, pulled the rest of them with her.

The five of them streamed out of the stone house, passing the iris beds and rose trellises and the courtyard of blossoming trees. With prodding from Azalea and Calla, Dalia gave up the room number at the hotel. Fifth floor.

Bay opened the door on the first knock. By the shift in her expression, Estrella knew she'd expected just Dalia.

The five of them rushed into the cloth-papered room.

Estrella shut the door behind them. She parted her lips to say what she had brought her cousins here for, to beg Bay to flee from them.

Don't think you're safe from us just because you grew up with us.

Don't die because we love you.

Don't let our hearts kill you.

But the words trailed off Estrella's tongue.

Paper covered every furniture surface in the hotel room. The desk. The night table. Even the bed, papers strewn over the unmade blankets.

Estrella drew closer, so slowly that Bay didn't stop her.

They were all copies. Reproductions of old photographs. Not just black-and-white but tintype, daguerreotype. And grainy copies of articles from newspapers that looked more than a century old.

The newspaper clippings were single column, the kind that got buried deep in the pages. They used words Estrella recognized, in some vague way that only came to mind when she thought of them together, as geological. *Overburden. Striation. Berm. Shear.* But she didn't know what any of them meant.

"Calla," Azalea said, handing articles to her youngest cousin.

The photos showed the low contrast of a scene that was all rock, a hollow in the ground that looked like it had enormous, ringing steps up the sides. Some showed the rings of that hollow as unbroken levels, like stacked bowls.

Others showed a wide ribbon of earth running from one edge down into the deep center, like a spilled liquid.

"What is all this?" Gloria asked.

Before Bay could answer, Calla said, "It's the sunken garden."

Estrella looked at it again. She studied the shape in different photos, the edges, the faint smudges of scrub grass and trees beyond.

Calla was right. She'd recognized it even without the flowers and vines and trees.

Bay's breath out sounded like the walls were sighing. "I told you I was still working it out. I just need time."

"Bay," Dalia said, her voice gentle as the brush of petals she'd grown herself.

The draft through the cracked window lifted the ends of Bay's hair and then let them fall back to her forehead.

"Bay," Dalia said again, laying her hand on the side of Bay's face.

In the way she said Bay's name, there was not pleading but urging, the assurance that to her and her cousins, Bay could tell these secrets.

"I was looking for something to get Reid to back off," Bay said, eyes flashing to all of them. "Unfiled taxes. Something like that. But when I started looking, I found out something happened at La Pradera. A long time ago. Before it was La Pradera."

"What happened?" Azalea asked.

Bay shook her head. "I don't know everything yet."

"Then tell us what you do know," Gloria said, matching Dalia's soft voice.

Bay straightened her shoulders, like this story was a thing she had to stand strong against. Whatever it was, she was buckling under the guilt of it.

"From what I could find, everyone thought it would be the best quarry in the country," Bay said.

"What quarry?" Gloria asked.

"Where the sunken garden is," Bay said. "It wasn't just some canyon. It was a quarry."

With those words, Estrella's memories of the sunken garden twisted and sharpened. The layers of petals fell aside. The pond streamed away. The wind stripped the trees. There was nothing left to imagine but the jagged stone beneath everything.

"They all said the overburden—the dirt and everything else covering the minerals—was thinner than they'd ever seen," Bay said. "That's why they were stripping the ground, to get at what was underneath. But they ignored how much of it wasn't structurally sound. There were faults and they knew it, and they didn't do anything to account for it."

Bay said each word like she was forcing them out. Estrella wanted to tell her this wasn't her fault. She didn't own this. She'd caught the dates on the newspapers, and this had been well over a hundred years ago.

"See the striations here." She set a finger against a photograph, the bands in the sides of the pit. "They're called benches. The part that drops down is the batter, the flat part's the berm. I don't know if you really understand how big this thing was. It's hard to tell with all the trees and the flower beds now."

She handed photographs to Calla and Gloria. "The benches are supposed to prevent rock falls from going all the way down the wall. That's to try to make it less dangerous for the miners and prevent damage to everything. Not always in that order though."

Estrella and Azalea clustered around Calla and Gloria, studying the striped benches.

"There are angles you're supposed to do all this at. Shallower angles. Especially if you have any structural weakness within the rock." Bay said each word with such pain, like she was watching it happen and could not reach out to stop it. "Faults. Shears. Anything like that. But they didn't do what the surveyors told them to do. They paid them off and just did whatever they wanted."

"They?" Gloria asked.

Bay's shoulders rounded. "The Briars. My family."

She gave them the photographs with the lines of the benches broken, that wide ribbon of earth. "They should have known, with walls that steep. They should've known this would happen." She swallowed hard enough that Estrella could also see the knot of it in her throat. "When it broke, the landslide was like nothing they'd ever seen. Millions of cubic meters of dirt and rock. Everyone in town thought it was an earthquake."

That was the band of earth. An avalanche, breaking the steps.

Gloria handed a photograph back to Bay. "Did everyone get out?"

Bay shut her eyes, shook her head, her jaw tight. "There's no count. No numbers."

"What do you mean?" Azalea asked.

"I mean I can't find numbers anywhere," Bay said. "My family buried this so deep I can't even find out how many miners died. All I can find are the photos and those articles saying some kind of accident happened. I had to go looking for death certificates. But I can't even find many of those."

The seam of a wallpaper panel was coming away from the wall, showing the yellowing glue underneath. Bay's fingers worried at the edge.

"All those lives," she said. "All those stories. And we hid it all."

Every word looked like a stone in Bay's pocket. She was more than a century removed from this, but still, the guilt had been passed down. No one else had taken it, so it had fallen to her, the Briar bastard, a burden tumbling down stone steps to the lowest point in this family.

Bay looked at Dalia, wincing like Dalia might slap her, or tell her she did not love her, or scream at her that her family were murderers and liars.

"This is what I come from," Bay said, her voice breaking into pieces as she confessed this to the woman she loved. "This is my family."

"Who rejected you," Azalea said. "Forget them. The things they did aren't yours."

"I've lived off Briar money," Bay said. "That makes me responsible."

"You lived off Marjorie's money," Calla said.

"I'm still a Briar," Bay said. "This is still mine."

"Then let's do something about it," Dalia said.

"How?" Bay asked. "It's done. Those men." She sank onto the edge of the bed, fingers raking through her hair. "Their blood is on our hands."

"It's not done," Gloria said. "You can tell the truth. Make sure everyone knows what happened."

"Are you kidding?" Azalea asked. "The Briars will kill her."

"Not if we have anything to say about it," Calla said.

Their voices receded against the striped wallpaper.

Estrella tried to listen. But the words floated round the room instead of reaching her. They patterned the bedspread. They stuck to the wallpaper. They caught on the white iron chandelier above them.

The dark earth on the boy she'd found in the sunken garden.

His clothes that seemed a hundred years out of date.

The half-starved look of an overworked boy.

The way he looked for things to do with his hands. The calluses on his fingers, rough as sand.

Everything Estrella had imagined about where he had come from fell away.

The force of it made her buckle toward the wall. She took slow, steadying breaths, but the world would not go still.

Dalia was again holding Bay's face in her hands, Bay's eyes shut. The other three were swearing that if Bay told the truth, they would scare Reid and every other Briar into thinking they were witches who would turn them into violets if they laid hands on her.

Estrella slipped from the room, down the stairs, across the open land that gave her a shortcut back to La Pradera.

She found Reid standing on the grass, lighting up a cigar he'd no doubt stolen from the collection Marjorie kept for guests. He'd changed out of his formal clothes, all traces of jacket and pocket square gone. But he looked like he'd dressed himself by pulling pants and a shirt out of the laundry, then grabbing the formal shoes he'd worn for the ball, probably left beside his bed.

How he looked didn't matter to him. In a man, not caring

was a draw, a mark of confidence. In Estrella, who'd worn her eyeliner until it smudged and her ball dress until it wilted, the same not-trying looked sloppy.

What shamed a girl was, in a boy, so often worth showing off.

Reid flicked the cigar. He threw embers over the ground. To him, this land was no different than a crystal ashtray.

The ash struck the earth, and anger gave Estrella words.

"You killed them," Estrella said.

He took in the sight of her, stained skirt and unbrushed hair.

He flicked another ember. "What?"

"Your family killed them." Her voice was rising, like a bird's call echoing off trees.

"What are you talking about?" he asked.

"Men died on your family's watch," she said. "And then you covered it up."

Reid crouched, putting out the cigar in the grass.

Estrella pressed her teeth together, like she could feel the burn on the ground.

Reid blew on the cigar. When it cooled, he tucked it into his pocket, rising to standing again.

He eyed her dress and smudged makeup.

"Clean up," he said. "Get some sleep."

How level the words came out startled her, charged but not angry. Low enough that the wind wove through them.

Reid started walking.

"Reid," Estrella called after him.

He kept walking.

"Stop," she said, letting her voice go.

She followed him past the fountains and trellises.

"Look at me," she said, and her voice turned to a yell.

Reid crossed the courtyard of blossoming trees. He was almost to the hedge wall when she caught up with him.

She grabbed his shoulder. She dug her fingers in so hard she could feel the heat of his skin through his shirt, and she wrenched him to make him turn around.

He did turn around, fast and hard.

He backhanded her, like he couldn't decide if he wanted to hit her or just flick her away.

She was close enough, and he'd let his hand fly fast enough that the impact landed hard. Open hand, his knuckles hitting her mouth.

Her lip split open, and the taste of her blood spread over her tongue.

Estrella stumbled, getting her balance back. Blood stung her lip.

"Nobody's killed anyone except you and your family," Reid said.

Estrella's heartbeat throbbed in her cut lip.

"You're the reason Bay's gone, aren't you?" Reid said.

Estrella spit out the blood in her mouth, the salt so strong on her tongue it was almost sweet. It struck the ground, and the shape of it looked like a trail of red starflowers. They shone on the grass.

She set the side of her thumb against her lip, blotting away the blood.

This was one thing she could use. They hadn't lost Bay, not yet. But Estrella could still frighten Reid with the stories and whispers about the Nomeolvides girls, their hearts as wild as they were dangerous.

"Not just me," Estrella said. "All of us."

She took a step forward, narrowing the gap between her and Reid.

In that moment, she was not just Estrella.

She was Calla, blushing too much to speak as she watched Bay's careful hands shape yew wood with a rasp and hand plane.

She was Azalea, embroidering Bay's initials into the hems of her pillowcases.

She was Gloria, stealing old tintype photos from Briar scrapbooks no one ever looked at, trying to work out which distant relatives Bay looked most like.

She was Dalia, her heart lit by the understanding that Bay was not just the one they all loved but also herself.

Estrella took another step, and Reid drew back, preserving the distance.

"That's what you think, isn't it?" Estrella asked, letting the sound of taunting slip into her voice. If she apologized for her own heart then she would make it tame, and small. But like this, it was wild, and limitless.

She could see him trying to twist his horror into rage, but Estrella could still find it, that fear.

Estrella was herself, a girl who had loved Bay even while Bay never considered her more than a charming little sister. She was a girl grateful for falling in love like that, because it taught her how. Because when she finally let go of this woman who did not love her back, it was to let her love Dalia. Because falling in love with a girl who feared nothing in this world had left her ready to love a boy whose heart had been broken before she ever touched him.

She was all of them, screaming for Bay to speed faster down the highway in Marjorie's wine-red four-door. She was the five of them holding their arms out of the windows, their hands riding the night air. She was all of them hushing one another's laughs and running through the dark as the engine cooled and creaked.

She was each of them, born with the possibility of flowers in their hands, but never feeling like living things themselves until they ran across La Pradera with Bay Briar. They were night-blooming girls, the grass damp under their bare feet and the stars above them as thick as spilled sugar.

"Who knows?" Estrella asked. "Maybe if you're lucky we'll all love you next."

She shoved him, palms against his shoulders. And with more fear than rage he threw the back of his hand across her face again. He struck her like she was a stinging insect to swat away.

The impact shook through her cheek and her forehead. The force opened the cut on her lip wider.

She lifted her chin, showing him the blood on her face, proof that she'd rattled him. Proof that even Briars could not ignore girls with flowers and death in their fingertips.

"What do you think they're thinking?" Reid asked. "The moment right before they're gone."

Blood dripped onto her tongue.

"Do you think they still love you?" Reid asked.

The dry feeling climbed back to Estrella's throat. She could not shove Reid's words away just because Bay was still alive. Fel was gone. The loss of him belonged to Estrella.

"Don't tell me you've never thought about it," Reid said.

The air carried the sour, bitter smell of her family's tears, a scent like salt and lemon rind in hot water. The faint stirring of every flower she and her family had ever given to La Pradera rushed back, the sound of their petals rising up like the flutter of a million wings.

For a hundred years, her family had put their hands in this ground, and it wanted to hold on to them so much it would never let them go.

Now voices drifted from the sunken garden, so faint Estrella could not make out the words. It was too many voices for her to count, braiding together and then unraveling, weaving into a solid veil of sound and then fraying back into innumerable voices.

Lost lovers.

Men killed and then disregarded.

They were flooding her until there was no room left for her own thoughts. Her tongue was the flame blue of an iris petal. Her skin was the rust silk of dahlias, and her hair and her eyes were handfuls of storm-damp ground. Her heart was a handful of raw buds, red as pomegranate seeds and slicked with rain.

What happened to the miners? She wanted to ask. But calling them *the miners* felt like disrespect. Not naming them was a betrayal to their lives and deaths.

She only knew the name of one.

"What happened to Fel?" she asked.

"You know what happened," Reid said. "You killed him."

"No, I didn't," she said.

"Was it fun?" Reid asked. "Making him disappear?"

"I never wanted that," she said, her voice splintering.

"Did you ever think of his family?" Reid asked. "Or did you not even ask if he had one?"

The ground looked like it was waving under her, billowing like a quilt.

She wanted to root herself here. She was close enough to reach out for her ocean of blue petals. She wanted to vanish into that sea of color, for it to swallow her, drink her. It was a wish that spun and grew until it had its own gravity, so heavy it dragged her to her hands and knees.

Reid's shadow fell over her.

"You killed him," he said.

Estrella kept her head down, so all she could see was the shimmer of blue petals. "I cared about him."

Even with nothing in her vision but ground, she wondered

if these words were a lie. Maybe her brutal heart's version of love was hate, and she didn't even realize.

Her cousins were life and enchantment. But she was all malice and knives.

"I loved him." The cracks in her voice deepened. It was more confession than defense.

Her heart was poison. It was a close tangle of thorns. Even when it held love, that love came sharp, and she didn't know how to offer it to anyone except with the edges out.

The Briars had killed Fel and all those men. And her family had killed men who came too close.

A wish flickered in her heart to become part of the ground. Fel was gone, and there was nowhere to mourn him. But he had once died in this ground, and now so could she.

It was the closest she could ever be to finding him again.

Her fingers sank into the bed of blue petals, and then into the soft ground. Blood fell from her lip, and the red dyed a forget-me-not petal.

The center of her flooded with every wish for things to be different.

For the treaties that had drawn new borders not to have been signed, so her family would not have lost their land and found they had nowhere to go but this graveyard. For them to never have been declared las hijas del aire or witches.

For La Pradera not to hold on to them so tight it drove the will out of them.

For the air to spin until it gave Fel back, his body and breath reappearing the way they had disappeared.

She wanted all this so much that when her hands sank further into the sand and met resistance, she could imagine what they were finding. Maybe they were meeting young, thin roots, or the closed fingers of unbloomed irises. But she could pretend they were not these things.

She could pretend they were hands.

THIRTY-TWO

He let himself fall into that ocean of lost voices. He was himself, and he was all these men.

They were boys who waited in the trees' shadows. Men who had kissed Nomeolvides women in the curves of hedges and under the ceiling of leaf-covered arbors.

And they were men and boys whose hearts were stained with blood and rust.

They were all woven from secrets they took with them into the ground.

But Estrella was drawing him back. This girl who had kept the carved wooden horses like they were her pets, and then buried one so deep it had called him to the surface.

Estrella. This girl who, in her blue dress against the green hills and the brick of the Briars' house, had looked like a small sky. A girl catching light in the folds of her skirt.

The girl whose hands had found him in the garden valley that had once been a quarry.

She had brought him back to life.

Now her blood, searing through the ground, reached him. Her voice burrowed down to where he drifted in the dark. Her hands found his, their fingers meeting in the sand. His brushed hers, and hers felt like cords of daylight.

Her heart felt strong and desperate enough to pull him back. Her mourning for everything her family had lost went down as deep as he had fallen.

The other voices whispered to him to follow her. Theirs was a story that needed to be told, and the land wanted it spoken as much as they did. They were the immigrants, the underaged, the ones left off role sheets. And they had been caught here, in the ages they had been when they died, freed neither by being found and given burials, nor by their families hearing what had become of them, nor by the truth ever being told.

None of those things had happened, so they had all carried it for more than a hundred years.

The ground shifted. Not a storm this time. The slow crawl of a wave, like blue petals spreading.

He did not realize he still had fingers, or a body. But he was rising up from that deep place. He had been drifting down toward his brother and all those other voices the ground had taken. But now he stopped, and gave into the feeling of his body floating toward the surface. He'd been a river stone, and now he was turning to foam on a sea.

The feeling of his own lungs came sudden and hard. It felt not like coming up from underwater, but like taking back the breath he'd had before. Earth fell from his lips. It drew back from his neck. It streamed away from his body like water. It ran off him as though he was a like magnet, and the dirt was filaments skittering away. Those currents of ground knew they did not belong on him anymore.

Her hands touched his forehead, and he realized he was skin and muscle again. She was brushing earth off his eyes as he coughed it out of his throat. She was sliding a palm under his neck and saying his name.

"Breathe," she said, and her own breath at the end of the word sounded like a whisper. "Breathe," she said again, and this time he felt the outline of the word on his temple, her mouth on his skin.

She slid her hand under his back. At her touch, his body sparked to life, first his skin and muscle, then the worn-down places around his heart. His chest trembled with trying to get his breath back.

The moon needled his eyes. A drop of rain, hot and sudden, struck his cheek, and he blinked.

Under that sudden light, he understood. He took with him what he'd learned in the dark, both things known and questions to ask. He brought it all to the surface.

THIRTY-THREE

The ground shifted and swirled. At first, she thought the ocean of blue petals was turning to water. Then she thought it was answering her wish to become part of it. It would break her into flowers, and make her part of the earth.

The blue and violet buckled, the flashes of forget-me-not petals and borraja rippling like a pond.

She thought she was imagining him, a boy from the earth. Petals and leaves and dirt still half covered him when she made out his shape. Black hair. Skin the soft brown of bare tree branches in winter. His eyelashes like dark stars.

He seemed like a thing she had imagined. She'd spun the black of his hair out of the night sky. She'd made up the brown of his skin from the brown of her own, and her cousins'. He'd been an illusion of La Pradera, a boy crafted out of her understanding that this was a place nightmares bloomed as easily as flowers.

The ground lied to her, the way the Briars had lied about the ground with the help of her hands and so many others.

Then petals and dirt blew aside, like the wind was drawing back sheer layers of a skirt. It pulled away from this boy as fast as if it had its own current. With the thinning of the blue and brown, the colors of him were close and true, his hair and skin and the pale violet of his mouth.

The breath came back into him, each inhale a gasp, each breath out sounding like coughing. She held him, put her mouth against his skin and told him to breathe.

"I'm sorry," she said, holding him close enough that she was speaking the words against his skin. "I'm sorry." Her own guilt, her wish for him to believe her, put cracks in the words. "I didn't know."

He hadn't opened his eyes. But his fingers caught in her hair, and with his whispered "I know," she understood that he recognized her by her touch and her voice.

Even with his skin damp from the ground, flecked with petals she'd made, he still smelled like blue mushrooms and wild grass, like the pond with its scent that made her dream of both stone and light.

Heat prickled her eyes. The life in him was water and warmth to everything dying in her. The hope in her, a dead-headed rosebush, woke and put out new green. It pushed out buds and shuddered into full color.

Estrella blinked, and a tear's heat and salt fell from her eyelashes. It struck the earth, and in its place a starflower broke through. It unfurled five soft-pointed pink petals. Its center held filaments of white pollen as fine as still-flaked snow.

The single flower spread into a vine, and then branched into a dozen more. Buds and leaves grew so fast the ground looked like it was bursting into blue and pink flames.

In the middle of that spreading ocean of petals, new color broke the blue and violet. Green rose up through the ground, growing into a tiny sapling. Its thin trunk wore few leaves. But it snaked into boughs and branches, and opened into flashes of color. It grew tall, and took on a willow's wide spread.

Tiny flowers fluttered over the branches, like wings landing. But instead of cream or soft pink, they were turquoise and teal. They were gold and green and lilac.

The colors of beads she had given to the pond, along with her wish that this boy would find everything he had lost.

THIRTY-FOUR

Fel opened his eyes, still bracing against the moon and the prickling light of stars. He moved his hands, and the feeling came back to each of his fingers.

The world resolved into forms.

A tree grew from Estrella's ocean of blue petals. The branches had the shape of cherry and almond trees in flower.

But instead of pink and white, this one had a dozen different colors. Blues and greens, golds and violets. Light purple petals climbed one branch, and blue-green flowers covered another bough. Green ones he thought were leaves cleared into blossoms. Blooms of pale gold petals trailed along the inner branches.

It was the remembered things he had told her, covered in all her wild color.

There was more to him now, more of his blood. He could reach his hand to Estrella's face, the moon brightening the edges of her hair.

With his thumb, he cleared a wet trail from her cheek. It led his eyes to her lips.

Her lip was bleeding. A gash cut across the pink red of her mouth. Blood was drying into the cracks of her lips.

Not like she'd bitten herself.

Like someone had hit her.

He felt a shadow moving closer.

Fel sat up. His chest tightened at the sudden shift, but the stirring of the ground underneath him kept him moving.

Reid stood near them, looking as startled to see Fel above the ground as he had to see him disappear into it.

Reid. This man whose family had killed and then covered everything over. This man who thought women like Estrella could be lent like candlesticks or cuff links, and struck like they were frozen ground.

Fel could see the tension shocking through Reid's hands. He looked ready, and afraid. Not of Estrella, with blood drying on her lip. Or Fel, with dirt and petals clinging to his skin, darkening the shirt he'd been wearing when Adán took him into the ground.

Reid was staring at that tree, that beautiful, unknowable tree with all its colors. It was no trick or performance. No pond of blue petals. It was not magic for him to put on display. It was stunning and terrifying as a statue of a saint.

It was damning Reid. Fel could see guilt moving across his face as the tree loomed and cast its shadow.

Reid's gaze struck them both but settled on Estrella.

"Your whole family," he said. "Do you know how close you were to getting killed for being witches before you came here?"

Estrella held on to Fel tighter, as though he needed guarding more than she did.

"We should've let them," Reid said.

Estrella gave against the threat, Reid's unspoken promise that if the town turned on the Nomeolvides women, if they hated and feared them, Reid would let them drive her family from this land, cast them out, murder them.

With herself, Estrella was reckless and unafraid, but she was as careful with her family as if they were glass.

Fel's body still felt like handfuls of ground. He had to brace against the earth underneath him to get back the feeling that he was on this side of it.

But he would kill this man. Even if he still felt himself crumbling like earth, he would kill him.

Estrella's family had been his when he had no family. This was his fight, too.

He pulled himself to standing. His steps felt unsteady, things he had to think about. He had to force his body into them, like he'd been startled awake from sleepwalking.

Estrella grabbed his arm, and he couldn't tell if she was trying to stop him or help him stand.

With each step, he felt more rooted in his own body, and he closed more space between him and Reid. There was current in his hands, half rage, half the untethered feeling of coming back to life.

Fel would kill this man. For his brother. For the other men. For the women who had become his family.

Steps struck the courtyard flagstones.

"Reid." Bay's voice rang out through the gardens.

Reid's stare flew and found her.

Bay stopped, catching her breath. In the distance, Estrella's cousins crossed La Pradera, the wind streaming their hair and skirts.

Reid studied Bay like he was watching her through a rain-blurred window. There was no flash of satin or fair hair, nothing pale or bright against the dark sky. In the place of blues and yellows there were browns and grays.

But he recognized her, her voice if not her clothes and her hair, cut and dyed. She put a haunted look into him, as though the voices that lived in the ground had gotten their fingers around his throat.

The sight of her deepened his fear. It shocked him into stillness.

"Reid," Bay said, moving closer. "Did you ever think about why they sent you here?"

The shadow and silver of clouds moved over Reid's face.

"This is the land of Briar disappointments," Bay said.

"I know that," Reid said, his voice unsteady. "Everyone knows that."

"Did you know we've disappeared, too?"

"What?" Reid looked down at his own body as though it might be vanishing.

"A long time ago." Bay unfolded papers from her back pocket, sheets that looked like copied newsprint. "More than a hundred years ago."

Fel tensed, waiting for her to tell the rest, not sure he wanted to hear the story of his own death and Adán's told like it was far history.

"The Briars who lived here went missing and nobody ever found them," Bay said.

Fel turned to Estrella. *What?* He'd meant to say it, not mouth it, but no sound came.

Estrella shook her head.

"Nobody knew what happened to them," Bay said. "People around here thought they'd skipped the country. That's one of a dozen theories the papers ran. But they just disappeared. I'm talking about their tea and their fountain pens left out on their desks and everything. They just disappeared, Reid."

"That's not true," he said, the sureness folding back into his voice. "You can't believe every story you hear. None of it's true. You're here, aren't you?"

Bay glanced at Fel and Estrella, as though these were things that should not be said in front of them.

"Look." Bay handed Reid the papers.

Reid's eyes moved over the print.

The only sign of him understanding was the pull of muscle between his jaw and his neck.

"It's not them," Bay said, looking first to Estrella and then to Reid. "It's the land."

"What are you talking about?" Reid asked.

"Something happened here," Bay said. "And the land's been taking people ever since. The stories, they all turned it into something about the women here, but it happened before they ever got here. The land took the men who lived here. Our family. Your family."

Fel watched Estrella, her lips parting as though she was breathing in Bay's words. He felt it, how neither of them expected Reid to believe Bay. To Reid, the Nomeolvides women were witches, an explanation so simple and clean he felt no need to adorn it.

But Bay, appearing with the wonder and terror of an angel, frightened him into believing.

"You know I'm right," Bay said. "You can tell me you don't, but you feel it." Bay looked toward Estrella. "The same way they feel everything in their family, you feel this. I can see it in you."

Reid handed the papers back. "Why are you telling me this?"

"Because I want you to know that our own family . . ."

Reid cut her off with a raised hand. "They are not your family."

"Fine," she said. "*Your* family. They sent you somewhere where there was a chance you could just vanish. They send their failures here hoping they'll stay out of the way, but you know what I think? I think they're hoping we'll just disappear. We won't be their problem anymore. Why else would they have started sending everyone they didn't want here? They knew.

They were willing to risk you and Marjorie's father and everyone else. They've been doing it for generations."

Pain started at the edges of Reid's face, gathering until it shut his eyes.

Fel hated this man, for hitting Estrella hard enough that her blood found Fel in the ground. For living off money made from the blood of men who had no other choice.

But for this second he saw him enough to recognize the understanding in Reid, his realizing how much his family counted him lost. He could hate him, and still see it.

Bay wouldn't let Fel kill Reid. Fel knew that, the rage dulling in his hands. But at least he had this, Reid's fear. If Bay would not let Fel use his hands against Reid, he could still use this, his fear, to keep him away from Estrella and her family.

"They want to get rid of you, Reid," Bay said. "One way or another."

Reid opened his eyes. "What happened here?"

Bay gave a short, pained whisper of a laugh. "*Your* family killed people. A lot of them. They died here. Almost a century and a half ago."

Fel saw neither shock nor recognition in Reid's face. Reid didn't know about the rock fall in the quarry. But he was also so unsurprised by the possibility that the Briars had blood and death on their souls, that Fel wondered how many others like him there were, how many quarries, how many lies spread so far and for so long they became true.

"Stay," Bay said. "Stay if you're ready to tell this story with me. If you're ready to take responsibility for what this family has done."

Bay's stare was so sure, so unbroken, that Fel understood the warning in her voice. This was her signal to Reid that if he stayed and lied about this, the land would have its vengeance on him the same as it had those vanished Briars.

For as long as it took for a cloud to pass over the moon, Fel thought he caught some sign of will and certainty on Reid's face. There was the possibility that he might become different than what his family had made him. And with that possibility came hope drifting off Bay, that this minute would make Reid into someone else. He might become someone who told the truth, who counted it as currency. He might turn into someone who made room for Bay in the world of his family, more brother than enemy.

But then the light came back, and Fel saw nothing but Reid's wish to brush all this off him. Bay noticed, her eyes shutting as those hopes fell from her hands. Her disappointment was so full and deep he could feel it. It made him want Dalia's hands on Bay as badly as he wanted Estrella's on him. Dalia, the girl who could pull Bay out of all these jagged, broken pieces without them cutting her. Estrella, the girl who called Fel back from the places where he got lost.

The Nomeolvides girls saved them as much as they destroyed them.

But to Reid, they were just witches. It was written in the way Estrella had drawn Fel out of the ground, in the tree of so many colors, in the way these women spoke a language that shifted and turned too often for anyone else to learn it.

Reid would run from this place. He would get as far away from all the death here as he could.

"You know now," Bay said. "So there's no pretending you don't."

Fel turned back to Estrella. But she was gone, and all three of them in the courtyard were left watching the space where she'd been.

THIRTY-FIVE

The truth ran over Estrella's skin, sharp as winter rain.

It hadn't been her family.

They had not brought this curse to La Pradera. They had thought their lovers had been disappearing long before they came here, back when they were las hijas del aire.

But it was the land.

Estrella and her cousins had given the land what they thought it wanted. Necklaces and bottles of perfume. Paper flowers and sugar hearts.

A carved wooden horse, painted blue, that called back the boy it once belonged to.

Estrella ran through the dark, her hands finding Dalia's shoulders.

"Has a woman ever disappeared?" she asked.

"What?" Dalia asked.

Now Estrella looked to her other three cousins. "Has a woman our family loved ever vanished?"

Gloria shook her head, hesitating. "I don't know."

"We never heard about it," Azalea said. "Do you really think they'd tell us?"

Estrella's understanding fell scattered and bright as the sparks off a bonfire.

"It's men," she said. "It's only men."

"What are you talking about?" Gloria asked.

"The land," Estrella said. "It doesn't take women. It takes men because it's men who died here. The miners. Our family helped hide their deaths, so the ground's been taking the men we love ever since."

"You're wrong," Calla said.

Estrella looked at her.

"This has nothing to do with La Pradera," Calla said. "The disappearing . . ." The words dissolved in the air. Even Calla couldn't say the raw truth of it, the disappearing of their loves, the vanishing of anyone they cared for too much. "It was happening to our family before we ever came here."

"Was it?" Estrella asked. She looked around at all her cousins. "Does anyone know that for sure? Do we even have stories about it that far back?"

They opened their mouths, considering speaking but then staying quiet.

"We accepted this as the way it's always been," Estrella said. "We thought we brought this curse here with us. But do we know that?"

She felt their four sets of eyes settle on her, listening but not yet understanding.

"We helped cover this up," Estrella said. "So it took something from us. It wanted us to answer for what we'd done. And it wanted our attention."

"It?" Calla asked.

Estrella looked down at her feet. "The ground. This place."

"But we didn't know about what happened," Azalea said. "Not until tonight."

"It doesn't matter," Estrella said. "We turned a graveyard into gardens."

Comprehension spread over Calla's face. "So it wouldn't let us leave."

Calla's words threw a new spray of embers across Estrella's thoughts.

La Pradera held them, made them sick if they tried to run, because it would not let them walk away from the truth they had veiled in so many flowers and leaves.

"That means it's not us," Azalea said, her face so soft and hopeful she looked younger than Calla. "We didn't kill them."

They traded glances, the language of having lived together so long they could speak to one another with their eyes.

Estrella wished she could pry the ground open like the shell of a pomegranate, spilling out its secrets like shining red seeds.

Beneath the sharp color of the flower beds and the gray of the flagstone paths, this land would always be its own. It would always hold its own rage, its own vengeance. Estrella and her cousins, and their mothers and grandmothers, could draw a hundred thousand blossoms from the earth, but it would never belong to them. It would never belong to the Briar family, either, even if, on paper, it was theirs.

If it had ever belonged to the Briars, it had gotten away from them when they buried the awful things that had happened here. Their own carelessness caused the rock fall, and by covering it, they had turned it into a worse violation against this ground.

This garden, and all the loss here, had haunted the Nomeolvides women, and none of them had realized. It had grabbed them, trying to speak of what it had witnessed. It had tried to make them see it.

The loss of their lovers had been less its wrath and more it trying to make them pay attention.

It wanted them to look deeper and see the stories buried here.

These unspoken things had their own pull. Spun together, they were heavy as a moon.

The colors of the sunken garden swirled around Estrella.

Of course La Pradera would not let them go.

A hundred years ago, Nomeolvides women had hidden the jagged rock of the quarry walls with so many trees and climbing flowers, no one could tell there had once been a landslide big enough to kill so many men. Her family had cast a veil of vines over the sunken garden, a place they had never thought of as more than a rocky canyon.

If they did not know how many lives the quarry had taken, those first Nomeolvides women on La Pradera would have thought they were doing nothing but tending land that could not be farmed. The steps of the quarry, broken by the rock fall, would have looked like nothing but forbidding ground.

They had turned this place from a graveyard into a fairy tale.

"Estrella?" Dalia said.

Even with the soft echo of Dalia's voice, all Estrella could see was this place they had made.

With dahlias and azaleas, calla lilies and morning glories, Estrella's cousins had painted this ground. With roses and countless bulb flowers, her mother and her cousins' mothers had kept this blood-soaked land a bright garden. With branches of blush and yellow flowers, her grandmother and great-aunts had spun this place from a tragedy to an enchantment.

They had given this place their hands. They had sealed the Briars' lie with so many petals they could not be counted. And for this, the land would not let them leave. It made them stay, hearing its voice. If they tried to run, it drew blood and pollen from their lungs.

They had to uncover the ground again. They had to let it speak and be seen.

They had to kill all the beauty they'd made.

Estrella ran down into the sunken garden, the place that had once been a quarry. She knelt next to one of the flower beds. She plunged her hands in, and dragged out a border of blue starflowers.

The rushing of steps on the stone stairs made her look up.

Bay and Fel and her cousins were following her down, her cousins watching Fel like he might be some figment of these gardens. An imagined boy.

Fel reached the path and then stopped. He watched her with his head a little tilted, like he hadn't decided whether he should stop her. She didn't blame him. She could see herself now, wild-eyed, her hair tangled as brambles.

She pulled stems so fast the indigo blossoms flew. Pink blooms and buds the color of dark wine fell to the dirt. Between flower beds, she dragged her fingers through the forget-me-nots dotting the grass.

She caught her breath. She found Fel's silhouette in shadow.

"Are you gonna help me or not?" she asked.

He took a few steps toward her. His uncertainty held him. He must have thought that tearing up these flowers, these gardens her family had made, was its own violation. She could read the hesitation in him.

She took his forearms and pulled him down with her.

This was his story, too, all that had been hidden under leaves and blooms.

He was slow pulling the first ones out. But when he saw the recklessness in her hands, the borraja arcing through the air, he tried again. This time he mirrored her, clutching the stems and tearing them away.

She went faster, grabbing not just at the stems but at the ground. Wet earth got under her fingernails and stained her dress. It dyed her shoes.

She and her family had made all this. She was not too delicate or clean to tear it all down.

Her cousins stood on the brick and stone paths. They
watched, eyes following Estrella's and Fel's hands. Azalea stood
with crossed arms. Calla kept near Gloria, Gloria's palm resting
on her shoulder.

Dalia's eyes landed on Bay. The look between them wove
so thick through the air Estrella thought she could reach in front
of her and touch it. It was invisible, but solid as the kind of satin
ribbon Estrella and her cousins once offered La Pradera.

Dalia dragged her hands through the ground like she was
stirring the surface of a pond, grasping at something that had
just slipped beneath the surface.

Their cousins reeled back. Dalia was ripping at flowers like
she was stamping out flames. Her fury turned to a thing that
looked like madness into a luring light. Estrella could see it on
her cousins' faces, their heads inclining toward her.

Dalia spun through the sunken garden, her hands fast as
moon-silver over water. Calla slid from Gloria's light hold. Gloria
trailed after, not to stop her but to join her. Azalea followed,
hands ready.

They took up flowers by the roots, the amethyst-colored
calla lilies, the bright azalea bushes, the pastel rounds of dahlias. They tore down the morning glory vines purpling the quarry
walls.

Dahlias spun like stars. Stalks of calla lilies in every color
from cream to near-black flew. Blue morning glories fell from

where they'd crawled up the balsam poplars. Azalea petals fell away from their centers.

They tore it all into a bright confetti. The petals caught in their hair and on their clothes.

Estrella felt the ground drawing back, like the sunken garden was taking a breath. She felt that breath spreading through the irises and hydrangeas and through all of them.

Their mothers and grandmothers appeared at the top of the sunken garden. Their faces showed their wonder as they recognized the lost Briar daughter in this auburn-haired stranger. They took in Fel, this brown-skinned boy with his sleeves still cuffed up, like he was a saint bearing sacred roses.

They watched him, this boy they thought had disappeared, earth flecking his skin. They watched Bay, this woman they had all claimed as their daughter. They watched their own children and grandchildren, each wrecked vine drawing both their horror and their thrill.

In the distance, Estrella found the far-off shape of her mother. She rushed down the stairs, and then was pulling at her own roses, tugging off enormous blooms. Dust-violet amnesia and yellow candlelight and pink secret garden roses tumbled from their stems.

Then Tía Jacinta was alongside her, picking bouquets of blue grape hyacinth like she was a little girl skipping through a wildflower field. Then Tía Azucena clutched at the day lilies. Even Tía Iris and Tía Hortensia followed, tearing at hello-darkness irises and a wall of blue and purple hydrangeas, the globes of tiny flowers spinning.

Lily magnolia and weeping cherry blossoms drifted over the quarry garden. The snow of pale petals swirled through the air.

The fever had caught even their grandmothers. They had followed their daughters and granddaughters, destroying the trees they had urged into flower. Abuela Mimosa and her branches of tiny yellow blossoms. Abuela Magnolia's sprawling white blooms. Abuela Lila's clusters of four-petaled lilacs. Abuela Flor's full-flowered cherry trees and Abuela Liria's wide-petaled lily trees.

Everything that cursed them had made a home of this ground. It had grown tendrils and shoots. It had twisted and curled, and shot out thorns. They had to dig their hands in as deep as the earth would let them. They could not free themselves by deadheading flowers and crushing leaves.

They would change nothing by picking flowers.

They had to rip out their fate by the roots.

The floor of the sunken garden spread over acres, and they scattered over its paths and lawns. They tore up so much of the ground that it helped them. It buckled and waved like an ocean.

Folds rose up in the earth like little mountains. They lifted what was left of the bulb flowers and hedges.

Those breaks in the earth took on forms Estrella recognized. Hands, arms, shoulders. Not like they were rising from under the ground.

Like the ground itself was making them.

Figures emerged from the earth the Nomeolvides women tore up. A man from the dirt beneath hydrangea bushes. Another from the stretch shaded by a weeping cherry tree. A third from under the iris beds.

A man with features Estrella recognized.

Near-black hair, flashing with the blue of a few caught forget-me-not petals.

Skin the color of sand when water left it mirror-wet.

A man who looked like an older version of Fel.

THIRTY-SIX

They were coming back, the men and boys lost so long ago. The ones with forged papers. The unaccounted for, the ones listed on roll sheets. The ones caught in the ages they had been because no one had ever laid their bodies or names or memory to rest.

For so long, the rumors had spoken for them. Their lives and deaths had not been spoken of, so the truth had been handed over to those who did not know. What had happened became twisted into stories about a family of women and their dangerous hearts.

Now, Estrella and her cousins were stripping away the gardens enough to let the land tell the truth. And the land was giving back those it had held, those everyone else had forgotten.

This was what Fel understood, that the force and rage in the Nomeolvides women was enough to tear down every bloom and vine.

But it also pulled those he had worked alongside back from the deep place he now knew.

Fel registered the shock moving through the women like water. But it did not slow them. They drew out boys Fel recognized, their clothes earth-stained, and men whose faces Fel had only ever seen stern and unmoving. But now they opened with wonder, like they had woken from sleep.

These were the men Fel had known. The ones who told him *It doesn't matter what we do, we're always gonna be breaker boys to them*, and *You wear this for your family*, and *Our mothers'll never know if we're in the ground.*

There was no gentleness in the women's hands. Only certainty. They pulled these lost men from the ground as hard as if they were dragging them out of the sea.

Bay followed Dalia to where she caught the ground moving, the stirring of the quarry beneath the garden. From this distance she almost looked like one of the men, plain trousers, suspenders, and a willingness to stay close to the ground as though it was her home.

But all this Fel only took in with half-second glances. All these lives flowed around him like a soundless storm. His hands and Estrella's were helping a man out of the ground near the deep pond. A man shrugging off dirt and grass.

Estrella did this with the same fierce resolution as tearing up the gardens. Fel knew she wasn't taking in the man's face. She was more set on getting him to the surface.

Fel's hands worked with the distance of helping a stranger.

His fingers numbed with each second of understanding who he was touching, the warmth of this man's body coming through the chill of the earth.

This man was a mirror of who Fel could be. This man had taught him to find blue mushrooms at dusk. He had been the one to tell him stories about the snows of cherry blossoms over los Pirineos, because Fel had been too young to remember.

They had inherited the same history, one of terraced gardens and wild olive trees that died in a hard frost. That shared history had helped Fel take this man with him, even when he had lost him.

Fel sensed the stares turning toward them, this matched set of brothers.

Now Estrella was watching them both.

Fel could see how they were different. Adán's brow bone harder, his skin one shade lighter brown. But to anyone watching, they were identical, set apart only by years.

It broke Fel open like a bud cracking its own green shell. He felt grown into this patch of ground, the two of them becoming twin trees that shared roots.

He wanted to thank Adán for how his face had never shown disappointment or judgment, not even when Fel had gotten the scars that marked him as a criminal. He wanted to say, because he had never said it before, that he had never thought how Adán loved was some sin or trespass. He wanted to tell Adán that he knew this was only the way his heart showed itself, careful and slow as the moon.

But Fel was silent. These things would not leave his tongue.

At Adán's hands on him, Fel startled. They were not children, and he felt it in their bodies. They hadn't been since they left their home of esparto-covered hills and frost-wrecked olive trees. They were both men grown by their country and broken by this place.

Adán's skin was damp from the earth. When he laughed, it was the humming of caballucos' wings.

He felt the hitch in his brother's stance and remembered that his right leg was just a little shorter than his left. Not enough that anyone noticed, but enough that after six days in the quarry he could not move enough to attend church on Sunday. The hem of one pant leg frayed to threads while the other held.

Fel remembered the times he'd tried blinking away the feeling of tears along his eyelashes, saying *I'm not crying.* Adán always held a kind laugh under his words when he said, *Yes, you are.* Not an accusation, an assurance that Adán thought no less of him.

Adán pulled away, hands still on Fel's arms, like he wanted to get a better look at him.

The other men found their footing on the ground, as though they had stepped off ships and needed their bearing on still land. When they saw Adán pulling Fel into him, they echoed it. They threw their arms around each other as though they were all brothers. The Nomeolvides women laughed because they could not help catching their shock and their joy at existing above ground.

The Nomeolvides grandmothers watched, clasping their hands as though they were praying but keeping their eyes open, small smiles lighting their faces.

Fel turned his head, finding the girl who'd touched him when the night sky was all blue horses. She was the wild will in this ground, her fingers both making and wrecking oceans of petals.

"Estrella," Fel said. "This is my brother."

THIRTY-SEVEN

The first things to come back were Gloria's glass earrings, Azalea's pewter spoon, Dalia's empty perfume bottle. They found them in the sunken garden, earth-darkened, but whole, the earrings set next to each other like they'd been left on a nightstand.

Then, Calla's paper flowers turned up like they were blooming from the hedges. Gloria's apron and Estrella's old dress washed up, drifting on the surface like floats of lily pads.

The Nomeolvides girls took these as signs that the land was forgiving them. These returned offerings were the ground's silent way of letting them go.

But then came things they did not recognize. A watch with a braided wristband caught on an arbor. A pair of dark velvet shoes, embroidered gold, appearing on the stone steps. Tiny jars of saffron threads and chili powder.

None of their mothers or grandmothers would claim them.

Not the necklace of silver leaves. Not the carved wooden comb with the scrolled handle. Not the satin purse embroidered with sea-colored beads. It made Estrella and her cousins wonder how many generations of Nomeolvides girls had done the same thing. How many hearts had lived with that same hope.

Now they had all pulled the work of their hands from the ground, and all the Briars except Bay had abandoned La Pradera. Even Reid would not come back, fearing this place now that he knew all his family had done, and all the wrath it held.

The Nomeolvides women would watch over this land. They would tell the truth of what had happened here, and they would let this land reclaim the acres of grass and flower borders and stone fountains. They would guide this place out from under more than a hundred years of betrayals so deep the Nomeolvides girls could not have imagined them.

Bay had told Fel and Adán and the other miners that they would live in the Briar house until they knew where they wanted to go next. "No arguments," she said. They would stay until they could chart their paths on maps, or find the far descendants of family members they'd once known.

When they had all blinked at her, she told them, "It's what my grandmother would have wanted."

The miners would tell their story. Bay, the girl who'd grown up as *the Briar bastard*, would help them. The truth of what this place had been before it was La Pradera would be spoken.

Each day Estrella and her cousins kept their eyes ready to find what La Pradera had given back, like they were spotting dyed eggs hidden in the grass. But then, one damp, chilled morning, Calla's father appeared in the low beds at the edge of the sunken garden. Then, days later, the traveling salesman Abuela Flor had loved showed up in the courtyard of blossoming trees. Then the map collector Gloria had counted as her father.

La Pradera gave them back, along with the possibility of who else might return to them.

It wasn't just men with bodies who slowly came back. Some nights, Estrella and her cousins caught faint silhouettes lifting off La Pradera like shadows, the spirits of those lost so long ago they were more ready to leave this world than join it again. They rose into the air. Some fled across the sky like winged creatures skittering off water. Others joined the shapes of women who seemed to appear from the highest magnolia branches. Heartbroken women already gone from this family.

"Why?" Calla asked, and in that single word they all understood the question. Why were these men not coming back to walk this ground like the miners? Why were they not reclaiming their bodies and lives and turning up in the gardens?

"Because everyone they want to follow is gone," Gloria said, her hand on Calla's shoulder. "It's been too long, so there's nothing else here for them." Her words were soft, not mournful. More like she was telling them all a nighttime story.

"It's a good thing," Azalea said, her voice so quiet and sure that she sounded like Gloria. "They're going off to find everyone they love."

The five of them watched the shadowed spirits rise from the

gardens. Then the shape and faint light of them disappeared into the gray sky.

Without ever speaking of it, the older Nomeolvides women called back to them the lovers they had once sent away, fearing they might vanish. The cousins hadn't heard anything about it from Azalea's grandmother until they saw her at the front gate, meeting a man as old as she was, their smiles shy. Then, close to sunrise, Estrella caught from her window the sight of Calla's grandmother embracing a woman whose hair was a mix of red and gray.

Estrella watched for Luisa, the woman whose name her mother had left unsaid for so long. She could not find the words to ask her mother, so instead she waited. They all waited, with the hope and wonder of how this land was thawing and warming to them.

All the grandmothers prayed into the grass beneath their feet and the sky above them, as grateful for the lovers returned to them as they were hopeful for others. When Estrella and her cousins and their mothers joined them under the darkening sky, she felt the force of all of them, true and heavy as some small star.

THIRTY-EIGHT

Estrella left him every caballuco she had, with a note saying he and his brother should keep them.

These carved wooden horses were what he had left, not just of his and Adán's wish that they would not die in the quarry, but of the dreams his brother had kept. Adán had always loved horses, from these figurines he played with as a child and the myths that came with them to Andalusians cantering over red earth.

Fel still was not sure how to speak to Adán. He'd wanted to see him again so much that now, when he could, he had no words to give him. Instead, he brought him the caballucos, wrapped in cloth that showed those flashes of yellow and orange, red and white and purple. The green one Estrella had found in Fel's pocket. The indigo one she had buried, bringing him back to life; it had turned up in the wrecked gardens, covered in dew that looked like drops of glass.

Estrella. This girl whose neck reminded him of the color of buckskin horses. This girl who'd done so well at avoiding him lately that new bursts of borraja were the only way he knew she hadn't run from La Pradera. The Nomeolvides women still had petals in their hands, but now they let them grow like wildflower fields, not ordered gardens.

Fel set the cloth in Adán's palms. Adán turned each small horse in his hands, his fingers tracing the dragonfly wings on their wooden backs. Their coats of paint had chipped, but their colors still showed.

Adán laughed. Fel did not understand why until his brother reached into his pocket and drew out an eighth caballuco, this one painted as black as their hair.

The one Adán kept in his pocket each day when they went down into the quarry.

Now Fel laughed with him, if for no reason but that his throat needed to remember how. He needed to fall back into how his laugh threaded with his brother's, two almost identical sounds. Like the Nomeolvides girls all talking at once.

He and Adán had no family anymore. They had only these things they could hold, and the stories they could tell.

Their Rifeña grandmother, born just outside Ceuta, had come from a family of flounder fishermen, always looking to the sea. Adán remembered her talking about it, when Fel had been too small to remember. The port sat so far on the tip of the peninsula that from the hill of her childhood home their grandmother could make out the far-off green of la Costa de la Luz. Later, she would tell her grandsons how she looked out on that horizon and knew her future husband was just beyond the land she could see, a young man harvesting cork in Cádiz.

Few believed her, this woman whose sisters called her dream-eyed, sentimental. While she halved lemons in the sunlight for leems, she would forget what she was doing, her fingers pausing on a yellow rind as she looked for shapes in the clouds.

But the Nomeolvides girls would have believed her. They would have seen the truth of it in the skill of her hands, so gentle she could rinse los azahares for orange blossom water without bruising the petals.

This much was still Adán's, and Fel's. Their hearts were nuez moscada, seeds encased in shells of red. Their bodies were maps of their family's blood. They were Cantabrian dragon-flies and Andalusian oaks. They were the teal water of Ceuta's harbors.

They were Adán's dreams of horses.

Adán set the black caballuco in Fel's hand.

"It's Alejandro," he said.

"What?" Fel asked, for a second thinking that Adán had named each caballuco, one more thing that had not yet come back to Fel.

"Your name," Adán said, a laugh in his voice. "It's Alejandro."

Alejandro. He remembered it, but hadn't thought of it. He had been Fel, and when his life before La Pradera came back to him, it had been with so much else that his name had fallen under.

"I've heard the women here call you Fel," Adán said. "And I like it. I like that you kept that part of our name. But I want to make sure you didn't forget your own. The one that's just yours."

THIRTY-NINE

All colors of torn-out flowers dotted the hills. Every stripe of color had been broken. Fountains stilled and trellises shrugged away their coats of climbing roses. Trees shed their blossoms, growing toward the sky. And in the days after, the land turned wild.

The stories Fel had told Estrella grew and flowered. Cherry and almond trees sprouted from the ground and wore coats of white and pink petals. Cork oaks spread from saplings into thickening trunks. Wild olive trees broke through the green hills, their leaves growing in like feathers.

Indigo mushrooms and stalks of unfamiliar flowers rose in their shadows. They grew tall and straight, the tan stems giving way to tiny brown flowers.

In all this new life, La Pradera had given Fel and his brother back a small piece of the land they had come from. A little of the life they'd had before found its way into these gardens. In these shade-growing flowers. In the perfume of almond and cherry blossoms. In the warm green and dust smell of olive trees.

Estrella knelt to the stalks of brown flowers. They looked like snapdragons, but spindlier. Instead of reds and yellows, these were all in tones of brown and gold. They looked photographed in sepia. Some were closed, their tops like hyacinth buds or tiny pinecones. But they were all drawn in those same browns.

"They're called bird's-nest orchids," Fel said.

She looked up, finding the boy she didn't know had been watching her.

"They grow wild in the woods," he said.

The way he looked at her made her feel like she was made of countless petals. Like her skin was the brown of orchids that grew in Cantabrian forests.

"Why are you avoiding me?" He said it without accusation or hurt. He just stood there, hands in his pockets.

His eyes followed the vines of blossoming almond and cherry branches, the petals blushing the wood. The bird's-nest orchids rose in soft brown stalks. Fairy rings of blue mushrooms covered the ground. Dandelions showed their wispy blossoms and greens.

He recognized these things. He knew them as belonging to his family. His stories had taken deep enough root here that they grew into things that could be touched.

If Estrella could keep her own brutal heart from finding him, she could keep him safe. She could guard the beautiful things locked inside him.

She opened her mouth to say she hadn't been avoiding him. That the stone house had been thrown into welcoming back lost men, and mourning ones who'd drifted up toward the stars. That the grandmothers and mothers were busied with how they would use the rumors of what had happened here to keep selling seeds and bulbs as though they were covered in gold. That at night Estrella and her cousins stood at the border of La Pradera, clasping hands, wondering if this land would still draw blood and pollen from them if, one day, they ran.

He felt it, the excuses building in her throat, and he gave her a smile of *Don't even try.*

The lies fell away.

"You shouldn't be with me, Fel," Estrella said.

He took a few steps toward her, the bird's-nest orchids brushing his calves. "Why?"

She shut her eyes tight, shaking her head. But the cherry and almond blossoms just got sweeter, and darker, an almost fall smell that the courtyard of flowering trees never let off. There, everything was perfume and light. Here, flowers smelled like wood and rain-slicked oranges.

You shouldn't be with me, because I helped turn the place you died into flower beds. This was the truth. But she could not bring the words to her lips. So she grabbed at any others in reach.

"We're las hijas del aire," she said.

"And my brother and I are immigrants with no family," he said.

"For years we didn't even exist on paper, Fel. You did."

"You want to talk about paper?" he asked. "On paper, I'm twenty-five. Or I was."

"What?" She couldn't help letting a laugh into her voice. He looked seventeen, eighteen maybe.

"It was so I could be twenty-one when I was fourteen," he said. "So my brother and I could both get the same jobs."

"Who believed you were twenty-one when you were fourteen?"

"Foremen who wanted to."

An indigo milk mushroom brushed her ankle, the cap the same blue violet as forget-me-nots. The color of her family's name. The shade of the wooden horse Estrella had buried in the sunken garden. The skirt Estrella had worn when Fel had first shown her indigo fairy rings.

That color, and her name, carried what she and her cousins had done, and what their mothers and grandmothers had done. The blue of their own name wore the stain of it all. The guilt was a weight in her hands as heavy as all those flowers yet to be made.

That guilt folded in on itself. It turned into a faceted thing made of edges and mirrors. It reflected back all the ways he had trusted her. She had believed she could protect him, that he needed her to, like he was a boy made from these gardens. But he'd had his own life, and death, and her family had buried it under everything beautiful.

She had never bothered to think of him as a boy with a story of his own, one that did not begin and end with her family.

"What we did to you," Estrella said.

"You didn't know," he said. "And Bay won't let the Briars hide this anymore."

A flicker of motion drew Estrella's eyes.

Among the olive trees, she could make out the shape of her cousin and Bay, the last Briar left at La Pradera.

Even with how long Estrella and her cousins had watched Bay, there was so much of her that Dalia had noticed before any of the rest of them had. Her watching eyes. Her ready hands. Her stance that held the vigilance of girls and the confidence of boys. Marjorie had passed down a little of herself to Bay.

The Nomeolvides girls had thought Bay belonged to them. She had always been theirs. And now they had let her go, not just so the one of them she loved most could love her, but so she could be her own.

The way Bay kissed Dalia, both of them parting each other's lips, pressing their hands so hard against each other's clothes it seemed like they could feel each other's skin through fabric, it was a thing Estrella envied them. There was so much hope and possibility held between them. Their love was something small but glimmering. They were careful with it, handling it like it was fragile as new ice. And now it was spiraling out and opening like frost flowers.

They shared the weight of two things yet to be done. Tell the truth about this place. Find the shape of a love they had kept to blushing glances for so long.

But Estrella and Fel. They were two sides of a war that had gone on under the earth for generations.

"We're dangerous, Fel," Estrella said. "I used to hate everyone who called us brujas, but they weren't wrong. We're poison." Her voice fell to a whisper. She couldn't wring anything louder from her throat. "I'm poison."

"And I'm a thief," he said. "Does it matter?"

"What?" she asked.

He shrugged one shoulder. For a second he looked like he was checking the land behind him.

But he meant his back, the scars she'd traced with her fingers in the dark.

"What did you think they were from?" he asked.

"What happened?"

"I stole fruit," he said. "Figs. I wanted to get them for my brother's birthday. Please don't tell Adán that part. He doesn't know what I was doing, he just knows I got caught trespassing."

Estrella took this, the small weight of him telling her something he could not tell his brother.

"I thought I was on land no one was taking care of," Fel said. "It looked like it." He held his laugh between his back teeth, as though it might soften the memory. "It wasn't. I was on the far edge of a rich man's property. There was so much of it he wasn't doing anything with a lot of it."

When Estrella had first seen Fel naked, when her hands had mapped the scars crossing his back, a deep place inside her had cracked. Now it shattered like a knot of glass.

"They did that to you for stealing fruit?" she asked.

He nodded. "Fifteen." Even saying the number made him wince. "They never told me if it was for my age or the number of figs I stole."

"You were fifteen and a court gave you that?"

"A court?" A laugh punctured the second word. "That wasn't how it worked. I got what the owner asked for. What rich men asked for was the law. He wanted to make sure I understood. I did."

The hope in her that he had no recollection of each lash on his back broke and crumbled.

"You remember it?" she asked.

"Oh, I remember it." His laugh was less bitter than pained. "I didn't know one man could own that much land. I didn't think men owned that much more land than they could farm. But I never made that mistake again."

His laugh was slight, but she felt the depth of it, the sad smile like there had been uncountable days and unmeasured darkness between now and that life he'd known.

"So that's what happened, if you've been wondering." He set one hand on her waist. His fingers slid onto her, then his palm, so slowly it felt like asking permission. "I won't let you call you or your family dangerous unless you're willing to call me a thief."

He didn't understand. Her family's legacy was sorrow. She didn't know what shape it would take now, but it was there, waiting in her blood. He was a buck in the woods, old enough to know the trees and the dark, but not old enough to realize that things smaller than he was could still be dangers. It wasn't just rich men and their quarries that could hurt him. She had been soft under his hands, but if he kept close, she would get her teeth and poison into him.

Even the flowers she grew would not stay under her hands. They made meadows out of rafters. They became oceans instead of gardens. There were things about her she wanted to make tame and mild, but they would not settle. They stayed fierce, defiant.

"Everything we touch, we wreck," she said. The truth of what had happened here. The men they loved. The women they adored and kept secret. "All of it."

His other hand started at the small of her back, fingertips first. They slid up to her shoulder blade, his palm laying flat against her.

"Then wreck me," he said.

He was doing this slowly enough that she could stop him. He was leaving room for her to say she did not want this. If she said it, he'd let go. If she couldn't say it, she could break away, ease his hands off her, with so little effort.

"I died," he said, "and you brought me back to life."

The sheet of cold air between them, the small distance she'd been keeping, thawed and heated. It turned as warm as his back while he slept.

She kissed his shirt, a place she had seen a scar crawl up to his shoulder. She wanted to give her own breath to every part of him that hurt, every piece of him still broken or bruised or left underground.

Her lips slid up the side of his neck. He bowed his head so the next time her mouth left his skin, he caught her lips with his.

He kissed her, and she was a world in bloom, her skin becoming starflowers. His tongue between her lips was borraja, that first bloom of hers that he'd taken into his mouth.

The sky over them lightened to gray blue. She kissed him hard enough that each time their lips broke, she heard him drawing in a thread of breath.

He kissed her until her tongue felt like it would burst into petals. He kissed her collarbone, his tongue tracing the path where her necklace had been. Her skin felt hot as the stars those beads had become.

The wind brought a rain of blue over their skin. Not the deep shade of borraja, or the lavender of forget-me-nots. Turquoise and blue green, petals from the tree of colors Fel had brought with him when he came back to her.

Years ago, her family had been forced off their own land, displaced by treaties and newly drawn borders. Rumors had followed them, and they'd been driven out of every town they tried to make their home. Their gift for holding earth in their hands had drawn suspicion, fear, scorn.

Wherever they lived, even now, they would have to give the ground flowers. That was a truth that stayed in their blood. Unless they wanted their gifts to decide when and how they showed themselves, they would have to bring into life the blooms waiting in their hands. If they refused, hundreds might show up in an attic or growing from wallpaper.

There were places that might hate them and the work of their hands. There were whispers that might follow them like shadows. There were women who might declare them witches and men who might chase them from their streets.

But there were also oceans and ice forests. There were deserts as red as foxes and forests of cork oaks and wild olive trees. There was this boy and his brother, and the land where they would care for horses, hills softened with meadow grasses.

There were hearts girls like her could love without fear of them vanishing. There was the five of them standing at the edge of La Pradera, their bare feet in the wet grass and the perfume of their names clinging to the hems of their slips.

There was so much ground they had never felt under their hands. There was the whole world, all its gardens still unseen.

ACKNOWLEDGMENTS

I surprised no one when I said I was writing a book about flowers. Especially not my mother and father, who when I was growing up had to put up with me wanting to visit the botanical gardens of every city we ever visited.

What surprised me was that this book about flowers also became a book about families. The ones we're born with, the ones we find, the ones we make. Families are where our stories start, and it's families who teach us how to bring our stories with us into the world.

I'm deeply grateful to those who've given me safe spaces to tell the stories I want to tell, and those who do the incredible work of making stories into books. Here, I'll name a few:

My agent, Taylor Martindale Kean, who I'm lucky to have as an advocate and a friend, and Full Circle Literary, for being a wonderful home for diverse voices.

My editor, Kat Brzozowski, for bringing me along on this next part of her adventures as an editor and for, with every note, helping this story find its heart.

Jean Feiwel, for welcoming me and the Nomeolvides girls to Feiwel & Friends.

For turning this story into a gorgeous book, art director Rich Deas and designer Danielle Mazzella di Bosco, who brilliantly brought La Pradera to life through the beautiful cover and interior.

Everyone at Feiwel & Friends and Macmillan Children's Publishing Group: Jon Yaged, Kim Waymer, Allison Verost, Liz Szabla, Angus Killick, Brittany Pearlman, Molly Brouillette, Melinda Ackell, Teresa Ferraiolo, Kathryn Little, Erica Ferguson, Romanie Rout; Katie Halata, Lucy Del Priore, Summer Ogata, and Melissa Croce of Macmillan Library; and the many more who do the magical work of creating books.

Wallieke Sutton, and everyone who gets the mail where it's going.

The brilliant writers whose insight helped shape this story: Tehlor Kay Mejia, my sister in countless shared jokes, who lent her brilliance to the earliest and latest versions of this book. Shveta Thakrar, for her caring spirit, and for teaching me to embrace the unexpected that so often holds the magic of stories. Mackenzi Lee, whose notes make my drafts better, and whose wit has brightened many days.

Fadwa Lahnin, for helping Fel and Adán's family come to life.

Dahlia Adler, for her friendship, humor, and heart, and for letting me use the Spanish version of her name for one of my favorite characters in this story.

My husband, for his attention to this strange fairy tale, his guidance on the genderqueer character who became a bigger part of this book with every draft, and for letting me lead him through the nighttime gardens that inspired the story.

My mother and father, who not only put up with every botanical garden visit but always encouraged me to learn all I could. My family, who were the first to teach me that we have to write our own stories.

Readers, always, for giving books lives of their own once they leave our hands.

GOFISH

ANNA-MARIE McLEMORE

What did you want to be when you grew up?
An astrophysicist or a fairy princess, depending on at what age you asked me.

When did you realize you wanted to be a writer?
I've always loved stories, but it wasn't until my early twenties that I thought maybe I could be a writer.

What's your most embarrassing childhood memory?
Getting a jaw widener put in right before I had to recite a poem in front of the whole school. I still cringe when I think of how hard it was to even talk!

What's your favorite childhood memory?
My father teaching me about astronomy.

As a young person, who did you look up to most?
My brothers.

What was your favorite thing about school?
When our teacher would read to us. I struggled with reading, but I always loved books, so read-aloud time, whether at school or with my family, was my favorite.

What were your hobbies as a kid? What are your hobbies now?

I Irish-danced as a kid, and I picked it back up recently. I can occasionally be found practicing a reel in the park.

Did you play sports as a kid?

I was mostly into dance, but I did like watching sports.

What was your first job, and what was your "worst" job?

My first job was as an administrative assistant, though I called myself a secretary because I thought it made me sound more glamorous, like the girls in old movies. I really liked that job. My "worst" job didn't come until later, when I had a boss who preferred her employees never talk to one another, only to her. I was so happy when I moved back to a job where I could get to know the people I was working with!

What book is on your nightstand now?

Fake Plastic Love by Kimberley Tait.

How did you celebrate publishing your first book?

By swimming in my mermaid tail!

Where do you write your books?

A desk where I keep an array of books and sticky notes, or, sometimes, outside.

What sparked your imagination for *Wild Beauty*?

The first spark for *Wild Beauty* began with the idea of gardens and secrets. Though the details of La Pradera are very much fiction, I drew a lot of inspiration from botanical gardens I visited growing up. They always felt like places that were not only beautiful but that held secrets I could only guess at. *Wild Beauty* came out of imagining what one estate's spectacular gardens might be hiding.

What challenges do you face in the writing process, and how do you overcome them?
There's always that moment when I realize a story may end up totally different than I imagined, but I try to have faith that's it's going to end up better and that I'll figure it out along the way.

What is your favorite word?
Luz, or *light*. It's my favorite word in both languages.

If you could live in any fictional world, what would it be?
I'm not sure I'd want to live there forever, but there are definitely some fairy tales whose worlds I'd love to visit.

Who is your favorite fictional character?
Daisy Buchanan or Tita de la Garza.

What was your favorite book when you were a kid? Do you have a favorite book now?
My dad had a book of Irish short stories he read to me, so that was my favorite. My favorite now is probably *The Little Prince*.

If you could travel in time, where would you go and what would you do?
I would go to Mexico a century ago and meet as many of my relatives as I could.

What's the best advice you have ever received about writing?
Write the stories of your heart, because they will be the truest and the most beautiful.

What advice do you wish someone had given you when you were younger?
You weren't asking for it.

Do you ever get writer's block? What do you do to get back on track?
If I get stuck, often taking in the work of other artists—whether that's books, visual art, music, or movies—inspires me and helps me look at what I'm working on from a different angle.

What do you want readers to remember about your books?
That girls of color and queer girls belong in fairy tales.

What would you do if you ever stopped writing?
Probably something in the theater. I worked with lighting as a teen.

If you were a superhero, what would your superpower be?
Breathing underwater. With a mermaid tail, of course.

Do you have any strange or funny habits? Did you when you were a kid?
I walked on my toes without meaning to do it, and I think sometimes I still do that. Maybe it's a short-girl habit.

What do you consider to be your greatest accomplishment?

Living openly as a queer woman. I know that's an easy decision for a lot of LGBTQ people, but for me, especially being Latina and coming from a traditional community, it took more conviction than I thought I had.

What would your readers be most surprised to learn about you?

I have all brothers and no sisters, which might surprise readers since I often write about families of women.

When sisters are rivals
and girls become swans,
no heart is safe.

ANNA-MARIE McLEMORE
AUTHOR OF *WILD BEAUTY*

Keep reading for an excerpt.

ROJA

Everyone has their own way of telling our story.

Some say it began generations ago, with a girl lured by the white birds in the woods. The moment she reached out a small hand toward their wind-fluffed feathers, a swan bit her, poisoning her blood.

Others say it started with a flock of swans gliding over our great-great-great-grandmother's house. They flew overhead at just the right moment to hear her cursing her own family's blood. So the swans cursed her, and all the daughters after her.

Some insist it was two sisters, squabbling for years over who was more beautiful. A bevy of swans in a nearby pond grew so weary of all the noise, and struck them with a spell that would take one of each of their daughters.

The worst one tells it this way: Once, a del Cisne woman—probably one of our great-great-great-grandmothers—stole a groom from his bride on their wedding day. The bride's family hated our bisabuela and her name so deeply they cursed her brown skin and her dark hair to become white feathers, and for the same fate to befall a del Cisne daughter every generation after.

These are the stories they tell, tales of winter storms or spiteful witches. Because when there is a family in which one of every two daughters grows an ink-black bill and a pale-feathered neck and snow-bright wings, people like to think they know why.

Few think to ask us.

This is the story we believe to be true:

A mother once raised her daughter among swans, hoping they would teach her their grace and beauty. And this daughter, with the swans for her sisters, grew lovely in both appearance and manner. When she married, she bore only sons, three and then five and then ten sons. And though she loved her sons, she wanted a daughter, so that she, too, could raise a girl with the grace of swans.

So she went to the swans she had once called her sisters.

"Please," she told them. "All I want is one daughter."

"We will give you better than one. You will have two," they said, with a magnanimous bow of their necks. "There will always be two daughters. But we will always take one back."

"Which will you take?" the woman asked.

They lowered their wings. "That will be for us to decide."

There may be as many versions of the story as there are daughters our family has lost to it. But this is the one my sister and I know. A woman wanting something so badly she did not understand the weight of the swans' pronouncement.

There will always be two daughters. But we will always take one back. The swans would take not just one of the woman's daughters, but one of her daughter's daughters, and one of her daughters, and one of hers. There would always be one daughter taken, and one left watching the sky in winter, wondering if a far-off flick of white was a coming snow or her lost sister.

Even when there were sons, there were always daughters alongside them, two sisters, whether they had brothers or not. Always two, always enough that the swans could take one and leave behind the other. My bisabuela had already raised three sons, sure she was too old for more children, when her daughters arrived. My great-great-aunt, intent on having one child, delivered, to her surprise, twin daughters. My second cousin thought she had defied the swans by having a single son and a single daughter, until the child thought to be a boy declared herself as the girl she had always been.

The way our aunt and our great-aunts tell it, our family never knows which daughter the swans will take.

But I've always known it would be me.

If I wanted to, I could believe everything was decided when we were born.

But I've always known it was earlier than that. And not just because the colors of girls are decided before they're born, though that's something I know to be true.

What I believe instead is that, in the moments of my sister and me becoming our own little lives, it was already written into us.

In the wisp of blood and not-yet-breath that was Blanca before she was born, there were already the beginnings of how her hair would grow as gold as October leaves.

Her eyes would be brown, the same as the rest of us, and that was something our mother would consider a great misfortune. But they were a brown as light as acacia honey, like amber. A brown that could be forgiven.

A few months after Blanca was born, I was a new wisp of blood and not-yet-breath. My own colors were already waiting. By then, Blanca had grown a crown of hair as fine and blond as a duckling's down. Her tiny hands patted the growing round of my mother's belly, where I was, slowly, becoming.

While my sister had a face as fair as the almonds my mother blanched each fall, mine would turn out as brown as the almond's skin, dark and delicate, that my mother swept off the counters. I would have eyes and hair as dark as the coffee grounds my father spread over his roses in winter.

My hair grew not only dark as those coffee grounds, but red. Not the copper or strawberry of green-eyed girls, but deep red, a red so dark it looked wet. It was a red that wouldn't take dye, not even the black walnut the señoras gave my mother. "Blood-soaked hair," they called it, my mother shuddering at the words, my father saying them back with as much pride as if they were a new knife, fine and just sharpened.

My father counted it as such a point of pride that he named me for it, setting his hand on my small forehead and declaring me *Roja* while my mother slept off a birth fever. The kind of birth fever, the señoras reminded me on my birthday every year, that Blanca hadn't given her.

If I wanted to, I could believe it was our colors that decided Blanca would be the gentle sister, pure and obliging, and I would be the cruel one, wicked and difficult. She would be the blessed daughter, the one the swans would spare. And I would be the one the swans would take.

But my sister saw our story ending another way.

BLANCA

I was five, maybe six when I first saw the swans. I remember because Roja was still having her tantrums, so she couldn't have been older than four. Our parents were trying to train them out of her, our mother by clutching her arm when she wailed for more than a few minutes, our father by crouching to meet her eyes and talking in a voice that was low, and neither harsh nor gentle.

"You can scream and cry if you want," he said. "But what you have in you is power."

His words were so level and sure, they made Roja quiet. Her tears froze on her cheeks.

"You let it wring you and throw you around like you're a doll," Papá said. "And if that's all you let it do, you'll be a fool forever. Because that power, that anger in you, that is the best thing you have." He gave her a nod as proud as if she were a son. "So claim it. Pick yourself up and use it."

My mother pulled me into the kitchen. Not like I was seeing something I shouldn't. More like she wanted to guard me from my sister. As though Roja might throw off shards of glass that would catch me if I got too close.

The kitchen still smelled like pomegranates from when my mother and I had split open the rinds that afternoon, spilling the jewels inside. Mamá had seemed happy, the two of us sitting at the table, her legs crossed at the ankles, my bare feet swinging off the chair. She was patient when my pudgy fingers squished the pith into the fruit. She laughed, rubbing sprays of red juice off my forehead and showing me how cutting the fruit into quarters and then plunging them into water made them give up their seeds.

Now Mamá stopped a few steps from the back door.

"Do you want to see them?" she asked.

I didn't know what she meant. I nodded anyway, nervous but thrilled by the promise of a grown-up secret.

From the living room came the flat sound of my sister driving her fists into the carpet. She wasn't crying anymore. Her face was against the floor. She had worn herself out.

The sound of her fist on the braided rug was as familiar as my own voice. I could almost smell the salt of her tears. The warmth of the wool under her flailing body. The thick vanilla of the hierbas in my father's pipe, which he lit as though to say he had nothing but bored patience, that he'd wait all night for her to pick herself up off the floor.

All these things smothered the pomegranate smell like a blanket over a flame.

My mother took me outside with her. The night air was a little sweet from the Ashbys' flowering trees, waking up from winter and turning blush-pink.

My mother must have smelled the swans' feathers on the air, because we had just set our feet onto the chilled ground when their shapes crossed the moon. The flashes of their silhouettes flickered over the gleaming round, and then they were gone.

They did not fly lower. They did not sweep down into the trees and toward our corner of the woods.

That, according to our great-aunts, would not be until Roja turned fifteen.

Then the swans would come for us. Los cisnes, birds as beautiful as they were terrifying. Their arrival always marked the season when they would decide which daughter would remain a girl, and which they would take.

From where my mother and I stood, those swans looked as distant as if they lived on the moon. That was what Roja and I would be to each other one day, after los cisnes finished with us. One of us would stay rooted to the ground, the other bound to the sky.

The thought of it felt like my veins being ripped from my heart. Roja was not just my blood. She was the sister who chased garden lizards like they were kittens, but hid in her bed every time a cricket got into our room. She saw my fear during thunderstorms and told me lightning was nothing but ribbons, no different from the ones we set in our hair, just made of stars.

I could not let that kind of distance spread between me and the girl I'd mapped the woods with, both of us learning them as well as each other's faces.

The next morning was still pale silver when I got Roja up out of bed. I buttoned her into the berry-red coat our father had bought her for Christmas, and I put on the cream wool one my mother had picked out for me. I brought her outside, and from the garden we took everything I thought might save us. White roses and red ones. Sour berries and sweet. Herbs with every kind of leaf.

We started with the herbs. I gave Roja the ones with rounded leaves, to smooth her out. I ate the ones with prickly edges that looked like ripped paper, so I'd grow sharper edges, too. Then the berries; I gave my sister the ripest ones while I let the sourest pucker my tongue, to make her the sweeter one.

And last, the roses. We slipped the petals onto our tongues like the communion wafers at church. I swallowed the red ones, and Roja the white, each of us eating the opposite of our names.

"Why are we doing this?" my sister asked. Not impatient. Not whining. Just because Papá had taught her to ask questions.

"If the swans can't tell us apart," I said, "they can't decide which of us to take."

PAGE

I'd heard how everyone talked about the del Cisne girls. At best, they whispered about them with a storyteller's thrall, like they might have about a lake filled with vicious mermaids.

The feathers are in them already; they're born with them under their skin. That's why their mother took them out of school last year, so everyone wouldn't see their wings coming in.

I heard when the moon's full their father doesn't sleep. That's how he gets all his work done.

Don't ever go into their house. Angel's trumpet and bittersweet berries grow through their floorboards.

At worst, they blamed the del Cisnes. If lavender bushes didn't take, or jam didn't thicken, mothers threw their hands up, shrugging that it must be swan season. If blond, water-eyed girls' barrel ringlets fell out before dances or ballet recitals, they hissed the name *del Cisne.*

I saw one of the del Cisne girls out in the woods once, after they weren't going to our school anymore.

She had hair almost like mine, but the yellow of hers was so vivid and rich that I couldn't think of it as anything but gold. It had weight and warmth, like the last threads of sunlight before the sky deepened.

But it wasn't her hair that stopped me.

It was her eyes, a brown so shining and deep I found their glint from across the forest pond. They caught the light even in the trees' shadows. Like blueberry honey, or the topaz on my mother's favorite bracelet. A hundred facets, brown and glimmering.

I watched her through the aspen leaves, their flickering yellow hiding and unveiling her.

She was looking out over the pond. I couldn't tell why. I kept waiting for her to skip stones or throw pennies in for wishes.

It got cooler and darker, and she buttoned the extra buttons on her sweater. When she crossed her arms over her chest like she was still cold, I knew she was about to go inside. Her family didn't live far. I didn't know that from following her. Everyone knew that, how the del Cisne girls lived in a house deep in the trees.

I waited for her to turn away from the pond, her hair fanning out in a sweep of gold.

But then her gaze lifted off the water. Her eyes moved across the screen of trees.

They stopped where I stood.

That brown caught me. Against the aspen-yellow of her hair, the color was as startling as it was beautiful. This girl was her own woods, gold and brown.

She didn't flinch. She didn't glare at me.

Her gaze didn't break even as leaves fluttered between us. Heat spread over the back of my neck, and I wondered if she'd known I was here the whole time.

YEARLING

The first time I ever talked to Page Ashby was when he found me in back of the school and hit me in the jaw.

He did it fast, no warning, and he did it while saying words my brain was too rattled to register. Something about how my grandmother had besmirched the honor of his grandmother. I didn't catch everything he said but I caught that much. He really did say it like that, too. *Besmirched her honor.* I half expected Page to pull out a glove, slap me in the face with it, and challenge me to a duel.

What, exactly, could Grandma Tess have done to *besmirch* anyone? Let alone Lynn Ashby. The only thing I could think of was something about the fruit the Ashbys grew. The best apples for a hundred miles came from their trees, and everyone knew it. Any insult to them was grave as cursing their mothers.

But Grandma Tess liked them as much as anyone else, and if she ever didn't, she wouldn't have mentioned it. *Not worth it all around,* she would've said.

Page Ashby stood in front of me, waiting. He was small, even adjusting for how I had two years on him, fourteen to his twelve. Under his overalls, he wore a plain shirt—white, cotton, the kind my mother said should never be seen in public because they were underwear. It darkened at the sleeve hems, the tint of dust and dirt off his family's orchard. His hair was light as the unfinished wood of the apple crates. It looked like he'd cut it himself, a try at a nondescript boy's cut that didn't look half bad in the front but went uneven in the back.

He stood with his hands in the pockets of his overalls. Unafraid, like he either knew I wouldn't fight back or was ready for it.

"You call that a hit?" I asked.

Sure, it had hurt at first, but the pain landed shallow, and faded fast. It was all snap and first impact. There was no force behind it, no solid path.

I wondered if the insult would make him hit me again, but he just blinked at me.

"Come on." I stood next to him. "Let's teach you to do this right."

"You're going to show me how to hit you better?" he asked.

"I hope not," I said. "But I can't let you go around doing that again."

He looked too surprised to argue.

"Show me how you make a fist."

He did.

"Do you want to break your thumb?" I asked.

"No."

"Then don't put it inside your fist."

He slipped it out and set it alongside his curled fingers.

"Didn't your father teach you this?" I asked.

"He's not really the fighting kind."

"Lucky you." My laugh was supposed to sound thoughtless, like shrugging something off, but it came out bitter. "Okay, now imagine going past whatever you're trying to hit. If it's me, you're not aiming for me, you're aiming for the brick behind me."

That was a trick Liam had taught me. Good of him, too, since he was usually the one I was trying to punch through.

Page charged his fist into the air in front of him, slow, but I could see him imagining it.

"Throw from your shoulder, not your arm," I said. "If you think too much about your hand, you end up bending your wrist."

He squared up his stance, unrounding his shoulders.

I stood in front of him. "Feel like trying again?"

"You want me to hit you in the face again?" he asked.

"How about you go for my arm?"

"What if I hurt you?"

That was a nice change from two minutes earlier. If Liam and I could have shut down our fights this fast, we would've both had time to learn the violin.

I touched my sleeve halfway between my shoulder and elbow. "You won't."

He did it. It hurt, the pain spreading out through the muscle in my arm.

"Better," I said.

He heard it in my voice, that pain I held at the back of my throat and the pride of knowing I'd taught him to do that.

"The next guy you sucker punch doesn't stand a chance," I said.

His face brightened into a smile.

"I'm Barclay," I said.

Page set his mouth like this was some kind of test. "I know."